# THE AUTHOR'S WIFE

First published in January 2026 by Barnacre Publishing
Cover Design by The Cover Collection

The moral right of Caroline Blake to be identified as the author of this work has been asserted in accordance with the Copyright, Designs and Patents Act 1988

This book is entirely a work of fiction. The names, characters, and incidents portrayed in it are entirely a work of fiction. Any resemblance to actual persons, living or dead, is entirely coincidental.

Copyright© Caroline Blake 2026

**All Rights Reserved**
No part of this book may be reproduced in any form,
by photocopying or by any
electronic or mechanical means,
including information storage or retrieval systems,
without permission in writing from both the copyright owner and the publisher of this book.

Paperback ISBN : 978-1-7393468-8-1

A CIP catalogue record of this book is available from the British Library

Instagram @caroline.blake.author

www.carolinemelodyblake.co.uk

*To my wonderfully supportive husband,
Darrell Blake*

**Other Books by Caroline Blake**

Just Breathe
Forever Hold Your Peace
Unexpected Storm
The Brief
An Unfortunate Situation
The Murder of Mrs Chadwick

## Chapter One

## Ivy

The minute Ivy steps off the ferry onto Holm Island, she is sure she has made a terrible mistake. She almost turns back to ask the ferryman to return her to the mainland. But she already knows this is the final crossing of the day. The anchor will be moored, and the ropes fastened tight. The ferryman will be looking forward to his dinner. Tonight, as the ferry stays here, then so must she.

Despite wanting to do an about-turn, she drags her small suitcase to the end of the short wooden pier, following the other foot passengers, where a local taxi driver is waiting for her by the side of a battered black Ford saloon, silently displaying a hand-written sign in front of his chest, which looks like it has been made from the inside of a cornflake box. *'Ivy Montclaire'* has been scribbled with a black permanent marker in a large cursive font. She wonders who wrote the note for him. A wife? A daughter? The writing is too feminine for it to have been him.

When she walks towards him and tells him her name, he takes her suitcase with a perfunctory nod and deposits it in the boot of the car. He doesn't say hello, comment on the weather, or ask her how she is. She is accustomed to chatty London cabbies. Their friendly smiles and polite questions are almost a trademark of the city. They always ask her about where she has been and whether she has had a nice day. They tell her little anecdotes about the famous people they have met, and she pretends to be interested — thankfully, not many people recognise her any longer, so she doesn't feel the need to make her way around the city incognito — and the journeys are generally pleasant ones. But she can tell this man isn't the type to be interested in her harrowing and extremely long journey from London all the way to the west coast of Scotland, or the purpose of her stay here on this small island, so she doesn't offer to tell him. He's terribly dour. But that's fine, as she is not in the mood for talking anyway.

The man is wearing an off-white knitted Aran jumper that looks as old as the hills, with faded corduroy trousers that probably used to be bottle green but are now the colour of weather-beaten moss. On his feet are sturdy brown boots, the type usually worn by hikers or farmers. But they are clean, Ivy notices. If they have been speckled with soil at any point, there is no evidence of their previous activity now. It isn't easy to guess his age; somewhere between forty and sixty. She knows from previous experience that all the men on the island are quickly aged by the constant assault of wind and rain, so she wouldn't be surprised to find that he is much younger than he looks.

He holds the rear passenger door open, and she climbs in. Her spine cracks and creaks as it sends shooting pains down the backs of her legs. She should have taken her painkillers an hour ago, but they are packed into the depths of her suitcase. Now she will have to wait until they get to the hotel.

The driver starts the engine, and they set off. She doesn't need to tell him she is going to Hollow Pines Hotel, although she does, just to be sure. The extremely helpful travel agent back in Beckenham assured her that she had sorted everything out, including all her train tickets, two nights at the hotel, and this taxi pick-up. Holm Island Taxis is the only taxi company on the island.

'You just need to make sure you're on the right ferry on the right day, and leave everything else to me,' the agent said as she gripped a sheet of paper as it shot out of the tabletop printer on the end of her desk. She folded it in half and handed it to Ivy with a smile. 'All the details of your trip are on there. You're going to have a fabulous time, I can guarantee it,' she said. It was she who suggested the wine tasting weekend. The hotel does them twice a year. 'They are really popular,' she told her. 'You're lucky to get one of the last available spaces.'

Ivy had wandered into the travel agency to escape a particularly vicious late summer downpour two weeks ago. Unsuitably dressed in a thin skirt and a white cotton blouse that was bound to become see-through with the mere hint of precipitation — and the days of her wanting to show her underwear to anyone are well and truly behind her — she thought she might take cover inside the doorway for just a few moments.

'Come and take a seat,' the kind travel agent said. 'You look drowned. Here, let me get you a towel to dry your hair.'

The agent disappeared through a door at the back of the shop and reappeared with a clean cotton tea towel, which she placed around her shoulders. Within minutes, as Ivy dabbed at her damp hair, she heard herself telling the agent that she had a momentous birthday coming up next month — her eightieth — and she wanted to treat herself. She had been shopping on the high street, but hadn't found anything she liked, apart from a cashmere cardigan in a beautiful baby pink, but the sleeves were far too long, and a delightful raincoat, the colour of soft morning mist, which she decided she didn't need. As she gazed around at the colourful brochures and holiday destination posters on the wall - one depicting a contented couple sharing tapas on a tiny round table, one showing a gaggle of women linking arms down a sunlit cobbled street, and the other of a young family running into the sea, all having the time of their lives - it occurred to her that Fate had led her there. She could have taken shelter in the dry cleaner's next door, or the coffee shop on the other side of the road, but she was there for a reason — so she could book a fanciful trip to the Italian Lakes or an exciting city break to Geneva or Vienna. It had been so long since she had dusted off her passport. She told herself that by the time the storm had passed and the sky was once again as blue as the Mediterranean, her holiday would be arranged.

When the travel agent told her about the wine weekend, she should have stopped her there. She should have explained that she couldn't possibly step foot onto Holm Island again, not as long as she lives. Even thinking about Scotland gives her palpitations. As the travel agent swivelled her laptop screen to show her how beautiful Hollow Pines Hotel is, and how she could amble around the gardens after breakfast, and, later, take a swim in their brand new pool, enjoy delicious food and wine, and even take a walk on the beach, which is only moments away from the back of the hotel, Ivy found herself in a state of silent acquiescence.

She didn't tell the agent that she had been there many times before, although the last time was nearly fifty years ago. She didn't tell her that she knows Hollow Pines like the back of her hand, although that was when it was a private home, not a hotel. She didn't tell her she was part of a couple then. When she gave her name — Miss Ivy Montclaire — there was no flicker of recognition. She decided the agent was too young to have heard of her and

Terence, everyone's favourite celebrity couple in the 1970s. The agent wouldn't have been born then.

The thought of Terence tugs at her heartstrings, and she, once again, questions her decision to come here. She knows her visit won't be the same as it used to be. How can it without her other half? Her reason for living. The love of her life.

Now, as the taxi jerks and jumps across treacherous potholes as it pulls away from the dock and joins the coast road, Ivy can feel her heart rate rising. Nothing has changed in all this time. It looks identical to the pictures in her memory. They pass the ancient pub and the row of fisherman's cottages with their front doors painted in the same bright pastel colours of fifty years ago. At the end of the row, there is a bench looking out to sea. It is still there. Old and weathered, but still standing.

She fumbles in her jacket pocket for her angina spray and squirts it under her tongue. She closes her eyes, ignoring the glorious view of the Hebridean waves bursting over the rocks on the shore. They are nothing new, and neither is this road. The memories are disturbingly vivid. She knows that in a mile, the road will sweep off to the left, away from the coast, inland towards the forest where the pine trees stand like sentinels on either side of the narrow road. Eventually, the forest begins to thin out again, allowing light to pass through the trees, scattering itself onto the road. From there, the road begins to climb and climb until eventually reaching the hotel at the top of the hill.

An image of Terence's old Morris Minor, the first time they brought the car, spluttering up the hill in first gear. The pair of them laughing, he telling her she needs to prepare herself for getting out and giving it a push. Both of them excited for their annual summer trip.

Another image of them shouting. Years later, the old car long gone. The darkness on the cliff top pressing in around them, the stars watching their angry exchange. Terence waving his arms in the air, like a horrid game of charades, his face red, his forehead shiny with sweat, despite the cold. Ivy screaming at him, pointing her finger at his chest. Her last, unforgettable words to him were so cruel.

She can feel the taxi beginning to climb. She knows where they are now, even with her eyes still tightly shut. She is pushed back in her seat. The road is smoother than she remembers. Perhaps it has recently been recovered as part of the hotel's renovation project. She takes a deep breath. She can feel the driver watching her through the rearview mirror. He must think she's asleep. She hopes he doesn't see the tears she is desperately trying to hide.

It is a mistake to come here. The ghost of Terence is on this island. She can feel him. She should be sipping mint tea in Limone by the side of Lake Garda right now, as she waits for her lunch — freshly caught fish and locally grown salad. She shouldn't be here, somewhere she has avoided all these years. The idea that she could somehow make her peace with the loss of poor Terence and fight her demons head-on is ridiculous. She has kept them buried all these years. Why has she chosen to face them now? What a stupid old woman she is. She will spend the night here and then go back home tomorrow. The concierge will arrange it for her if she asks. She feels slightly better at the prospect of having to spend only one night at Hollow Pines.

Then, as the taxi takes a familiar sharp bend, another memory hits her. Kneeling in the middle of the road in the pitch dark. She remembers choosing a specific spot, just after the bend, where a speeding car couldn't possibly miss her. Nobody sticks to the speed limits around here. Her hands were clasped tightly across the back of her head as her forehead and her knees pushed into the road. Child's pose. Except that it wasn't the gentle, resting posture after a yoga session. Tiny stones dug into her young skin, but she bore the pain as a penance while she waited for an inevitable impact. She doesn't know how long she was there. Not long. Maybe ten minutes, although it felt like hours.

The driver of the car stopped just inches from her taught body.

'What the bloody hell…' she heard him exclaim as he clambered out of his car. He was English, but she didn't recognise his voice as someone who was staying at the house. The engine was still running; the driver's door left open to the horizontal whipping rain. He grabbed her elbow and pulled her to her feet.

'Are you okay?' he asked. She couldn't tell whether he was angry or concerned. A bit of both, probably.

Of course, she isn't okay, she wanted to tell him. Do normal people lie in the road waiting to be driven over?

'What are you doing?' he shouted over the noise of rain hammering on the bonnet and roof of his car. A small red one. 'I nearly killed you.'

Yes, but you didn't, she thought.

She wished he had.

## Chapter Two

## Catrina

Six weeks ago, when Catrina opened the message in the new group chat Simone had created on WhatsApp named *Aged to Perfection*, her heart sank. For a while, Simone had been talking about a blow-out thirty-fifth birthday celebration at the end of September, and Catrina was looking forward to a girls-only weekend in Barcelona or Valencia - a posh five-star hotel, where they could sip strawberry-decorated Prosecco cocktails and giggle like they were back in high school. A wine-tasting weekend on a remote Scottish Island, where autumn is brief and winter is long, was not something she ever expected Simone to suggest.

'Because I have aged like a fine wine,' said the message, 'I would love you and Ryan to join me and Troy at the Hollow Pines hotel, Holm Island on Friday, 19th September. They will have a selection of the best wines and Champagnes paired with delicious food. Please say yes?'

Simone's husband, Troy, immediately posted a response in the group. 'Thank goodness she has finally decided on something. Now, I can go back to watching the footy and only pretending to listen.' He followed the message with a laughing face emoji to dissolve the sting.

'A selection of the best wines and Champagnes paired with delicious food?' Catrina replied. 'What do you know about those?' What she really wanted to say was, 'Where in the hell are we going, and why are you inviting Ryan and Troy? I thought it would just be girls.'

'Do you like that? I copied it from their website,' Simone replied, with the same laughing face emoji Troy had just used. 'But it will be fun. What do you think? Two nights away, doing absolutely nothing but eating and drinking.'

It is true, Catrina loves eating and drinking, and Simone knows that. But she was hoping for tapas and sangria in the sun with the girls, not haggis and sherry in the pissing down rain with boys.

'Of course, I will be there,' she replied. 'It sounds fun. Who else is going?'

'Just us four.'

Catrina wasn't sure whether that was better or worse than going with a large group. In a group, she could blend into the background, disappear to her room for an hour if she felt like it, and she wouldn't be missed. But the thought of her two best friends and her new boyfriend checking on her every move and making sure she was enjoying herself felt like too much pressure. But then again, she was glad Simone hadn't invited her family, as she didn't want to spend the weekend having to be sociable with Simone's parents and her supercilious high-flying sisters. They always made her feel inadequate and insecure, as though a job as a barista should only ever be a stepping stone to something better. A job for students on their way up the career ladder. They might be right, but Catrina enjoys her job and has no ambition to join them on their corporate hamster wheels.

When Simone rang her a few minutes later, she feigned enthusiasm and told her she couldn't wait. It would be brilliant. Yes, a break in Scotland is something different. We'll love it. Yes, she was *so* excited to try all the different wines - they are both Prosecco aficionados, but she agreed it would be interesting to try something different and learn about the regions where each wine was made. Simone assured her that they didn't have to spit them out. Whatever the snooty sommelier told them - she didn't care that they were the expert - she would not be spitting out her wine. Never in a million years.

'I presume you'll want to bring Ryan?' asked Simone. 'You know Troy loves him. Well, I love him, too, but if you bring him, the blokes can chat in the bar and watch football while we go to the pool.'

'They have a pool? An indoor one, I hope,' said Catrina. 'Scotland can be pretty wild in September.'

'Yes,' laughed Simone, 'of course, it's indoors, but who knows, I might skip the pool and go to the sea. Wild swimming is a thing, you know? Everyone's doing it these days.'

'Not in Manchester, they're not,' said Catrina. She couldn't help laughing at her friend's girlish enthusiasm. 'You give it a try, though, if you want. I'll hold your towel and take the video of you shivering as your lips turn blue.'

'I know we talked about Barcelona,' said Simone, 'but I saw a reel from this hotel on Instagram, and it's five-star luxury all round. Plus, we've never been to Scotland, have we?'

Catrina assured her that it was a great idea. After all, it was Simone's birthday, so it was her choice. As the weeks passed, Catrina began to warm to the idea.

Now, as she holds onto Ryan's hand in the dimly-lit, wooden-clad hotel reception, after the choppy crossing on the rusting old ferry, from which her stomach is just recovering, she is beginning to enjoy myself. It will be nice spending the whole weekend with Ryan, she thinks. This is their first trip away together.

Simone was right when she said Catrina can't keep putting her life on hold just because Lucas is no longer around. She can't keep holding Ryan at arm's length either; she knows that. She doesn't want to lose him. He is a lovely man. He is kind and generous, and in the three months they have been dating, they haven't yet had a cross word. He is good-looking, too, not in a Chris Hemsworth obvious way - his muscles don't burst out of his shirt, and his jawline isn't as strong - but his blue eyes twinkle with mischief, and he makes her laugh every day.

Catrina has to face facts: Lucas, the love of her life, isn't coming back. As Simone keeps telling her, it's been almost a year and, although she will never forget him, she needs to move on.

'So which one of you is the birthday girl?' asks the man behind the reception desk. He has an endearing Scottish accent, elongating 'you' and rolling the r in 'girl'. He dips his chin and peers over his round glasses at Catrina and Simone.

'It's me,' says Simone, demurely. 'But I won't tell you the number. You know you should never ask a lady her age?'

She giggles. Simone is a Black woman of Caribbean heritage, and despite having a husband more handsome than Idris Elba, she has always had a penchant for tall, stocky white men with ginger hair and brown eyes, ever since she dated that rugby player during her first year at university. This man, being exactly her type, brings the hint of a blush to her cheeks. His name badge shows that he is called 'Andrew'. Simone locks eyes with him. Catrina digs her surreptitiously on her back, which causes her to giggle even more. Simone flicks her a sideways look and winks, which confirms she is just having a bit of fun. Fortunately, Troy is on the other side of the room, reading the faded labels of dozens of bottles of whisky displayed in a tall, glass cabinet, and is oblivious to his wife's shenanigans.

'So, Catrina Blackwood and Mr Ryan Johnson are in room twelve, right at the back of the hotel, and Simone and Troy Bailey are in room eleven,' says Andrew. He flashes them a friendly smile. 'I made sure to give you adjacent rooms. I'm sure you will love them. Both rooms are up on the third floor.' Andrew pushes two key cards across the counter. Catrina picks them up while Simone signs the guest information sheet for them. 'Those rooms have the best views of the garden and the cliffs at the back of the hotel,' says Andrew. 'On a clear day, you can see right across the bay to the mainland. Not today, though, I'm sorry to say. The clouds are moving in thick and fast.'

'It might clear up later, do you think?' asks Simone. 'I haven't checked the forecast, but I've heard that Scottish weather is changeable, isn't it? Like four seasons in one day.'

'Aye, it's true, one minute it's raining cats and dogs, and the next minute the sun is out again. But, by the look of those clouds, they are set for the day.'

Catrina follows Andrew's gaze and looks out through the floor-to-ceiling picture window at the side of the revolving front door. The patches of clear sky are quickly diminishing as a blanket of clouds is blown towards the hotel.

'However, tomorrow might be a different story,' he says. 'When you open your curtains, who can tell what you might get? That's the beauty of Scotland.'

Troy returns to the desk, reading aloud from a leaflet he has picked up from somewhere. 'It says here that this place was built in 1903 by a whisky baron named Arthur

MacDonald.' He laughs. 'Everyone in Scotland is called Mac-Something, aren't they?'

Andrew laughs and tells them he is a MacDonald, too, a descendant of the original family. Troy continues to read as he grabs his and Simone's suitcase by the handle and pushes it towards the lift. 'Once a stately retreat built in 1903 by a wealthy whisky baron, Arthur MacDonald, because of its isolated location, Hollow Pines stood as the crown jewel of Holm Island for many years. During its lifetime, the house has been frequented by poets, artists, musicians, and aristocrats. It is here that the famous author, Terence Nightingale, wrote his Sunday Times bestselling novel *The Swirling Sea Mist* following romantic cliff top walks with his wife, the star of West End and Broadway theatre, Ivy Montclaire. The hotel is still owned by the MacDonald family and was restored and converted into a hotel in 1995.'

The lift doors open. Catrina and Simone step inside, followed by Troy and Ryan. Simone pushes the button for the third floor.

'You know, Terence Nightingale only became famous because he died shortly after writing that book?' says Ryan. 'The one about the swirling sea mist. He fell off the cliff, apparently. Smashed into smithereens on the rocks on the beach below.'

'No, really?' says Simone. 'That's awful.'

Ryan shrugs. 'We all have to die somehow, and at least his name lives on. There was a devastating storm in 1976, and he got caught up in it. He mysteriously disappeared after dinner and was found dead the next day when the search party was sent out to find him.'

'What a tragic way to go,' says Simone. 'His poor wife.'

'There was talk that the howling, hollowing wind that whispered through the pine forest at the front of the house was actually the ghost of Terence Nightingale calling out for help,' says Ryan. 'The family was frightened to set foot inside the house after dark, so they stopped coming. The house was boarded up for decades. It was only recently that the house was converted to a hotel.'

The lift doors open. They step out onto a luscious green tartan carpet. The narrow corridor is dark, lit only by a smattering of brass table lamps on square tables outside each door. Ripe for being knocked over after an enthusiastic wine tasting event. Room twelve is directly in front of the lift door. Room eleven is to its left. The dark mahogany doors and brass numbers are polished to a high sheen. It's old-fashioned, twee, and absolutely perfect.

'Really?' asks Simone. 'So, they called it Hollow Pines after the ghost?' Her eyes are wide and filled with excitement.

Ryan winks at Catrina and squeezes her hand. 'Yes,' he says. 'Why not?'

'You're so full of shit,' says Catrina. 'Hollow Pines is the name of the original house. Don't listen to him, Simone. He's trying to scare you. There are no ghosts around here.'

'You daft sod,' says Simone. 'I believed you for a minute.'

'He's making it all up,' says Catrina.

Troy lifts his palm, and Ryan gives him a high five. 'Great story, mate,' he says. 'See you in the bar in ten?'

'Make it five,' says Ryan, 'I'm gasping for a drink.'

'I'll get you back for that,' says Simone, taking a swing at him with her handbag.

## Chapter Three

## Ivy

Ivy has visited a fair few country house hotels that used to be someone's home. Most of them are sympathetically and tastefully done, redecorated, like they all are, in ubiquitous creams and whites with shiny tiled floors. Polished mirrors tend to sit behind the bar. Tasteful paintings by local artists tend to be hung behind the reception desk. There might be a discreet price tag hanging from the bottom right-hand corner, if anyone cared to ask the price. All traces of the former home are usually expunged. But to Ivy, Hollow Pines still feels like it used to. From the outside, it doesn't look much different, but when you have loved a place as a family home and spent many happy summers in it as a beloved guest of its owners, it is difficult to see it in any other light.

The huge sign at the bottom of the stone steps leading to the front door seems false; a prank, planted there by mischievous children, stolen from the real *Hollow Pines Hotel* down the road. Even the various bistro sets - round glass tables and cast iron chairs with colourful cushions dotted about the front porch - don't convince her. But she must confront the truth. This is no longer a private residence. This is no longer 1976. She is no longer amongst friends. She is here alone.

The taxi driver, taciturn and disinterested as he was throughout the journey here, has now decided he wants a conversation. Having hauled Ivy's suitcase from the boot of his car, he is clutching the handle as he gazes up at Hollow Pines. He looks enchanted and slightly overawed by the grandeur of the building, like a small child staring at his favourite kindergarten teacher, about to pass her an apple.

'It's a braw bit of architecture,' he says. 'It's over two hundred years old, you know. My daughter was wed here.'

'Oh, how nice,' says Ivy.

She begins to climb the stone steps, leaving him and his reverie on the gravel driveway. She is not interested in his daughter or her wedding. She wants to get to her room and lock herself away until she can leave tomorrow. The weather seems to be taking a turn for the worse, predictable for this time of year, she supposes, and despite her thick, woollen winter coat, she feels a distinct chill around her neck. All the more reason to go home. It is definitely ten degrees warmer back in London.

A middle-aged couple is sharing a pot of tea at one of the bistro tables. Small plates have the remnants of cake crumbs, and Ivy suddenly has a yearning to be met at the door with the promise of a warm drink and a slice of homemade cake. A sudden gust of wind shoots the lady's napkin from her knee onto the floor, and she chuckles as she bends to retrieve it. Her husband laughs too. Ivy turns away. She has seen enough of the couple's happiness, reminding her of how it used to be with her and Terence.

She pauses to catch her breath and turns back. The taxi driver is smiling to himself, snapping a photograph of the hotel on his phone. She ignores him and carries on.

At the top of the steps, she is dismayed to find the old front door is gone, replaced by one of those infernal glass circular ones. The ones that revolve. She hates them. There is never enough room inside each of the miniature cells. Ungainly shuffling whilst in close proximity to strangers is never elegant. She steps inside. Seconds later, she finds herself in the Great Hall, at least that's what they used to call it. The sweeping wooden staircase in the middle is still as grand as ever. Polished and gleaming. A large parlour palm sits in a deep blue ceramic pot halfway up, where the stairs bend to the left and right, on their way to the first floor. On the wall halfway up the stairs, Ivy spots the huge painting of the stag on the edge of a forest. He is roaring into the air, his head thrown back, mouth open, his breath visible in the cold dawn air. She always loved that painting. Barbara offered it to her once. She said she could take it home and hang it in her London flat above the fireplace. But Ivy told her it wouldn't be at home there, like it is here.

Her mind flashes with images of long-ago parties: a mountain of precariously stacked Champagne glasses, cigarettes held aloft between two scarlet-painted fingers, air-kisses, cloying perfume, loud music, and even louder conversation and laughter. Someone's arms entwined around someone else's legs on the stairs. She can almost feel them; the memory is so vivid. People always tended to congregate in the Great Hall. It is such a beautiful space.

'Good morning, welcome to the Hollow Pines Hotel. My name is Andrew MacDonald. May I take your name?'

Ivy notices the small reception desk on the left side of the room, sympathetically made to look as though it has always been part of the house. The wood is stained a deep brown to match the aged staircase. At one end of the desk sits a huge glass vase bursting with beautiful dahlias in rich autumnal tones of burgundy red, coral, and cream. She wonders if there is now a florist on the island. There never used to be, much to Barbara's constant chagrin.

The man behind the reception desk offers her a smile. It is warm and friendly, not corporate and forced. He has a look of Hugh about him, she thinks. The red hair, the sharp jaw line, the wide smile. He is the image of him, and it takes a second for her brain to compute that this is not the nineteen seventies. Hugh is an old man now. She wonders whether this younger version is related to him or whether she is imagining the resemblance. He has the same surname, but there must be hundreds of MacDonalds in this area. He could be his son. Or more likely his grandson. Time is shifting quicker than the dawn mist. Inside, Ivy still feels thirty-four, Hugh and Barbara are still the extravagant hosts, and Terence is still here, by her side in the Great Hall, helping her up the stairs with her luggage, then kissing her in the bedroom, twirling her around in the Ceilidh after dinner, lighting her cigarette as they rest for a moment between dances. Loving her.

'It's Ivy Montclaire,' she tells the Hugh-lookalike. She wants to ask him about his family tree, but decides to bide her time.

'Miss Montclaire.' His face lights up. He emerges from behind the reception desk, and now he is here, in front of her, taking both of Ivy's hands in his, as though they are lifelong friends. She wants to embrace him as though he were Hugh. She is expecting Barbara to appear at any moment and pull her into her soft bosom, suffocating her with her signature scent - a mixture of Elnett hairspray and Charlie perfume. That's what she loved about Barbara; she could have afforded the most expensive, luxurious perfume in the world, but she wanted to be ordinary. She wasn't showy. Charlie suited her perfectly. She wore it for years.

'My mother is a huge fan of yours,' says Andrew. 'She will be here later, if you wouldn't mind signing an autograph for her, it would make her day, I know it would. Would that be okay?'

'Of course, of course,' says Ivy, gently pulling her hands free, on the pretence of searching for her glasses in her handbag.

Andrew strolls back behind the desk. 'When she heard you were on the guest list, she wanted me to tell you she is a huge fan of the theatre, and she even went to Stratford to see you in that play.'

*That play?* 'Macbeth,' she reminds him. It was her finest hour. The pinnacle of her career. But who wouldn't be successful, riding on the waves of such brilliant words? Her job was easy. The script did all the hard work for her.

'Yes, that's the one.' He has the grace to blush.

'Don't worry, I know Shakespeare isn't for everyone,' she says. She doubts this young man has The Bard at the top of his favourites list, and she doesn't judge him for that.

'I'm not a fan, but my mother loves him,' he says. 'I haven't seen it, I'm afraid, but I heard you were fantastic.'

He begins to tap on the computer. Ivy is sure the words *back in the day* are on the tip of his tongue, but he doesn't say them.

'Do you mind me asking?' says Ivy, 'Are you related to Hugh and Barbara MacDonald? They used to live here many years ago.'

'Yes, my grandparents,' he says with a fond smile that suggests a close family bond.

'That's nice,' she says. 'On your father's side?'

'Yes, that's right.'

Barbara always wanted a boy, and Ivy is glad she had one. Being besotted with Hugh as she was, she would have adored a miniature version of him. Ivy wants to ask him how his grandparents are. She hasn't seen them since that summer, fifty years ago. If they walked in now, would they recognise each other? People say that age can be cruel to beautiful women, taking away their firm skin and glamour, leaving them with lined faces and drooping breasts, bending their spines and forcing arthritic feet into ugly shoes. But Barbara will still be stunning, Ivy knows she will. Her beauty shone from her soul, like sunlight breaking through soft rain clouds.

Andrew busies himself preparing Ivy's key card and printing the guest information sheet, which he asks her to sign. He doesn't ask her how she knows his grandparents. He doesn't have to. The stories about her and Terence and the parties thrown by Hugh and Barbara have been told a thousand times. Newspapers and magazines fought for exclusive snippets about the extravagant parties at Hollow Pines, filled with artists, writers, and musicians. Salacious gossip sold then, just as it does now.

'Your room is at the top of the house,' says Andrew, 'The third floor, just as you asked. I hope you enjoy your stay.'

Ivy specifically asked for a room on the third floor, which used to be where the staff slept when Hugh and Barbara were the owners of Hollow Pines. She wanted to be sure she wouldn't be accosted by unpleasant memories, which she would be if she opened a familiar bedroom door. The third floor is one part of the house she has never been to. She also asked for a room at the front, overlooking the pine forest, and the hotel's sweeping driveway. She and Terence used to sleep in the *White Room* at the back of the house on the second floor. Each of the bedrooms was named after a colour in those days. Hugh assured them that the *White Room* had the best view of the coastline and the sea beyond, and he was right. The corner bay window gave them an almost panoramic view of the cliffs and the steep grassy path leading down to the rocky shore. Ivy spent many hours lounging there in an armchair, her knees covered with a scratchy tartan blanket, sipping black coffee and knocking back headache pills after a late night, while Terence lay on the bed, his forearm draped across his eyes, a shield from the morning sun. Later, hangovers were compared and contrasted over breakfast in the dining room, which, actually, was more like lunchtime, by the time everyone was in a fit state to get themselves dressed, where more steaming coffee was poured from silver pots by ever-attentive staff into fine white porcelain cups. They nibbled on triangles of crustless toast, served with slivers of smoked salmon and a quarter of a lemon. They giggled, remembering the events of the previous night - quietly at first, until they began to feel better. When their stomachs were lined with good food, and the pills had shifted the headaches, they would start to become raucous again. Someone would have to shout to be heard. Someone would shout back. Shrieks of laughter would pierce their tender skulls, but youth allowed them to tolerate it. They bounced back from hangovers quickly and efficiently, ready to party again.

In those days, Ivy thrived on the companionship and noise that great friends brought. Nowadays, she is quite content to go for days and days without speaking to a soul.

The revolving door bursts into life, and the taxi driver and Ivy's suitcase are thrust into the hotel. She discreetly presses a ten-pound note into his hand, which he takes with an obsequious nod of the head. To her, the quiet journey was worth every penny.

'Thank you. I'll leave you in the capable hands of young Andrew, here,' he says. He seems to have come out of his shell now and is actually smiling. He glances around the room. Ivy can see he is transported to another world - the world of his daughter's wedding. She can imagine him as the proud father-of-the-bride, dressed in his family's tartan kilt, patent shoes polished, and jacket brushed. He would have been nervous about giving his speech, probably. His wife would have poured him a large whisky – liquid confidence in a glass - to get him through the ordeal. They both have fond memories of this place, it seems. Although Ivy has traumatic memories, too. Horrible, visceral memories.

The taxi driver tells her it was lovely to meet her and wishes her a nice stay. As he is leaving, she wants to shout after him to come back.

'Don't leave my suitcase here.'

'Don't leave me here.'

'I have changed my mind.'

'I want to go home.'

'Is there somewhere else I can stay for the night?'

'Can we leave now?'

Instead, she smiles at Andrew, signs the guest information sheet, and then follows his direction to the lift.

# Chapter Four

# Catrina

It doesn't take long for Catrina to unpack her stuff in the hotel room. She hasn't brought much with her. She hangs a dress in the wardrobe, puts her swimming costume, t-shirts and jumper (well, she didn't know what the weather would be doing, so she packed for all occasions) together with a spare pair of jeans in one of the deep drawers of an old pine chest. She then deposits her makeup bag on a shelf in the bathroom. The whole thing takes less than two minutes. Nevertheless, Ryan is begging her to hurry up. He *needs* a drink. He is perched on the edge of the bed like a racehorse jockey about to set off at The Derby. He wants to win the *How Much Booze Can You Handle?* race with Troy. The sign of a man, apparently. Neither of them will admit there is a competition, but Catrina knows there will be, and both of them will want to claim the prize. They have had an early start and a long journey, but his eagerness to start on the alcohol grates on her nerves. It shouldn't. They are here on a wine tasting weekend after all. Plenty of alcohol will be consumed over the weekend. By tonight, they will all be full to the rafters with it. So she takes a deep breath, counts to three, and tells herself to have more tolerance. Deep breath in, full breath out. Deep breath in, full breath out.

It doesn't seem to be working.

She is still irritated.

'I think I'm going to take a bath,' she tells him.

'What, now?' he says.

'Have you seen the bathroom? It's beyond luxurious, and there's a top-of-the-range bath oil with my name on it.' She gives him her biggest smile, which he once told her he can't resist. Okay, they were on a date in a candle-lit restaurant at the time, and they hadn't known each other long. They were in that 'can't wait to rip your clothes off' stage. But still, it's worth a try to get her own way and a little time to herself. She can see the disappointment in his face. He knows she is being distant. In all the months they have been together, he has never asked Catrina whether she still has feelings for Lucas, whether she is over him or not, but Catrina knows he wonders about it at times. He must do. Now, it is one of those times. If she were him, she would be wondering it, too. It's only natural that when someone has a significant ex, the new partner will be a little cautious. She waits for the barrage of questions – Is everything okay? What have I done wrong? Do you want to talk? - but they don't come.

This is the first time Catrina has been away without Lucas, after being with him for five years. Any fool would wonder how she was coping without him. On the surface, it might look like she has moved on, but the reality is, she hasn't. Not really. How could she move on so quickly? She has only been without him for eleven months. Next month will be the anniversary, which Catrina is dreading with all her heart.

She would love to talk to Ryan about Lucas. He knows the basic facts, but since their initial conversation on one of their early dates, when she told him what happened, Lucas's name hasn't been mentioned. She wishes Ryan would just ask her about him, face the Lucas-shaped elephant in the room. Maybe he doesn't want to because, if he did, he knows she couldn't lie to him, she thinks. She would have to tell him that, deep down, she still loves Lucas. Of course, she does. They were together for a long time; they shared a house; they had plans to get married, to have a future together. Love like that doesn't die so easily, does it?

'Well, if you're sure,' says Ryan. 'Do you want me to wait for you, or....?'

'No, no,' she walks over to him, into the gap at the end of his sentence, and he stands, arms open wide. She steps into his bear hug and wraps her arms around his neck. She gives him a long kiss, which she hopes conveys the message that he has nothing to worry about. She is with him now and will give him her full attention. At least she will try. 'I'll be half an hour, tops,' she says. 'I just feel a bit grubby after the journey, that's all. You know how I love a bath.'

'Okay, my darling, I'll see you in the bar. You take your time. Enjoy your bath.'

Damn it. Why does he have to be so nice? It makes her feel even more guilty than she already does.

When he's gone, Catrina messages Simone and tells her she needs a bit of space, but she won't be long. Simone sends a red heart emoji. She doesn't need to say anything else. She knows how Catrina feels about Lucas, and she knows this trip will be difficult for her. Catrina hasn't been anywhere since Lucas went missing last October. In the first few months, she was reluctant to leave the house at all, except to go to work, in case he suddenly reappeared and couldn't get in because he had lost his key somewhere along the way. She wanted to make sure she would be at home to welcome him. She bought extra milk for his coffee, and then poured it down the sink when it went out of date, before going to the corner shop and buying another litre bottle. She made sure to always have a stack of his favourite beer and kept their Sky Sports subscription for six months before cancelling it.

Troy was devastated when he went missing, too. Lucas was his best friend. The four of them were close, Simone and Troy, and Catrina and Lucas. They went on double dates at least once a month. They talked about having kids soon and bringing them up together, like cousins who weren't related. They had their future lives planned out, and Lucas's disappearance shook them all.

Simone and Troy have always wanted two or three kids. They have been trying for the past few months. Every time Catrina's WhatsApp pings with a message from Simone, she is expecting a photo of the little blue line in a pregnancy test. After Lucas disappeared, Simone and Troy began their family plans, leaving Catrina behind.

'Troy and I are trying for a baby,' said Simone. 'I mean, it might be ages before anything happens, but we have to start soon if he wants me to pop out two or three.'

Catrina gave a defensive laugh as Simone's eyes pleaded for her friend's consent. They were in a café in Manchester, each of them had bags of shopping at their feet. The January sales had long since finished. Simone had dragged Catrina out on the pretence that she needed some new summer stuff. 'I know you hate the sales,' she said, 'but they're done now and all the fresh stock is in.' What she meant was, it's time to stop moping around every weekend and get your arse off the sofa and into the outside air.

'You're going to be the best mum in the world,' Catrina told her. 'I hope you manage to get pregnant really quickly because I'm broody as hell and there's nobody else I know who has a baby for me to borrow.'

'We'll be roping you in for babysitting duties, don't you worry,' said Simone, with tears in her eyes. 'I hope it happens quickly, too, although not too quickly. I don't want a Christmas baby. I always feel sorry for people who have December birthdays. Everyone is too busy organising Christmas to give attention to their birthdays, and then they end up getting two presents in one. It isn't fair, is it?'

They were both born in September, which meant they were among the oldest in the class at school. Cartrina's mum told her never to have a baby in autumn or winter, as it meant having to wait an extra year to get them to school. Another year of expensive nursery fees. A summer baby was much cheaper. But Catrina knew that telling Simone to wait was futile. Lucas's sudden disappearance had awakened a fear in her, which is probably in everyone, that life can change at any time, and you have to make the most of every moment. Hence, the expensive weekend trip to Scotland, which most people would have saved for their fortieth birthday, not their inconsequential thirty-fifth.

Catrina lowers herself into the bath and splashes her arms with the coconut-and-lime scented water. The summer smell of the bath oil doesn't match the hotel's vibe, not one little bit. They seem to have got everything else right - the bagpipe music playing in the reception area, turned down low so it isn't overpowering; the tartan carpets; the wool throw on the bottom of the bed, and the whisky room-service menu in case you wanted a night-cap. But the bath oil is definitely more befitting of a tropical beach hotel. But she isn't complaining. It is beautiful and reminds her of sun cream.

She closes her eyes. She remembers her last holiday with Lucas, two weeks in a five-star hotel in Santorini. On the first evening, after a long, cool shower, they got dressed up and walked along the beach road, taking their time to choose somewhere special for dinner. Most of the restaurants had tables outside on the pavement, and some were actually on the beach. They chose a place that was busy with the locals. The sun had set, and the scorching heat of the day had cooled to a pleasantly tolerable warmth. Lucas ordered grilled octopus in a dressing of olive oil, lemon, and oregano, and Catrina had lobster spaghetti with a rich garlic and tomato sauce. It was the most delicious meal she had ever had. She can still remember what they were wearing. He had a white linen shirt over black linen shorts, and she wore a mint green sundress from Monsoon – ankle-length with tiny shoestring straps – with gold flat sandals.

'You look beautiful,' he said as they clinked their wine glasses together. 'Here's to a happy holiday.'

And it was a happy holiday. They went for slow jogs in the mornings, ate a late breakfast, and spent lazy afternoons by the pool. They held hands as they walked along the beach in their swimwear, before getting changed for an evening out. They hired a car and drove around the island, marvelling at the white-washed houses and tiny blue-topped churches. Then they climbed the steep steps on the Caldera cliffs and posed for photographs with the stunning view behind them.

Ryan's job as a teacher meant that he had to holiday in August, so wherever they went, they generally paid extra to stay in an exclusive adults-only hotel. He loved kids, but he didn't want to spend two weeks sunbathing next to a pool full of inflatable toys and lilos. He wanted peace. He wanted to listen to the sound of the birds, with the sea in the background.

The first time he told Catrina that he wanted to stay somewhere quiet, she laughed, thinking he was joking. It seemed contradictory. He was usually such a party animal - loud, boisterous, like an excitable puppy. Always the last man standing at a wedding or someone's party.

'The only noise I want to hear is the waiter's voice asking me if I want another drink,' he said.

'You're an old man in a young man's body,' she laughed. 'Are we going to be surrounded by pensioners?'

'Yes, hopefully,' he said. 'In my experience, they are well-behaved and civilised, and they sit and read all day without being a nuisance to anyone around them.'

So, over the years, she left it to him to choose the resort and the hotel. She told herself she wasn't fussy, as long as they were together. If he was happy, she was happy. She did have some reservations, but she didn't share them with him. She didn't tell him that she enjoyed the noise around the pool, that she loved seeing kids splashing in the pool and screaming with laughter, and that she loved the loud music from the pool bar, especially the foreign music that they didn't get to hear in Britain. She didn't want silence. She would rather sit up on her sun-lounger and watch the goings-on around them than lie horizontal with her eyes closed, missing everything, seeing nothing. But after their first trip together, she had to admit that she had never felt more relaxed. She could feel her soul thanking her for the peace. She didn't have the usual dread of having to go back to work. When the time came, she was ready for work. Her batteries were well and truly recharged.

Now, she pulls the bath plug with her toe and watches as the warm water swirls away, carrying her memories with it. It doesn't do any good to keep living in the past. Don't they say look back, but don't stare? She climbs out of the bath and wraps herself in one of the soft white towels.

Ryan is the one waiting for her in the bar, not Lucas. She needs to remember that.

## Chapter Five

## Ivy

If the hotel hadn't been full, and Ivy weren't such a people pleaser, she would have asked to be moved to another room. Taking the chance of being allocated a room she used to stay in with Terence is surely better than being in room number thirteen, she thinks as she steps out of the lift. But here she is, standing in what used to be the staff corridor on the third floor, about to spend a weekend in the unluckiest room in a hotel with more memories than she is ready to face. This trip has to be one of the worst decisions she has ever made. Her heart races. She is going to need another angina spray if she isn't careful. She tells herself to calm down as she pushes the door open. She is just being overly superstitious. Nothing bad is going to happen to her. Hugh and Barbara would never have had a *Room Thirteen* if they were in charge, but it doesn't mean she will be beset with bad luck. She might even enjoy the evening if she allows herself to, and before you know it, it will be tomorrow, and she can go home.

She is pleasantly surprised by the spaciousness of the room. Despite the fact that the walls are painted a deep, ocean blue, and the carpet is gunmetal grey, the room is light and airy thanks to two large bay windows. They are separated by a ceiling beam, which she concludes means that two rooms must have been knocked into one. In the old house, staff sleeping quarters would never have been as generous as this. Under one of the windows is a two-seater crimson velvet sofa sprinkled with various cushions that are decorated with woodland animals – hares, hedgehogs, and stags. She daren't sit in it; her old bones would never allow her to get out. A low wooden coffee table stands on a sheepskin rug between the end of the bed and the sofa. Leaving her suitcase by the door, she pulls off her shoes and sinks her toes into the delicious feel of the wool. On one end of the coffee table, a young spider plant sits in a baby-pink-coloured plant pot. At the other end is a small pile of paperback books, with a printed card that reads *Please visit our library on the ground floor for more books*. The books are dog-eared and well-read, and there are a couple that take her fancy, so she moves them to the bedside table and wanders over to the other window.

The view from the front of the hotel might not be as pleasant as that at the back, which looks out onto the cliffs, but Ivy prefers it. She is thankful they had a room to accommodate her wishes. Here, she can't hear the crashing waves of the sea, reminding her of the place where Terence died: just the gentle wind pushing its way between the pines, and the occasional car when its tyres crunch the gravel on the long driveway, reminding her that she isn't entirely alone.

She flops onto the king-size bed. The duvet cover is white and silky soft, the bottom half of which is covered by a woollen blanket, the same green tartan as the carpet in the corridor. MacDonald, Lord of the Isles. Hugh's family tartan. She runs her fingers over the various shades of green and down the white lines that separate the squares. She can see Hugh, one Midsummer's Eve in his MacDonald tartan kilt, his white shirt open at the neck, revealing the top of his hairy chest, holding his wine glass high above his head as he proposed a toast before dinner. His fingers precariously slipping from the stem before gripping it again. Red wine sloshing onto his steak and onto the pristine tablecloth. Barbara shrieking with laughter as she dabbed at it with her napkin, then flicking the red-stained napkin at Hugh's bare legs in mock admonishment.

'Friends, Romans, countrymen,' Hugh bellowed over the noise. 'Oi, quiet now. You there, shush. Trying to be serious here. Let's make a toast.' He stepped back, stumbling over nothing but his own feet. He looked down at them, concentrating hard. He took a cautious step forward, moving closer to the table, where he clung to the tablecloth like an adrift sailor being thrown a lifebuoy.

'Steady, old man,' someone shouted.

'Am perfectly steady, fank you very mush,' he slurred. His glazed eyes searched the faces at the table, but unable to find the advice-giver, he collapsed back onto his chair, a giggling heap of drunkenness. His toast was forgotten as they all tucked into the delicious meal. More wine was poured into his glass by one of the staff. That was one of the rules of Hollow Pines - nobody should ever get to the bottom of an empty glass. Nobody ever did.

Ivy reads from the information pack on the coffee table that dinner is to be served in the main dining room to the right of the staircase. It reads, '*6.30 for 7.*'

'*6.30 for 7*'. Whenever she hears the phrase, she thinks of Terence. He used to hate that wording.

'What time do they want us there, six-thirty or seven?' he complained on their first trip to Hollow Pines. It was the summer of 1970.

'Well, it's just what Barbara said, they want us there at six-thirty, so we're ready to eat at seven.'

'So just say six-thirty, then everyone knows what's what.'

'It's flexible,' said Ivy. 'You can arrive whenever you like, between six-thirty and seven.'

'Bloody ridiculous,' he grumbled.

He had been in a bad mood for months, all year in fact. The swinging sixties were over, and Terence was dragged into the seventies kicking and screaming. He was thirty that year and was dreading it. Ivy still had five years to go.

'I don't want to be thirty,' he persistently told her, as though saying it often and loud would make it true. 'I am not ready to be an adult. I want to be twenty-one still, just getting the key to my parents' front door. I don't want to say goodbye to my youth.'

They were in his tiny one-bedroom flat in Fulham, squashed together on his single armchair that he had picked up from the charity shop at the end of the road, when midnight arrived on 30th April, bringing with it Terence's birthday on the first day of May. Neither of them had any money in those days. He was a low-paid journalist working for a not particularly popular rag. She was an aspiring actress, although she spent more of her working hours behind the bar at the Dog & Duck than she did on the stage. They had been dating for a year and a half by then, spending every moment together, friends and family temporarily sidelined, as though snatched time between their work commitments was too precious to spend with anyone other than each other. He took a drag on his cigarette and closed his eyes as he blew out the smoke. Ivy listened to his mantel clock chime twelve.

'That's it then,' he said. 'Midnight. I'm officially old.'

Ivy began to sing *Bridge Over Troubled Waters*, collapsing into giggles after only a couple of lines.

'It isn't funny,' he said. 'There *are* tears in my eyes. Look.

And times *are* rough.' He pushed himself away from her and marched to the door. 'I'm going to bed,' he said. Then, 'Are you coming?' as though he had just remembered his manners.

The proposal she had expected as he turned thirty didn't come. She told herself to be patient. They hadn't been dating long, not really. Everyone knew that weddings were expensive and her parents didn't have enough money to foot the bill. She and Terence would need to save for it. She would think long and hard about how to broach the subject.

She followed him desolately, her mood now matching his. Suddenly, she was tired. Her joy snuffed out like a birthday candle. As she climbed into bed, she stubbed her toe on his gift, which she had hidden underneath the bed for him to open first thing in the morning. A portable typewriter in its brown, faux-leather case, complete with a handle. It was crimson red; his favourite colour. She had been saving for three months, shoving pound notes underneath the mattress at every opportunity, and was excited to give it to him. As she closed her eyes, she prayed that he would be in a better mood when he woke up.

That summer, the typewriter made the journey with them on their first trip to Hollow Pines, and every afternoon, while Ivy languished in the bath before their evening meal, Terence would bash out the last few chapters of what would later become his first novel.

With just two days to go before they were due to go home, he typed those precious words *The End*. He pulled his glasses off and threw them into the air. They landed on the soft eiderdown on the bed. Ivy came out of the bathroom just as he was pulling the sheet of paper out of the typewriter.

'I've done it, I've done it. I've finally typed *The End*.'

He picked her up and swirled her around effortlessly.

The bath towel and the last lines of his book were discarded as he pulled her onto the bed. His previously grumpy mood had finally lifted. That night, when the two of them were late for dinner, Hugh and Barbara didn't bat an eyelid. They were the most gracious hosts. That summer, Ivy was just getting to know them, but already felt like they were lifelong friends.

# Chapter Six

## Ivy – June 1972

On Midsummer's night, they danced on the rear patio through the night. Hugh and Barbara had invited dozens of people to their party – friends from the island and two of Hugh's cousins. The house was full and extremely noisy. The record player and its two speakers had been pushed towards the open French doors of the drawing room, and the men took turns to flip the vinyl over or nudge the needle when it stuck. Piles of records were stacked in a cardboard box, waiting to be played.

Nobody seemed to notice when the sun finally went down shortly after ten-thirty. At some point, candles were lit and placed in the middle of the outdoor dining table. Blankets had appeared, but it was so warm - heat mainly generated by alcohol and dancing - that they were cast aside and lay in various heaps on the flagstones.

When dawn appeared at four-thirty, Ivy suggested coffee and took herself off to the kitchen to make some, leaving Terence on a swing-seat with one of Hugh's cousins, a lanky young woman, not long out of college, who fancied herself as a model. The persistent flicking of her hair and the crossing of her legs were irritating to the women, but mesmerising to the men, most of whom had been watching her throughout the night.

At one stage earlier in the evening, she had tossed her platform shoes into the flower border, lifted her skirt high, and skipped across the lawn, twirling around like Giselle waiting for the disguised Duke of Albrecht. Ivy caught Barbara's eyes, and they smiled conspiratorially as Barbara rolled her eyes. Ivy watched Terence watching the dancer. But Terence had always been sensitive, spiritual even, and as soon as he felt Ivy's eyes on him, he looked over to her and smiled. He waggled his forefinger in a *come-hither* fashion and winked. Ivy shot over to him, and within minutes, he was hers again. His temporary waywardness forgiven. She couldn't blame him for looking, not really. Men are hard-wired to be drawn to the beauty of a woman, aren't they? As they stood close, hip to hip, he began to run his fingers up the back of her top, and her bare skin goosebumped at his touch. As he kissed her neck, thoughts of the Giselle-wannabe were dismissed.

Later, in the kitchen, as Ivy filled the kettle with water for the coffee, she watched Terence through the dusty window above the sink. She had to stand on tiptoes, as her shoes, like the ballerina's, had long since been discarded somewhere. Terence was laughing. The ballerina laughed, too. Which one of them had told the hilarious anecdote, Ivy couldn't tell, but the young woman found whatever it was so hilarious that she had to balance herself by holding tightly onto Terence's knee. She was sitting back on the swing-seat, kicking her delicate legs to and fro, her toes accidentally (on purpose) making contact with Terence's calf every now and then.

Ivy watched the ballerina's hand as it stayed on Terence's knee a second too long. Two seconds. Three seconds. Then it began to move up his thigh. She wasn't laughing by this time. She was pouting. Her young chin lifted her face towards Terence's. Another flick of the hair, which was immediately blown back into her face by the warm summer wind. Terence wanted to move it, to tuck it behind her ear out of the way, Ivy could tell. That's what he did with her. He loved long hair. She watched his indecisive hand, waiting for the movement that would signify betrayal.

'Sandra, there you are!' Barbara appeared at their side. Terence sat up straight, as though caught red-handed doing something naughty. His indiscretion showed as two circles of pink in his cheeks. 'I've been looking for you,' said Barbara. She grabbed Sandra's wrist and pulled her to her feet. No longer Giselle – just plain Sandra.

Ivy thanked Barbara afterwards. In the early morning, when most of the guests had said goodnight and staggered to their rooms, she and Barbara were sipping their second, or maybe third, coffee in the drawing room. The French doors were still open, reaching out into a new day. The temperature had dropped, and they had each reached for a blanket, which they had strewn around their shoulders. Ivy wasn't tired. She often found it hard to sleep until she had fully sobered up. She told Barbara what she had seen through the kitchen window. She saw Terence's hesitation. He wanted to touch Sandra. He was entranced by her. Barbara called the girl a witch, which Ivy said was a bit harsh. Barbara laughed, and they both knew that Ivy was only saying that to be polite. Ivy thought she was a witch, too.

'Flirting with someone else's man like that,' said Barbara, 'not on my watch, let me tell you. The little minx was sent to her room with a flea in her ear.'

'She's a little old to be sent to her room, don't you think?' said Ivy.

'I dinnae care,' said Barbara. 'She went on her own accord when I told her how alcohol and late nights would impact her complexion, so on this occasion, I did nae have to get the pistols out.' Barbara's accent was more pronounced when it was just the two of them, which made Ivy laugh.

She put her coffee cup down on the side table and tossed the blanket onto the floor. 'I'm ready for my bed now,' she said. 'Are you coming up?'

'Aye,' said Barbara. They held each other's hands as they slowly stumbled their way upstairs. 'You've got a good one there,' she said as they parted at the door to the *White Room*. Barbara and Hugh's room was the *Lilac Room*, further down the corridor. 'He wouldn't have taken her up on any offer, you know that, don't you?'

'Yes, I know, I know,' said Ivy, nodding vigorously, more to convince myself than to convince Barbara. As she opened the bedroom door, she was almost shocked to see Terence fast asleep on top of the bed. Part of her didn't think he would be there. She expected him to have followed Sandra to her room. He was snoring softly, still fully clothed, except for his shoes. She took a folded blanket from the top of the wardrobe, shook it out, and covered him with it. She unzipped her dress, stepped out of it, and lay beside him, tucking herself into his back.

'What time is it?' he whispered. He turned his head and his breath smelt like whisky.

'Shhh, go back to sleep,' she said.

'I love you,' he whispered. Within seconds, he was back to sleep, his breathing deep and regular.

In the morning, young Sandra was quiet, subdued, even. She appeared at breakfast with no makeup and her unbrushed hair tied into a high ponytail. As she took a slice of toast from the pile in the middle of the table and began to spread it with butter and strawberry jam, Ivy saw her for what she was - a woman much younger than her, and some might say more attractive, but no threat. Not really. In the cold light of day, she was much more ordinary than the temptress she had appeared to be the night before. She was small - a good couple of inches smaller than Ivy, which made her feel better. Terence always said how much he loved the fact that Ivy was tall and elegant. He didn't want to strain his neck to kiss her standing up. They were equal in so many ways. Terence said good morning to her, as they all did, but then continued his conversation with Hugh.

The perceived threat was over. Ivy didn't know why she had worried in the first place.

## Chapter Seven

## Catrina

Catrina tries to shake thoughts of Lucas from her head as she gets dressed after her bath. The truth is, she is tired of carrying the weight of Lucas-related sadness. She wants to shake him off and feel free. She is tired of missing him. She wants to enjoy this weekend, for her sake and for Simone's. She doesn't want to ruin her friend's birthday weekend by being miserable. She will feel better after a few glasses of wine, she tells herself.

In her mind, she has been treating Ryan as second best, and from now on, this has to stop. He gets on well with Troy and Simone, her parents and her brother love him, so she should be thankful that she has met such a kind and caring man; they are thin on the ground once you reach thirty-five. All the good ones have already been snapped up and marched down the aisle quicker than you can say 'dating profile.'

She knows that Simone worries about her and is giving her all the time in the world to get over Lucas. She is the best friend anyone could wish for, but Catrina also knows that Simone's patience doesn't come from a bottomless pit. It will run out one day, it is bound to. She sends her another message to let her know that she is on my way and will see her in the bar shortly. While she has her phone in her hand, she sends a message to Tom, her brother, telling him they have arrived safely in Scotland and the hotel is lovely. She adds that he should bring Lottie here one day. She would love it.

Tom was one of the last people to see Lucas before he disappeared. A group of them had gone to London for Tom's stag party one weekend last October. There were ten of them, mainly Tom's friends from work, Catrina and Tom's dad, and Lucas. Initially, Lucas wasn't sure about going. He complained that he wouldn't know any of Tom's friends and was worried that Tom would feel obliged to 'babysit' him, to make sure he was enjoying himself. He said he didn't want to be a burden, so it would be better if he declined the invitation. Catrina told him that was nonsense and persuaded him to go, something she has tortured herself about ever since. After all, if he hadn't gone to London, he might still be here with her.

Of course, Tom would tell her that was rubbish. Yes, that weekend was the last social event where Lucas was seen, but he would have gone missing whether or not he had gone to London. If that's what someone wants to do, nobody can persuade them to change their mind. He is right, of course. It seems that, for whatever reason, Lucas wanted to go missing, which is exactly what he did. If he hadn't gone that weekend, he would have gone the next.

Is it better for Catrina that he is missing, and not dead? Initially, she thought it was. For months, she lived with hope every day, which is surely a better bedfellow than despair. Although the truth is, now she isn't entirely sure. Hope is deceiving. Hope lies to you, tells you what you want to hear, like an unfaithful boyfriend. Hope makes you think one thing when the opposite is true. Hope gaslights.

Sometimes, she wishes Lucas had died. At least she

could learn to live with the finality of it all. Now, all she lives with are questions. Lucas wasn't - isn't - the type to disappear off the face of the earth. Why would he? He didn't have any money problems. He wasn't depressed. He had a good relationship with Catrina and with his family, and he had a good job as a Science teacher at a school less than three miles away from where they lived. An easy commute, lots of school holidays, and nice middle-class kids, from what he told her. No dreaded Ofsted inspections and discipline issues. Why would he go missing? Why would he abandon his life? Why would he abandon her?

She had explained to the police woman who visited his parents' house in Preston that he wasn't the type to do this. He loved her. They loved each other. Why would he leave her?

'Why would he leave any of us?' his mum had said. Animosity filled the living room as she glared at Catrina; the love and closeness they had built over the past five years were destroyed in a moment, like tower blocks reduced to rubble in a demolition.

Lucas's dad gripped her hand. 'He wouldn't, love, we know that,' he said. 'He would never leave us in limbo like this.'

'They must have had a row,' his mum said, pointing to Catrina, who was sitting on the sofa on the other side of the living room. His mum had dark shadows beneath her swollen red eyes. A crumpled tissue was being twisted and pulled apart by her fingers. 'They weren't on the best of terms. Ask her. She can tell you. They were always bickering.'

The police woman and Lucas's parents waited for Catrina to elucidate, to tell them how she and Lucas had argued and how he had threatened to leave the toxic relationship he found himself trapped in. But it wasn't true.

They loved each other. They were happy. His mum didn't understand their banter, which was never taken seriously by either of them. They certainly weren't the bickering type. They had their future planned. Catrina tried to explain to his mum that everything was fine between them, but she refused to believe it. It was easier for her to have someone to blame.

'Tell me again about your last conversation with him,' the police woman said.

Catrina had gone over the story countless times, with Lucas's family, her family, the police from London, and now the police in Preston, but she was happy to tell them again. Anything to help.

'I rang him in the early hours of the morning,' said Catrina. She opened her phone, located the call log, and held it up for the police woman to see. 'Sunday morning, 20th October. Look, outgoing call, less than two minutes long.'

The police woman noted down the time of 02:34. 'That's very late to be calling someone,' she said. 'Was that arranged between the two of you, that you would ring at that time?'

'No, but I was missing him. I thought he might be awake, you know, having just come out of a nightclub or something.'

'Checking up on him, more like,' said Lucas's mother. 'You didn't trust him, did you?'

The police woman waited for Catrina to respond.

'That's not true,' she said. 'I did trust him. I wanted to speak to him, that's all.'

'What did he say exactly?' asked the police woman.

'Well, I asked him if he was awake, and he laughed and said he hadn't been, but he was now. He hadn't turned his phone to silent. It's something we both do. If one of us is out, we keep our phones on until we are both home safely, in case we need each other.'

The police woman nodded. 'Go on.'

'I asked him if he was drunk, and he said only a little bit. He wasn't happy, though, like I expected him to be after a good night out. I could tell there was something wrong. I expected him to tell me that he had had an argument with one of the lads, and there had been a fight or something. You know what stag parties can be like?'

The police woman continued to scribble in her book. 'Yes, I do,' she said. 'You see plenty of them in my job, unfortunately.'

'So I asked him how his night had been, and he started crying, and said he wasn't coming home.' Catrina stifled a sob; took a deep breath. 'His exact words to me were, "I'm not coming home, Catrina. I'm sorry. Tell my parents that I love them, but I'm not coming home."'

'Why didn't he ring me?' cried his mum.

'I don't know, Sue,' she said. 'I don't know.'

'Carry on,' said the police woman gently. 'What else did he say?'

Catrina took another deep breath. 'I have never heard him cry before, in all the years we have been together, and I almost laughed because I thought he was drunk. I told him not to be ridiculous. He had train tickets booked for later that day, sometime in the afternoon; they all did. They were all coming home together.'

'What did *he* say?' repeated the police woman.

'He said, "I'm not being ridiculous. Goodbye, Catrina," and he hung up.'

'She's lying,' Lucas's mum shouted. 'I don't believe her. Why didn't he message me? Why didn't he ring me? You must have had an argument. There's got to be more to it. You just don't want to admit to it. This is your fault. This is all your fault.'

She pushed herself out of the chair and ran from the room. Catrina listened to her slippered footsteps running upstairs. The slam of the bathroom door reverberated down her spine like a crack of thunder.

Lucas's dad followed his wife upstairs. The police woman, seemingly impassive to the trauma they were engulfed in, continued to examine Catrina's phone. No doubt she had seen it all before, families imploding before her eyes like cities crumbling in an earthquake.

'I'm not lying,' Catrina told the police woman. She nodded. Catrina wasn't sure whether that was confirmation that she believed her, or merely confirmation that she had heard her. The only thing she knew to be true was that Lucas had not come home with Tom and their dad, and the rest of the blokes from the stag party. His bank cards, his phone, and all his clothes were found in his hotel room. His passport had disappeared from his bedside table at their house, where it was usually kept, which told her that he had planned the whole thing. The strange thing is, there has been no trace of him since he was seen leaving the hotel in Mayfair shortly after their phone call. CCTV had shown him disappearing into a crowd pouring out of a nightclub close to the hotel. After that - nothing.

Catrina has often wondered how long he had planned it. Nobody can disappear in London without being traced by the thousands of cameras everywhere. He must have changed his clothes somewhere. He must have changed his appearance: a false beard, a wig, a hat pulled low over his eyes. Who knows?

After a week of no contact, Tom told her to forget him. He had called round after work to see how she was. He was furious that his stag party had now been tainted and, if Lucas didn't show up soon, his wedding would be tainted too. His wife-to-be, Lottie, would be furious if anything ruined her big day, he said, the day she had been planning since she was a little girl. Lucas was acting like a selfish prick.

'Oh, fuck off, Tom,' Catrina had screamed at him. 'The love of my life has gone missing, and all you can think about is your bloody wedding.'

'No, that's not…'

'Get out! Get out of my house!' She pushed him angrily towards the door, and he slunk away. He gave her a backward glance as she slammed the door behind him. His face was full of contrition and hurt. Catrina should have pulled the door back open and begged him to come inside and finish his coffee, but she let him go. He drove away while she slid to the hall floor, wrapped her arms around her knees, and sobbed.

Half an hour later, Lottie was at the door. Catrina didn't answer at first, but Lottie lifted the letterbox and peered inside.

'Catrina, let me in,' she said. 'I can see you. You can't sit in the hall all night; it's freezing. You know when you get cold, the blood supply to your face disappears, and over time, it damages your capillaries. You'll look like an old lady in no time. Trust me. No amount of expensive face creams will be able to reverse the damage.'

Catrina managed a smile. As she opened the door, Lottie pulled her into a warm embrace and wrapped Catrina in her arms. She stroked the back of her head as she leaned on her shoulder and wept. She told Catrina what an insensitive wanker Tom could be at times. He didn't mean what he said.

'My wedding won't be ruined,' she said. 'He shouldn't have said that. Yes, it will be sad if Lucas isn't there, but we will get on with it, won't we? Who knows, that might be the day he decides to turn up, and if he does, we will treat him like the Prodigal Boyfriend, feed him fatted calf and make him welcome.'

Tom and Lottie were married on 2nd November, two weeks after Lucas disappeared. The wedding was as expected – extremely emotional. Catrina did her best to keep it together – the day wasn't about her, and she didn't want to be the centre of attention. As it was, she felt too many eyes on her throughout the day; friends, aunties, her mum checking on her every few minutes, ready to pounce with tissues and a glass of wine if there was any trace of tears. After the meal, when the lights were lowered and the DJ began to play his set, and the dance floor began to fill, Tom and Lottie went to her and gave their blessing for her to leave early, if she wanted to. They said she could sneak away while everyone was distracted by Beyoncé. Nobody would notice. Locking herself in her hotel room with a giant bar of chocolate and Netflix for company sounded more appealing to Catrina than anything in the world, but she wouldn't do it. She kissed them both and told them she appreciated their concern and loved them dearly, but she wanted to stay to the end.

'Yay,' said Lottie, as she dragged Catrina to the dance floor. *Should Have Put a Ring On It* was just starting. Instead of crumbling, she did her best Beyoncé impression and gradually began to enjoy herself.

Lucas didn't do his Prodigal Boyfriend appearance. Not that day, or any day since.

# Chapter Eight

# Ivy

Ivy can hear loud voices and laughter in the corridor on the other side of the door. She used to love this time at Hollow Pines, just before the start of the evening, when the house was filled with anticipation and hope. It is almost six-thirty now. She is ready, wearing a calf-length woollen dress, the colour of autumn heather, with thick black tights and black leather shoes. If she is quick, she could join the other guests she can hear on the other side of the door. That way, she won't have to arrive in the dining room alone. But in the time it takes for her to make a decision, they have gone. She hears the gentle ping of the lift as it arrives to take them downstairs. As their voices taper off, she is left in silence. Once again alone.

    She drops her gold necklace onto the bedside table. Her attempts at fastening it have failed; her arthritic fingers aren't conducive to delicate movements these days. Her fingers touch her neck involuntarily. It feels bare without jewellery, but there's nothing she can do. If Terence were with her, he would do it for her, but she has to accept that it is time for this particular necklace, with its tiny clasp, to be confined to her jewellery box. Terence used to love fastening her necklaces, not because Ivy couldn't do them, but because, he said, he loved to kiss the back of her neck as she held her hair out of the way. She remembers the string of pearls he bought her for her thirtieth birthday. She wanted to wear them immediately. She took them out of their box and held them tight while he fastened them, her eyes closed as she concentrated on his kisses.

The telephone next to Ivy's bed startles her from her memory back to the present.

'Good evening, Miss Montclaire,' says a young woman. 'We will be serving dinner at seven o'clock. Will you be joining us?'

'Yes, of course,' says Ivy. 'I'll be right there.'

It is almost five to seven by the time she reaches the dining room. Time slipped away from her again. Her being-fashionably-late days are over, and as she creeps into the room, following the waiter to her allocated table, she hopes nobody will notice.

'Here you are,' says the waiter, indicating a table where three young women and two men are already seated. He pulls out her chair, and she sits down to a chorus of greetings from her fellow diners.

'Hello, I'm Catrina,' says the woman next to her. 'This is my boyfriend, Ryan, and my best friend, Simone, and her husband, Troy.' Ivy nods hello to everyone.

'I'm Beth-Ann,' says the woman directly to her left.

'Good to meet you all,' says Ivy. 'I'm hopeless with names, but I will try my best to remember everyone. It isn't just because I'm old. I've always been the same.'

They all laugh politely.

'Why don't we go around the table and say one interesting thing about ourselves? That way, you might be able to remember who we are,' says Catrina.

'I doubt it, but it sounds like fun,' says Ivy.

She remembers Hugh and Barbara used to do something

similar when they had a group of people who didn't know each other. In those days, they had to say silly things such as the most bizarre place they had found themselves after a night out, or the most notorious nightclub they had been thrown out of. Terence tended to win that one.

'I'll start,' says Catrina. 'I'm Catrina and I work in a coffee shop in Manchester. Contrary to popular belief, I'm not named after the lady in the famous rock band.'

Ivy doesn't understand what she's talking about, but laughs with the others anyway.

'My name is Ryan, and my claim to fame is that I once asked the most beautiful woman out on a date.' He looks at Catrina, and everyone groans. 'Anyway, she said no, so I asked Catrina out instead.'

The table erupts with laughter, and Catrina punches Ryan's arm. Ivy instantly decides that she likes him.

'I'm Simone, and I'm a teacher. Tomorrow is my birthday, hence the trip here. I intend to drink nothing but wine all weekend long. Fortunately for me, Monday is an inset day, so I have plenty of time to recover.'

'I'm Troy, and as Simone's husband, it looks like I'll be the sober, responsible one who has to look after this reprobate. I'm a solicitor from Manchester, so I'm that kind of guy. An upstanding citizen.' He laughs, showing straight, white teeth. He's extremely handsome, thinks Ivy.

'Never in a million years,' says Simone. 'Don't listen to him.'

'I'm Beth-Ann,' says the woman next to her, 'and I am a travel writer.'

She looks like someone who would have a glamorous job. Designer glasses nestle in her thick, chestnut hair, which flows onto her shoulders in soft curls. Her fingers are adorned with gold rings set with various stones – a ruby, an opal, and a huge sapphire surrounded by sparkling diamonds, like the one Prince Charles gave to Lady Diana when they got engaged. Her forehead has the shine of someone who regularly has Botox treatments. There are women like her all over London. The type who wear sunglasses when it isn't sunny and who would be appalled to be spotted choosing something from the reduced section in Waitrose.

'Pleased to meet you,' says Ivy.

'I'm here to write an article about the wine weekend for *The Independent Traveller* magazine,' says Beth-Ann. She looks at Ivy, nodding enthusiastically, apparently waiting for her to say she is a loyal reader. Ivy doesn't tell her that she never heard of it - she knows from Terence that writers have delicate egos. 'I usually specialise in city hotels in London and Europe,' she says, 'but I'm trying boutique hotels in the British countryside, starting with the Scottish islands.'

Is this what this is, a boutique hotel? Is that what Hugh and Barbara would like it to be called? Ivy wonders what Barbara thinks of the place now. Surely she would love it. She would love to see the dining room filled with life and laughter, as it is tonight. As it used to be in the seventies. Barbara often told her that the house deserved to be filled with people. It was too beautiful to be empty. It needed to be admired. She said that in the winter, after the parties were over and the revellers had gone back home, she could feel the atmosphere shift. The house seemed forlorn, sad that the laughter and music were no longer there.

Before the conversation can progress and Ivy can give them her interesting fact, they are interrupted by a couple of waiting staff. The older one explains that tonight they will be served an Australian menu, with a crisp, white Australian wine. He places king prawns covered in creamy garlic sauce in front of them, while the other waiter pours a splash of Tasmanian sparkling wine into glasses, telling the group how the pairing has been chosen. Something about a light body and fruit notes, and acidity cutting through the richness of the sauce. Hugh and Barbara would laugh, thinks Ivy. Everyone expected them to be wine snobs - they certainly had the money to buy the best bottles - but they weren't at all. Drink whatever you want with whatever you want, they would tell everyone. Bottles of red, white, and rosé were gathered in the middle of the dining table back then. As one bottle emptied, it was immediately replaced by another from their extensive wine cellar.

Ivy takes a sip of the wine, just to be sociable. Alcohol doesn't mix well with her painkillers, so she needs to take it easy. Another thing Hugh and Barbara would laugh at - how old age interferes with social plans.

The two men slug their wine in one mouthful, and Ryan asks Catrina to catch the waiter's eye so that they can have a top-up. She tells him that it doesn't work like that. He will have to wait for the next course and the next wine, which will be something different. Her tone is that of a mother reprimanding a feckless teenager at a family wedding, knowing that too much alcohol will lead to embarrassment for them both. Ivy wonders how long the couple has been together. Catrina is wearing the forced smile of someone at the end of her relationship tolerance level. Every now and then, her eyes flick to the door and then over her shoulder to the other diners, and back again. Ivy wonders who she is looking for.

One thing is certain: the man sitting next to her isn't the object of her attention.

## Chapter Nine

## Ivy

It is almost ten o'clock by the time Ivy and her dining companions leave the dining table. By now, most of the hotel guests are drunk. The women are giggly, the men are lascivious and flirty with them. Just how it should be, thinks Ivy. Just how it used to be at Hugh and Barbara's parties.

Andrew had appeared at her table as the main course was being taken away and introduced Ivy to his mother, Hugh and Barbara's daughter-in-law, which led to gasps and a barrage of questions from her new friends at the table about who she was, or more exactly, who she had been. When giving the interesting fact about herself, she had simply said that she had lived in the same house in Beckenham for thirty-three years, and there really wasn't much else to say.

'This lady is the famous Ivy Montclaire,' declared Andrew's mother, as Ivy signed her autograph on the back of an old photograph she had brought with her. 'A legend of the theatre; a national treasure.'

Catrina, Simone, and Beth-Ann all admitted to being in love with the theatre, which was a joy to Ivy's ears. They asked her if she had been in anything they may have seen.

Ivy told them about the honour of playing Lady Macbeth at Stratford, but that was many years ago, in the nineteen-eighties, before they were born. She had also played Sybil Birling from *An Inspector Calls* in the West End. Surprisingly, only Simone had heard of J.B. Priestley. She had studied English Literature and Drama at university. She told Ivy she had spent all her spare money on going to the theatre, and she still goes whenever she can. They have such wonderful theatres in Manchester. Giving Ivy an apologetic smile, she said she had never seen An Inspector Calls on the stage, but she loved the film, so Ivy did what women do, and played down her part, literally, by telling her it was only a short run and Simone would have been far too young to see it at the time. In reality, the play was a great success and ran for months. Extra days kept being added to the schedule as tickets sold out, again and again.

Ivy wanted to spend more time with Andrew and his mother, so she could ask them about Hugh and Barbara. Where are they? Are they well? Will they be coming this weekend? But Andrew, seeing she was being bombarded with questions from all around the table, said he didn't mean to interrupt and that he would see her around. Ivy reluctantly allowed them to leave; his mother clutching the signed photograph to her chest, a broad smile on her face.

Andrew isn't behind the reception desk now. Ivy swallows down her disappointment, telling herself she shouldn't expect him to still be working at such a late hour. He can't be on duty night and day. In his place is a plastic sign that reads *Reception Desk Closed.* A tall man in a dark suit, white shirt, and a MacDonald Lord of the Isles tartan tie, as smart as any of the doormen at The Savoy, is guarding the front door. The night watchman. He holds his arms behind his back, his back straight. Ivy wonders whether he is a failed policeman or a soldier, the drill sergeant's commands still ringing in his ears.

For a second, she contemplates asking him when Andrew will be next on duty, but she doesn't want to be any trouble. What does she expect Andrew to do? Telephone his grandparents and tell them an old friend is staying at the family hotel? Will they race here from wherever they are and leap across the fifty-year chasm? It's unlikely, she knows that. She tells herself that if she and Hugh and Barbara had wanted to keep in touch with each other over the years, they would have. The fact that she now doesn't know where they are living, or whether they are in fact still alive, means their friendship died a long time ago. She is wise enough to acknowledge that much, if not all, of the fault for that lies at her door.

'We're having a nightcap in the bar,' says Simone. 'Would you like to join us?'

Their men, Ivy can't remember their names off the top of her head, are already halfway there. Catrina is trailing behind, staring at her phone as she walks. The door to the bar is open, and laughter and the clink of glasses trickles out. She can almost smell the whisky from here.

'Are you a whisky drinker?' asks Ivy. Simone gives her a look that tells her she should know better. Whisky is for old people. Certainly not for sophisticated women such as her. 'Stupid question,' says Ivy with a laugh.

'Why?' says Simone. 'You saying I can't handle something strong?'

Her question, together with a delicately raised eyebrow and a mischievous smile, is a challenge that, fifty years earlier, Ivy would have very gladly taken. She would have strutted into the bar, arm in arm with Simone, and poured two or three fingers of the amber liquid into crystal tumblers, not wishing to be outdone by the men. Although she used to insist on ice with her whisky, which Hugh told her was an abomination, an insult to the master distiller. When she once told him the ice was necessary to soothe the fire at the back of her throat, Hugh had laughed and topped up her glass.

'Get that down you, girl. The fire's the best bit,' he said.

Then he put *Light My Fire* by The Doors on the record player and twirled her around until she was dizzy.

'I haven't had whisky since the summer of 1976,' she says. 'You know when there are associations with certain things…'

'Oh, I do,' says Simone. 'One night, my eighteenth, I think it was, or maybe Catrina's eighteenth, I can't remember now, anyway, we both got so drunk on vodka and orange, trying to be grown-up and ladylike, that I can't touch the stuff now. The smell of it makes me want to vomit.'

'My association with whisky is more to do with people than being drunk,' says Ivy.

'Oh, I see. Did your husband drink it? Is that what you mean?' asks Simone. 'I'm sorry, I shouldn't have asked.' Her hand shoots to her mouth, but it's too late, the question has already bolted, like the proverbial horse from its stable. 'It's just that Troy picked up a leaflet from over there that mentioned you were Terence Nightingale's wife, and you used to visit here back in the day. I know that tragically, he died here. I'm so sorry.' She grasps Ivy's arm, and Ivy covers Simone's hand with her own.

Ivy looks over to where Simone had gestured and sees a wire rack of various leaflets. Details about Terence must be in there somewhere, along with suggested tourist attractions to visit on the island. They have always been entertainment, the pair of them. She should be used to it by now, but it still pains her that people are gossiping about his death as though he were a fictional character and they are part of a book club. Terence was real. Her love for him was real. She wonders whether there will ever be a time when he isn't talked about by strangers.

'Thank you, dear. But actually, it isn't just about Terence. He didn't particularly like whisky; he just drank it to be sociable. But a group of friends - oh, it's silly, isn't it?' Ivy stops walking. She doesn't want to go any nearer to the bar. There are so many memories in this place. In the bar, in particular. She has faced enough for one day. 'I'm going to call it a night,' she says.

'Yes, of course,' says Simone. 'It was lovely to meet you. I'll probably see you tomorrow at breakfast, or maybe lunchtime at the wine tasting?'

Ivy can't be bothered to explain that she may have left by then. 'Yes, of course,' she says. 'Good night. It was lovely to meet you, too.'

Simone catches up with Catrina, who shows her a photograph on her phone, which they both laugh about. Their men are at the bar where their girlfriends join them. Ivy watches as they climb onto bar stools. The barman pushes a bowl of nuts towards them and nods as he listens to their drinks order.

From what she can see through the open door, the room is barely recognisable from the one she remembers it to be. Barbara's white leather corner sofa and two matching chairs – the height of fashion in the seventies - have been replaced by black leather tub chairs. Dozens of them are dotted around the room, surrounding low circular coffee tables. The eruption of fiery orange and yellow flowers on the old wallpaper has been extinguished by a cool grey paint. The disco ball is no longer dangling from the ceiling, but has been replaced by dozens of tiny spotlights.

A mirrored bar runs almost half the length of the room, about twelve or fifteen feet long. Ivy can see three bar staff behind it, two men and a woman, all wearing the hotel's black t-shirts with *Hollow Pines* stitched into the top left-hand corner. She wonders what Hugh would think of this room now. It was once his favourite room in the house. He had commissioned a bar from a local craftsman, just a short one, nothing fancy. There was only room for one person behind it. Made from a mixture of teak and pine with a black Formica top, it was his pride and joy. He proclaimed Hollow Pines to be the only house on Holm Island to have one. It was placed at an angle to the corner of the room, forming a triangular space behind it. Bottles of vodka, gin, wine, and whisky were stacked on a high glass shelf on the wall. The shelf underneath held glasses of various shapes and sizes. There were always two buckets of ice in readiness on the bar itself.

They spent hours and hours in that room, with Hugh behind the bar preparing drinks. He always welcomed his guests in with magnanimity and warmth. What was his was to be shared. Cigars and cigarettes were freely available, and the staff deposited crisps and nuts on all the side tables around the room, despite the fact that everyone had just ploughed their way through a three-course feast.

'Who's choosing the first record?' Hugh would say. 'Tonight, I think the honour should go to my lovely wife.'

Sometimes it was Ivy, sometimes another female guest, but more often than not, it was Barbara. The room would break into applause, as though Barbara had been gifted an OBE, and they would wait expectantly while she flicked through the collection of vinyl LPs. The first choice of record depicted the mood for the night. Disco, glam rock or Motown soul were the favourites to get the party started. Terence was always the first to start dancing, drunk or not. Ivy loved that about him. He didn't need whisky to get him into a party mood.

She can't face the bar tonight, nor is she ready for sleep. Decades of late nights in the theatre mean that she is unable to sleep this side of midnight more often than not. She makes her way back through the Great Hall to the library on the other side of the staircase. She glances at the leaflet Simone mentioned, but is not interested in reading it. Much has been said about her and Terence over the years; in their heyday, they were often in the Sunday papers for one reason or another, especially after their wedding. After Terence's death, even more so.

Afterwards, Ivy moved through life on a storm of caprice - booking flights to Europe for short stays in expensive hotels, moving house at least once a year, whizzing around London in an open-top sports car, whatever the weather, and then moving to New York for a time. It was gold dust for the paparazzi. She couldn't keep track of herself sometimes, so goodness knows how they managed it. Maybe that was the point. Staying still gave her time to think about what she had done. About Terence. About her future life without him.

The thought of his tragic death being printed in the hotel leaflet has shaken Ivy more than she wants to admit. After her initial wobble this morning, she thought she was settling in, getting used to being here. But now she is sure that she wants to go home tomorrow.

She finds the library where it has always been, cushioned between the dining room to the front and the drawing room to the back of the old house. As she pushes open the door, she can see that this seems to be another room that has been knocked through to the room next door, which means that Barbara's intimate drawing room, with its Chesterfield sofas, sheepskin rugs, and trendy black-and-white Marilyn Monroe prints, the location of many parties, with the French doors open onto the rear garden, has been sacrificed. But now the library, which previously had only one small window looking out to the side of the house, is airy and light and at least fifteen feet long. Ivy is delighted to see that the drawing room's old French doors are still there.

It is raining quite heavily now, although there doesn't seem to be any wind yet. Maybe that will come later. Wind and rain are best friends and rarely parted on this Scottish island, from what Ivy can remember. She has forgotten how quickly the weather can change in Scotland. One minute pleasant and warm, the next cold and unforgiving.

She shivers at the thought of the storm on Terence's last night here. It was ferocious. Everyone said they hadn't experienced a storm like it, not in living memory. She has always hated storms since then, especially those accompanied by strong winds. Thunder and lightning have been known to force her to bed.

She turns her back on the window and concentrates on the excellent selection of books. Fiction from every author you would want to read is displayed alphabetically in floor-to-ceiling wooden bookshelves, their spines creating a kaleidoscope of colour. Non-fiction, too. Books on cookery, gardening, psychology, history, and fashion. Each section is clearly marked, but the signage is so discreet that the whole blends seamlessly, like branches of a great tree of knowledge.

It's a beautiful room, designed, it seems, to invite lingering. The shelves line every wall, their warm, polished wood reaching to the high ceilings. Small tables and generously cushioned armchairs are scattered in quiet clusters, ready and waiting for a solitary reader or a group engaging in hushed conversation over cups of hot coffee. Dotted around the room, huge plant pots in various shades of blue, from icy pale to a deep, majestic blue, hold healthy parlour palms arching gracefully toward the light. On a couple of the tables, sit smaller begonias with glossy, dark green leaves speckled in white, their patterns echoing the marbled paper of antique bindings. On the windowsill which was once the old, smaller library sits a single white orchid in a round, white porcelain bowl, its delicate blooms standing like a piece of living sculpture against the glass. Whoever has designed this space has created a lush and welcoming atmosphere.

Ivy chooses a book about National Trust properties and sits down to read in one of the high-backed armchairs. She is no more than three or four pages into the book when her peace is broken by a visitor. It's Catrina. She slams the door shut behind her. Her biscuit coloured hair has fallen loose from its ponytail, and long strands of it fall around her neck. Ivy can see that she has been crying and wonders what she has to be sad about when she is here with her boyfriend to celebrate her best friend's birthday. She wonders why she isn't with them in the bar.

'I'm sorry to interrupt,' says Catrina. 'I didn't know anyone would be here. I just need a minute.'

Ivy welcomes her in and passes her a tissue from her bag.

The rain throws itself at the window and weeps down the glass.

# Chapter Ten

# Catrina

Catrina didn't think anyone would be in the library. Her initial reaction is to do an about-turn and leave, but Ivy insists that she sit down *to gather herself together*. She scrambles in her bag for a tissue, which Catrina takes gratefully. Ivy doesn't ask her why she is crying. She simply gives her the space to calm down.

Catrina can see that a book is open on Ivy's knee. Whether she is reading it or whether she is waiting for Catrina to begin talking in her own time, she isn't sure. Ivy's face is filled with warm concern. Catrina can see her eyes glistening with unshed tears. She's an empath, clearly. Now, Catrina feels bad for causing Ivy to reflect her emotions, and she assures her that she is okay.

'Ryan's drunk,' says Catrina, as she wipes her eyes with the scrunched-up tissue. 'But that's not why I'm crying.' She laughs. 'He irritated me, that's all, so I came to get myself a book, to get away from him for a minute. He wanted a drink on the front porch. He was trying to drag me outside to do some *stargazing*, but have you seen the weather?'

'Yes, rain and wind are frequent visitors in Scotland, I'm afraid,' says Ivy. 'You certainly won't be able to see any stars tonight.'

'He's gone upstairs to the room, sulking because I told him he'd had enough to drink. He told me I was *up my own arse* and I should *calm down.*'

'That's not a very kind thing to say to a woman, is it?' says Ivy. 'In my experience, when a man tells a woman to calm down, it has entirely the opposite effect.'

'Yes! Can you say that louder for those at the back?' says Catrina. 'Honestly, men have a lot to learn about women, don't they?'

'Indeed,' says Ivy, nodding sagely.

'Wow, listen to that rain. It's coming down with some force. I knew we should have gone to Barcelona,' says Catrina. 'Somewhere warm and dry.'

Ivy laughs. 'Yes, Barcelona is beautiful. I haven't been to the Sagrada Familia for many years. I envisaged a trip to Italy,' she says. 'It was the travel agent who persuaded me to come back here.'

She gazes out at the rain, which is drumming against the window to the side of them and on the French door at the back of the room. Catrina can see a hundred memories dance in the older woman's eyes. She would love to ask her about them. She wants to know more about her life as an actress and her relationship with Terence Nightingale. They must have been an incredibly glamorous couple. It is clear to see that Ivy was once very beautiful. She has the poise and elegance of someone who has been used to attention. Her sleek, silver bobbed hair shines in the light of the desk lamp beside her. Her face carries some wrinkles, but she is still a good-looking woman. Her clothes look expensive and tailored. No doubt from some exclusive boutique in London that Catrina would never be able to afford to buy from.

'You've been here before, have you?' asks Catrina. She knows Ivy was a frequent visitor to Hollow Pines back in the seventies, and she also knows that Terence died here – the facts are printed on the hotel leaflet for the world to see - but she doesn't want Ivy to know that she has been reading up about her, like some kind of stalker.

Ivy nods. 'I've been here many times,' she says. 'I used to come here with my husband, Terence. He was a close friend of Hugh, a photographer he met in London, who owned this magnificent house in the seventies. We used to come here every summer for a few weeks. It was divine. Some of the best days of my life were spent right here.'

Catrina looks down at Ivy's arthritic hands, which are clasped tightly together. She notices a slim gold ring on her wedding finger. 'It's a beautiful hotel,' she says, 'so I can only imagine how lovely it would have been as a private home. Has it changed much since you were last here?'

'Not extensively, no. The bare bones are the same. This was the library back then, but it ended there.' Ivy gestures to the ceiling where a beam crosses the room. 'They have knocked into this other room, which used to be the drawing room. Barbara and I - that's Hugh's wife - used to have coffee in here, looking out at the view. It's not easy to see at this time of night, but it really is something to behold. At the end of the long garden, you can see… Well, you'll see it for yourself in the morning, if you haven't already done so, there's a path that leads to the beach.'

'When were you …'

'Oh, I haven't been back since 1976,' Ivy says quickly, anticipating the question. 'Anyway, enough about me. I'd like to know why a lovely young lady like yourself is shedding tears. You haven't been on the gin, have you? Always makes me maudlin, that stuff.'

Catrina laughs. 'No, I haven't touched any gin, although I've probably had too much wine.' She sits back in the chair. She might as well get comfortable. She has a long story to tell, and something tells her Ivy is a good listener. She is not ready to go to bed yet. She would rather give Ryan enough time to get to sleep before she goes up. She doesn't want to talk to him anymore tonight.

So, she begins to tell Ivy about Lucas, about the once-in-a-lifetime love that she thought would sustain her through her whole life. She tells her how close they were, how they told each other everything. At least she thought she did. She tells her about his romantic proposal in their kitchen as Catrina was frying eggs one Sunday morning for breakfast. Lucas knew that she would have been mortified with one of those public proposals in a bustling restaurant, or shown on the big screen at a football match, what should be a private moment, witnessed and critiqued by dozens of strangers. He didn't have a ring. He said that he intended to get one; he had seen one in the jeweller's in town but hadn't bought it yet, as he had planned to ask her the following week on her birthday. But he couldn't wait, he said with a cheeky smile. Catrina looked so cute in her threadbare, Marks and Spencer navy blue t-shirt nightie that he couldn't help himself. It was the most romantic thing ever.

'But then he disappeared,' she says. 'On my brother's stag party, of all things, last October. He was in London for the weekend. We spoke on the phone in the early hours of the morning, and he said he wouldn't be coming home. Just like that.'

'And you haven't seen him since?' asks Ivy. She passes Catrina another tissue, as the first one is sodden with tears.

'No, I haven't seen him or heard from him,' she says. She wipes her eyes and nose. 'I'm sorry, I shouldn't be burdening you with all this. I hope I haven't dragged your mood down. We are on holiday, after all. We should be having a good time.'

'Don't be so silly,' says Ivy. 'I don't think my mood

could get any lower, if I'm honest.'

'Really? Oh, I'm sorry to hear that. Are you okay? Are you in pain?'

Ivy looks at her hands and rubs her swollen knuckles swiftly. 'No, no. Well, a little, but I'm used to that. I keep popping the pills, you know?' She taps an expensive-looking leather handbag at her side, tucked between her leg and the arm of the chair. 'I'm just finding it more difficult to be here than I envisaged. I shouldn't have come.'

'Would you like to talk about it? I mean, I don't want to be intrusive, but…'

'Oh, my dear, you're not being intrusive,' she says. 'Don't worry.' She pauses, then says, 'I think I would like to talk about it, actually. I rarely talk to anyone about Terence these days.'

She tells Catrina about Terence Nightingale, the famous author. The man who wrote five best-selling novels, three of which were in the Sunday Times Top 100 chart. He finished his most famous novel, *The Swirling Sea Mist,* right here, in this very house, she says. She has noticed a copy of it on the bookcase over there. She points to the opposite wall. She tells her of their once-in-a-lifetime love that she thought would sustain them both for their whole life. She tells her about Terence's romantic proposal, like something out of a film. They were in Rome. They had eaten in a small, family-run restaurant in the heart of the city. They took a walk through the cobbled streets, then stopped to perch on the edge of the Trevi Fountain for a while. She had thrown a coin into the water and wished they could always be so in love. On the way back to the hotel, he pulled her into an alley, got down on one knee, and handed her a ring - a beautiful solitaire the size of a strawberry.

'Well, that's a slight hyperbole, but it was huge,' she says. 'I was so nervous to wear it.' She holds out her left hand, examining the ring finger. 'But then I lost him, too. He died here in July 1976. Not in this house. Out there, on the cliff.' She flicks her hand to the window behind her. 'I don't wear the engagement ring now, but I still have it. Safely tucked away at home.'

'It seems like we both lost our loves,' says Catrina. 'I'm so sorry. How old was he then?'

'Just thirty-six,' says Ivy.

'That's so young,' says Catrina. 'The same age as Lucas. Just a year older than me and Simone. How tragic. Did you find someone else to love? Please tell me you did.' She leans forward on her chair, elbows resting on her knees. She can do more internet searching when she returns to the room; there seems to be plenty of information about Ivy Montclaire. But she would rather hear it from the woman herself. She would love to know about her life. She would love to hear about how happy a new man made her after she had experienced the tragedy of Terence's death. She can't imagine what Ivy has been through; the love of her life, her husband, went out for a walk and never returned. Slipping and falling off a cliff is such a preventable death. She can't imagine how she would have felt being told the news, and having to pack up her things, and his, and make the journey home without him. It must have been utterly traumatic.

'No,' says Ivy. 'I never looked for anyone else. Nobody could compare to Terence.'

'I'm sorry,' says Catrina. What else can she say? She sits back in her chair, feeling suddenly despondent, which is bizarre as she hardly knows this woman.

'I've had a good life,' says Ivy. 'My career has been everything to me, and I've been extremely fortunate. But my mother used to say that nobody in life has everything they want. The trick is to be content with what you have.'

'That's very good advice.'

Catrina wanders over to the French doors and watches the rain as it courses down the glass. She focuses on a single drop and follows it with her fingertip as it races against the drops on either side. A silly activity she used to do as a teenager while she listened to music in her bedroom, her homework lying untouched on the bedroom floor. She still finds it calming, almost meditative, just as she did then.

'I saw someone this afternoon who is the image of Lucas.' She turns to Ivy, who is watching her intently. 'When I looked out of the window upstairs, he was in the garden. Someone who works here. Did that ever happen to you? I mean, did you see people who reminded you of Terence, who looked just like him?'

'All the time, dear. All the time.'

Catrina returns to her chair and flops down, suddenly exhausted. 'It's disconcerting, isn't it? I wish it didn't keep happening. My stomach flipped over, and for a moment, I thought it was him. It wasn't, of course.' She doesn't tell Ivy that she sees someone almost every day who looks like Lucas. In the city centre on the way to work, in the supermarket, driving past a car on the motorway. She is on the lookout for him constantly. She wants to shout his name in the street and see who turns around. She would do anything to see his face again, just one more time.

The library door flies open.

'Catrina, here you are. I've been looking for you.' It's Ryan. He squints across the room. He must have taken his contact lenses out. 'Oh, hello, Ivy,' he says as he comes nearer.

'Hello, again,' says Ivy. She hauls herself out of the chair, leaning heavily on the arms. 'I'll be off now, leave you two alone.'

She moves slowly and with difficulty, and Catrina wants

to ask her if she's okay, but her instinct tells her not to. Ivy doesn't seem to be the type of woman who has welcomed old age and the aches and pains that accompany it. She pats Catrina's shoulder as she passes. Ryan runs back to the door and holds it open for her, and then slumps down in her empty chair.

'I woke up and you weren't there,' he says, petulantly. 'I was getting worried about you.'

'I told you I was going to find a book,' Catrina tells him. 'You know I find it hard to get to sleep without reading, and I've forgotten to bring my Kindle.' She tries to keep the impatience out of her voice.

'I don't remember,' he says. He stands and holds out his hand. 'Are you coming?'

'Yes, I'm coming,' she says. She gives him her hand, and he pulls her up from her chair. She still hasn't chosen a book. She picks up the one Ivy left behind, deciding to come back tomorrow if she doesn't like it, to choose another one. Maybe Ivy will be here, and they can continue their reminiscence.

## Chapter Eleven

## Ivy – December 1968

'I'm not a novel writer,' Terence told Ivy the first time they met. He was sitting at the bar at the pub, where she worked, the Dog & Duck. It was a miserable, wet December evening. Reasonable people were tucked up inside their own homes, warm and dry, dressing gowns tight around their middle, feet pushed into sheepskin slippers, a cup of tea on the arm of their chair. Only a handful of hard-core regulars were in the pub, those who wouldn't miss their nightly beers for all the tea in China. Two of them were playing darts in the snug, their cigarettes filling the small room with grey smoke. The other one, an elderly man in his seventies, was sitting by the open coal fire reading a folded newspaper. His collie dog, Stan, was curled at his feet. His half pint glass of Guinness was empty, but he only ever bought one drink, so Ivy didn't bother asking him if he would like another. He would go home when she told him the pub was closed and that the landlord was ready to lock the door.

Ivy was polishing pint glasses that had long since had all their finger marks eliminated, looking busy so she didn't have to walk away from the handsome man who had decided he needed someone to talk to after a long day at the office.

'But my head is full of stories, of characters – all different kinds of people,' said Terence. 'I can see them, as clear as if they are standing right here beside me.' They both looked at the empty barstool by his side and then laughed when their eyes met again.

'I am sure you would be able to write a book, if you really tried,' said Ivy, as though it would be the simplest thing ever. 'Just break it down into chapters, one scene at a time.'

'Do you really think so?' said Terence. 'It's not the same as writing for a newspaper.' He leaned across the bar, the elbows of his jacket resting on the soggy beer mats, soaking up the spilled beer, waiting for her to give him the encouragement he was looking for.

'Well, all you can do is try,' she said. 'If you already have your characters, and you have the beginnings of a story, all you have to do is put them together and see what happens.'

He laughed heartily. 'That's it. Yes, I think you're on to something.' He drained his glass of beer and slammed it down on the bar. 'I'm going to be an author one day. I think that deserves another beer. What can I get you? I'm sorry, I don't think I know your name.'

'It's Ivy,' she said. She held out her hand for him to shake. He clasped it in his, his eyes meeting hers, and kissed her knuckles with his soft lips.

'My name is Terence,' he said. 'Pleased to meet you.'

'You too, Terence,' she said. 'I'll have a Bacardi and Coke.' She wasn't a fan of Bacardi but wanted him to think she was sophisticated. She wanted him to know that she was more than the run-of-the-mill barmaid who drank half pints of lager and lime. She was better than that. This was only her part-time job. A means to an end.

'Can I come to your first book signing?' she asked.

'Absolutely,' he said. He handed her a pound note and told her to keep the change. 'I would love you to be there.'

That night, he walked her home after her shift had finished. They sheltered underneath her tiny umbrella, which he held above their heads, her arm linked into his, their hips occasionally bumping together. As they walked, she told him about the many auditions she had attended and the small part she had played at the Charing Cross Theatre a couple of months earlier. She had no more than half a dozen lines, but she had delivered them well. At least, that's what her biggest fans told her - her mum, dad, and younger sister, who grinned up at her from the middle of the front row.

'I knew you were an actress,' said Terence. 'I could tell. You have that *je ne sais quoi*. Something special that I can't quite put my finger on. Let me take you out to dinner, and you can tell me all about yourself. I want to know what your dreams for the future are.'

That was the most romantic thing Ivy had ever heard. 'That will be lovely,' she said, without hesitation. 'You can share your ideas for your first book.'

Their first date was the following Saturday night, shortly before Christmas. Terence took her for dinner in a candlelit French restaurant in Soho. As he had requested, Ivy told him about her dream of being an actress. He topped up her glass with Chianti and assured her that one day she would be. He said she was too beautiful to hide her light under a bushel. The stage was perfect for her, or rather, she was perfect for the stage. Ivy had never been called perfect before. Her heart sang all the way home, and on her front doorstep, they shared their first kiss.

'Can I take you out again?' he asked.

'I'll have to check my diary,' said Ivy. He kissed her again, long and slow. 'I think I'm free all week,' she said, desperate to see him again, and not caring that she might have to cancel a shift in the pub to fit in with his schedule.

The following month was when Terence met Hugh whilst working. Hugh was a freelance photographer, and their paths had crossed at The Beatles' rooftop concert in Savile Row, London, which Terence was covering for the newspaper he worked for at the time. After hours of waiting around, they began chatting and, as soon as their work was done, they went for dinner and drinks with a group of other journalists. They were firm friends ever since. Hugh, like Terence, had been living in a small one-bedroom flat in London, the difference being that he was also the owner of the magnificent Hollow Pines on Holm Island, which he had inherited and where he spent most of his free time with his beloved Barbara.

He told Terence that he and Barbara loved to fill the house with friends and family in the summer, and invited Terence and a lady-friend to make the trip to Holm Island. Terence told Hugh about Ivy, the delightful young lady who worked behind the bar of his local pub. He said he was besotted with her and was determined to make her his wife one day, and he would be honoured to take her to Holm Island.

## Chapter Twelve

## Catrina

'So, what did you think of last night's wine?' asks Ryan.

Catrina is still in bed, sleepy and comfortable beneath the duck feather quilt. Ryan places a mug of steaming black coffee on her bedside table and climbs back in beside her. He puts his arm around her neck, and she settles her head on his chest. 'The wine was good,' she says. 'Too good, actually. I've got an awful headache. I'm not used to drinking so much.'

Ryan laughs. 'You're such a lightweight. You need to get rid of that hangover before lunch. We've got another three wines to taste.'

'I know,' she groans. 'Maybe we should ask for smaller glasses this time.'

'You don't have to drink it all,' says Ryan. 'Just have a mouthful. I don't think they're giving us too much, really, but I can always finish yours off for you.'

Catrina sips her coffee so she doesn't say anything she'll regret. *We're on a wine weekend*, she reminds herself. *What did I expect, that he would drink sparkling water?* She knows she's being unreasonable. It isn't as though Ryan is a heavy drinker. He isn't at all. Still, she feels on edge. *It's all me, it's all me, it's all me*, she chants silently in her head. Everyone was drunk last night, including her, if she's honest, which explains why she was so emotional. She doesn't know why Ryan being tipsy irritated her so much. He has so many good qualities. She wouldn't be here with him otherwise. She isn't one of those women desperate to be part of a couple. She is with Ryan because she likes him. She knows she should apologise for last night, but somehow she can't find the right words.

As they drink their coffee and Ryan flicks through the television channels, searching for something that isn't news, she tries to focus on what Lucas used to do to irritate her. Simone said she read somewhere, in some self-help book - she's always reading those - that if you focus on the negative aspects of the man you were in a relationship with, removing all rose-tinted glasses, it will make the break-up easier.

'I know it's not a break-up,' she had said. 'Don't look at me like that.'

'But I don't want to get over him,' Catrina said.

They were in Simone's back garden. It was one of those beautiful late spring days that promise a glorious summer. Troy was out, and Catrina was enjoying her company until they started talking about Lucas. She almost stormed out, except that she knew that would hurt her friend's feelings, so she asked Simone to tell her more about what she had read. Catrina knew Simone's heart was in the right place and that she wanted what was best for her.

'Well, it's human nature to focus on the good things, isn't it? When people look back on history, they always think it was better. My grandma tells me how good it was in the fifties when she was a teenager. The good old days, she says. I keep telling her, Grandma, you lived in Jamaica then, of course, you have fond memories, dancing in the sunshine, splashing in the warm sea, living with your parents, with no bills to pay. But...'

'What are you saying, that my relationship with Lucas wasn't as good as all that?' said Catrina, interrupting her.

'What? No, I'm not saying that at all.' In one quick movement, Simone jumped out of her deckchair and knelt in front of her. She grasped both her hands. Catrina could see tears in her friend's eyes, and her own fell then. 'I know you loved Lucas,' said Simone. 'Just take him off the pedestal once in a while. If you keep him there, how can anyone else get a chance to get on it?'

Her words stuck. Ryan is nowhere near the pedestal, but he is never going to climb up there if Lucas won't relinquish his place.

Now, as she lies in bed, she thinks about how Lucas would have dealt with this weekend. The very idea of drinking wine on three consecutive days would not have been something he would entertain. Lucas was so judgmental about drinking, always preaching about how many calories were in a particular drink. Apparently, an espresso martini is slightly better for you than a Long Island Iced Tea, if you didn't take into account the caffeine content. Honestly, Lucas had a way of stripping the pleasure out of food and drink with a single disapproving glance. A slight rise in his eyebrows and a tilt of his chin meant *I'm watching you. Do you have any idea how long you will need to run to burn that off?* Yes, she did know, because he made sure to tell her.

Simone used to say that if Troy policed her drinks like that, she would drink more, just to annoy him, even if it meant she had to deal with the hangover from Hell the next day. But Lucas didn't mean any harm by it. He was looking out for Catrina's health, that's all. She wonders what he would say if he knew that she hadn't been for a run since last October, since his disappearance. Running isn't something she ever particularly enjoyed. She just enjoyed being with him, so his hobby became hers; his fitness regime became hers.

'Shall we order a room-service breakfast?' asks Ryan, interrupting her thoughts. He plays with her hair. The intimate gesture pierces her with guilt, like Cupid's misplaced arrow. She feels bad for crying about Lucas last night, for still missing him. Ryan is just as good as Lucas ever was. 'Do you think it's too late for that?' he says. 'Maybe we should have hung the menu outside the door last night.'

'I'm not sure what the protocol is, but it's Simone's birthday today, so shall I give her a call and see what she wants to do? She might want us to eat together, or she might want to have a quiet breakfast with Troy.'

'Sure,' says Ryan.

She sits up and reaches for her phone. Ryan sips his coffee while he waits for her and Simone to decide on the breakfast plans. He is so easy-going. Lucas would have had her up and out before now, jogging around the hotel grounds before the sun had barely had time to rise – anathema to what she would want to be doing. Having a lazy morning in bed is more Catrina's style, and Ryan's style, too.

'Oh, Simone has beaten me to it,' she says. 'There's a message here, sent about five minutes ago. She said *Shall we meet for breakfast at nine*? Is that okay?'

'Yes, if that's fine by you, it's fine by me,' says Ryan.

She sends Simone a voice note, singing Happy Birthday in her morning croaky voice, and telling her they will knock on her door when they are ready.

Twenty minutes later, she is dressed and ready. Ryan is still in the shower. She knocks on the bathroom door and tells him she is going next door to Simone and Troy's room, as she wants to give Simone her birthday present before they go down to breakfast.

'Okay, my love,' shouts Ryan over the noise of the running water.

She grabs Simone's carefully wrapped gift and leaves the room.

It's then that she sees him. As soon as she opens the door. It's the same man she saw yesterday, the one she told Ivy about, who is the image of Lucas. He caught her eye as she looked out at the view from the bedroom window after her bath, taking her breath away as he disappeared behind some trees. He has his back to her now, rummaging in what looks like a linen cupboard at the end of the corridor next to a utility staircase. She imagines it would have been originally built for the servants to use when this was a grand private home. A metal four-wheeled trolley beside him is stacked with clean towels and bedding, which he is neatly putting away in the cupboard.

'Good morning,' she says. Her hand is about to knock on Simone and Troy's bedroom door, raised in the air expectantly. She is being stupid, waiting for him to turn around and speak to her. She knows it isn't Lucas. Logic tells her so. Why, then, is she so desperate to glimpse the face of a man who might look a little bit like him? She doesn't need a therapist to tell her that it is bizarre behaviour. She mentally admonishes herself for being so pathetic and for being somehow unfaithful and disloyal to Ryan.

The man doesn't respond. Maybe he hasn't heard her. Maybe he's wearing earphones, listening to music or a book as he works.

But there is something about his posture that says otherwise. It has changed subtly. He seems to have frozen. His hands are still, his feet firmly planted on the carpet. Then, suddenly, he bolts. He dashes down the staircase, leaving the trolley and the open cupboard door behind.

Without thinking, she sprints after him, down the corridor, down the stairs to the floor below. She peers along the darkened hallway. He is nowhere to be seen. She dashes back to the stairwell and looks up and down the metal staircase. She stands still, listening for footsteps running down to the ground floor. But it's silent. He's gone.

Feeling incredibly stupid, she climbs the stairs back to the third floor.

In Simone's room, she wishes her a happy birthday and watches as she opens the tiny box containing her present. A pair of gold earrings from her favourite jewellers on King Street, Manchester.

'Oh, they're little bees,' she squeals. 'I love them, thank you.' She flings her arms around Catrina and hugs her tightly. 'You know I've had my eye on these, don't you?'

Catrina waits until she has put them in and admired herself in the full-length mirror before she tells her about the Lucas-lookalike in the hotel.

'I'm sorry about that,' says Simone. She gives Catrina a sad smile and squeezes her hand.

'What do you mean?'

'Well, I'm sorry that you've seen someone who looks like him. It must have been a shock, having the memory of him thrust upon you like that. To be fair, though, all white men his age look alike, don't they? Cropped hair, going a bit thin on top. Compensating by growing some stubble.' Simone strokes her chin and laughs, and Catrina forces herself to laugh, too. She isn't wrong. This is exactly what Lucas looks like. At least, that's what he looked like when Catrina last saw him, almost a year ago. Who knows what he looks like now? He could have dyed his light-brown hair jet black, or orange, or sky blue pink for all she knows.

'It's not him, is it? Do you think it might be?' Catrina can feel her heart rate rising at the thought of Lucas being in the same hotel. She wants Simone to tell her that she is being ridiculous, to quieten the little voice in her head that is screaming *It is him, it is him.* 'I mean, he wouldn't be working in a hotel, would he? Not as a porter or cleaner, surely? Not when he's been a teacher all his life.'

'Of course, it's not him,' says Simone. 'Although it's not as though he can go back to being a teacher, is it? Don't you think that if he got himself a job, the police would have traced him by now? He'd have to pay national insurance and tax and stuff, wouldn't he?'

'Who would?' Troy ambles out of the bathroom, followed by a rich, smoky scent of oud and bergamot and steam from his hot shower.

'Man, how much aftershave have you splashed around in there?' Simone waves her hands in front of her face, like she's dramatically batting away a pernicious insect.

'Just enough for you, babe, I know you love it,' says Troy. He scoops Simone into his arms and swings her around the room while she laughs and demands to be put down.

Then Ryan is knocking on the door, and amid the clamour to get downstairs for breakfast, the conversation about Lucas is somehow forgotten.

But as Catrina pretends to study the breakfast menu, knowing full well that she will order her usual breakfast of scrambled eggs on toast, she can't help scanning the dining room for the mysterious employee. Most of the staff here are young, between twenty and twenty-five, which is usual in hospitality. The oldest person in the room is a man aged about fifty whose job is to greet guests at the door and note their room number on a sheet of paper. There is nobody here who looks remotely like Lucas.

She thinks about what Simone has said about Lucas not

being a teacher anymore. She is right, of course. If he worked at a school, they would want to see his identification documents. He would be registered with the HMRC. So, that means a cash-in-hand job would be his only option. Somewhere like this. Somewhere he could work for the summer season and then move on. Somewhere where he isn't likely to be found by any of his friends or family.

She wants to tell Simone what she's thinking, but she can't while Troy and Ryan are at the table. She whips her phone from her jeans pocket and sends a message, hiding her phone under the tablecloth.

*I think that man is Lucas.*

Simone looks at her phone and then at Catrina. She shakes her head imperceptibly.

Catrina sends another message. *It could be him. He ran off down the staircase when he heard my voice.*

Simone reads it, but then puts her phone face down on the table and ignores me.

Catrina sends another. *Why would he do that? It's odd.*

'Everything alright, babe?' asks Troy, indicating her phone.

'Yes, just someone from work,' says Simone. 'I don't need to reply right now. It's nothing. Anyone want more tea?'

She smiles as she fills Catrina's cup with fresh tea, as though this were a normal day. As though there is no possibility that Lucas might be here. As though Catrina's world isn't about to collapse into an emotional whirlwind.

## Chapter Thirteen

## Ivy

Good morning, Miss Montclaire,' says Andrew as the lift doors open and Ivy steps out into the Great Hall on the ground floor. He is back on duty behind the reception desk.

'Good morning, Andrew,' she says. 'Are you well?'

'Doing grand, thank you very much,' he says. 'Are you going for breakfast?'

'No, I'm not at all hungry this morning, although I wouldn't mind a coffee. I think I'll get one and bring it out here, if that's okay.'

She spots a couple of large, easy chairs in front of a floor-to-ceiling window, next to the revolving front door. Covered in the MacDonald Lord of the Isles tartan, they are high-backed with tiny mahogany feet, and the plump seat cushion looks extremely comfortable. The perfect place to sit and pretend to read for an hour or so, while watching the comings and goings of the hotel.

'Grand idea. You sit right there,' says Andrew. 'I'll get you a coffee from the dining room and bring it out. Milk and sugar?'

'Just milk, thank you. Hot, if they have it.'

'Of course,' he says.

He disappears into the dining room and returns within a few minutes, carrying a large white cup of steaming coffee on a delicate saucer, together with a plate of shortbread biscuits cut into tiny triangles. He puts them down on the small round table between the chairs. 'I thought you might like these. Chef makes them herself from a family recipe that she wouldn't share if you pinned her down and threatened to tickle her to death.'

As he laughs, two small pink circles appear on his cheeks, which slowly spread to his ears. Ivy is immediately transported back to the seventies. 'You remind me so much of your grandfather,' she says. 'You have the same laugh and the same red hair, although I see you have brown eyes. His eyes were as blue as a baby's.'

Andrew rubs a hand over his hair. 'I get my eye colour from my mother,' he says.

Ivy nods. 'Yes, I noticed. She's a very beautiful lady.' She wants to ask him whether his mother lives nearby or whether she is a visiting guest at the hotel. She wants to ask him about his grandparents and where they live, but the words stick in her throat and come out as a cough. She takes a sip of her hot coffee as Andrew fusses and asks whether she needs a glass of water. She assures him she is fine. He looks panicked. The last thing he needs is for an eighty-year-old lady keeling over in the middle of his hotel reception. That wouldn't be good for business at all. He wanders back to his desk before making Ivy promise to shout him over if she needs anything.

She sits back, her head resting on the back of her chair. Last night's rain has cleared, and the clouds have almost disappeared, leaving a powder blue sky. The view out of the front of the house – or rather hotel, Ivy reminds herself, although she still thinks of it as Hugh and Barbara's house – is always beautiful in the mornings. It is north-facing and captures the morning sun like an artist's painting. She remembers this time of day in past summers, the front garden and driveway would shimmer with dappled sunlight. The pine trees would sway in a gentle breeze. She would often sit out there on the porch with Barbara if it were warm enough, chattering for hours, along with the sparrows, great tits, and Scottish crossbills, until the sun moved down the side of the house and the shade became too chilly, forcing them back indoors.

In those days, they didn't have these comfortable armchairs inside the Great Hall. Back then, the hall was quite dark, with small, square windows on either side of a solid wooden door, painted a glossy black on the inside, which Barbara decided would be elegant. And it certainly was. The chandelier was always lit, as it is now, spreading sparkles of rainbow light onto the floor. It was perfect for parties.

Ivy cannot stop her memory from wandering to the night Terence died, when they had one of their biggest arguments on that front porch. Right there in front of where she is sitting now. She tries to block it out by opening her paperback book, putting on her reading glasses, and beginning to read. After a few minutes, it is clear she won't be able to concentrate, so she gives up and closes her book. She sips her coffee as she watches the birds scampering about outside, pecking at the soil for worms.

That day with Terence hadn't started well. From the moment she woke, Ivy had a feeling they were going to have cross words at some point before they went to bed. She could feel the air between them, heavy and tense, as it flexed its muscles, ready for a fight.

Terence had been unusually quiet during the train journey from London that morning. By then, they had become regular visitors to Scotland and tended to sit opposite each other on the train, allowing them both to have a window seat and enjoy the magnificent view of the countryside as they travelled. In recent months, moments together had been few and far between, and Ivy was particularly looking forward to their holiday. She had been working six nights a week. She had a leading role in *A Streetcar Named Desire* at the Young Vic and often didn't get home until after midnight, by which time Terence was asleep. He liked to get up early to write when he was at his most creative, so they were like ships passing in the night, each with their own schedule.

Their train didn't leave London until eleven thirty-five, so they had plenty of spare time in the morning. As Terence climbed out of bed, Ivy reached over to him, grabbed the waistband of his pyjamas, and asked him to lie back down. He shook her off, saying he had things to do.

She dozed for another hour, by which time he was dressed, packed and ready to leave. The weekend broadsheet was spread across the kitchen table next to a pot of cold tea, and Terence was seemingly concentrating on the crossword, head down, his pencil hovering over the page when Ivy walked into the kitchen. She made fresh tea and gathered and folded underwear and shirts that had been drying on the clothes horse overnight. He nodded now and then and appeared to listen as she chatted about nothing in particular.

With an armful of laundry, she kissed his forehead and told him she was going for a shower. She was a little disappointed that he didn't pull her onto his knee and push his hands inside her dressing gown, but she told herself there would be plenty of time for intimacy when they reached Hollow Pines.

On the train, she asked him if he was okay, if there was anything on his mind, but he said no. He claimed to be absorbed in his book and told her he had the beginnings of a headache. Even then, she wasn't worried. She couldn't think that there would be anything wrong. His latest book had reasonable reviews, and he had recently done a book signing at Hatchards, which was a full house, so he had nothing to be morose about. They were on their way to Holm Island for two weeks of revelry and rest in equal measures. Everything would be fine.

When they arrived, Hugh and Barbara greeted them at the door and introduced them to the group of their friends who were joining them for the weekend. Terence's mood changed then, like someone had flicked a switch inside his head. He became perfectly amicable, friendly and talkative. His usual self. Hugh pushed a tumbler of whisky into his hand, and they spent a pleasant hour in the bar before making their way upstairs to unpack and change for dinner. But in the room, the switch flicked back. Terence was once again cold and continued to ignore Ivy. There was no sign of the *bon ami* in the bar. She knew she had to have it out with him, but he continued to deny that there was anything wrong.

As soon as the desert was cleared away after dinner, she leaned over to him and whispered that they needed to talk. Leaving her napkin on her chair, she left the room, knowing he would follow her into the Great Hall.

'Enough is enough now, Terence,' Ivy snapped at him as soon as the dining room door had closed behind him. 'What the bloody hell is going on?'

'I don't know what you mean,' he said.

The way he raised his head in defiance told her she wasn't wrong. She knew she wasn't imagining things. In those days, she was pretty astute to the workings of a man's mind. She knew they didn't think the same as women. They are two very different species, after all. Women talk more.

Their feelings aren't alien to them. They are used to them changing with the ebb and flow of hormones, and if something bothers them, they find someone to chat to, to offload. Men - Terence, in particular - run from emotions like young colts run from a cowboy, until they are lassoed and forced to face them.

'You have hardly spoken to me all day,' said Ivy. 'You wouldn't stay in bed this morning…'

'I. Had. Things. To. Do,' he said.

He threw each word at her like a dart. She backed away and clung onto the newel post at the bottom of the stairs as his words unbalanced her. He looked so handsome in his tuxedo. Black always suited him, especially when he had a summer tan, and she wanted to take him in her arms and kiss him and end whatever silly feud was simmering between them. She didn't want to listen to his hurtful words. She wanted soft whispers of love and desire that tickled her neck as he held her close to him.

Suddenly, the dining room door flew open. A young waiter dashed through the hall and into the kitchen at the back of the house.

'He'll be back in a few minutes with the coffee,' said Ivy. 'Can we talk somewhere else, somewhere more private? You know how people gossip about us.'

They both looked at the hall window. The peach-pink of the sky promised a stunning sunset. She remembers thinking that they couldn't possibly argue in front of such a romantic sky. It would be sacrilege, like bickering in church. It simply isn't done. Within moments, surely they would be in each other's arms again. Whatever had been bothering Terence, whatever misunderstanding he was burdened with, would be ironed out. A short walk around the grounds, holding hands and remarking on how beautiful the heather looked on the distant hills, at its best in the summer, would bring them back together.

But it didn't work out that way.

Ivy returned to the house alone.

Terence was never seen again.

Ivy became a widow that night.

'Andrew! Andrew, please can you....'

'Yes, Miss Montclaire, what is it?' Andrew dashes to Ivy's side and kneels beside the chair. 'Are you alright? You look pale. Gosh, your hand is as cold as ice.'

Her heart is racing.

*I wish I were anywhere but here. I wish I had never sheltered in the travel agents that day. I should have put my head down and battled through the rain. It wouldn't have done me any harm. I would have been home in ten or fifteen minutes, changing into dry clothes while the kettle boiled. Then I wouldn't be here, on this Godforsaken island. Memories are bombarding me in every room. It's too much.*

'I want to go home,' she says. 'I shouldn't have come.'

'You want to go home?'

'Yes, please, Andrew. Can you order a taxi for me? I presume there's a ferry crossing this afternoon. I'll take that.'

'Let me make a call,' he says.

As Andrew runs back to the reception desk, Ivy tries to remember where there might be a decent hotel on the mainland, apart from the Thistlewood House Hotel, where she had once stayed with Terence. She doesn't want to go there. There will be another one, surely. Somewhere she can stay for the night. Anywhere will do. She will get the train back to London tomorrow afternoon as planned. Whatever happens, she can't stay here another minute.

'Miss Montclaire,' says Andrew. 'I'm sorry, but this afternoon's ferry has been cancelled. The weather forecast for later is terrible, I'm afraid. There's a storm coming.'

She closes her eyes and rests her head on the back of the chair. She has been here often enough to know that the ferry is at the mercy of the weather. Just because the sky is blue now doesn't mean it won't be gunmetal grey within an hour. If the sea is rough, the crossing is too dangerous to attempt in a boat, even one as large as the ferry.

It appears that she is staying here another night, whether she likes it or not.

## Chapter Fourteen

## Ivy – July 1976

'The sunset is stunning tonight, isn't it?' Ivy said as they stepped onto the front porch on that terrible night. Terence's last night.

All artistic people love nature, and he was no exception. He took notice of his surroundings everywhere, but especially when they were at Hollow Pines. In the height of the summer, the beautiful flowers, majestic trees, and the distant, stunning mountains entranced him. He loved to listen to the chatter of the birds, the babble of the flowing river and the whisper of wind through the pines. Ivy was sure that whatever was bothering him would pale into insignificance as soon as he connected to nature again. But how wrong she was.

'Is that what you've brought me out here to talk about? Really?'

'Oh, Terence, stop being such a drama queen. It doesn't suit you, not one little bit. Spit it out, whatever's bothering you, and let's get it over with.' She was beginning to get angry now. He was acting like a whiny child.

'Hey, you two, is everything alright?' Ivy turned to see Barbara standing in the doorway. The chandelier behind her highlighted her blonde, carefully curled hair like a halo. She held her wine glass aloft, waving it around as she beckoned them back inside. 'Hugh has opened the brandy,' she said. 'Want one?'

'That would be lovely,' said Ivy. She knew that if she declined, Barbara would persist. 'We won't be long. Just getting some air.'

She looked over to Terence, who was leaning on the wooden balustrade surrounding the porch, his back to Barbara.

'You okay, hen?' Barbara mouthed. Ivy nodded. Barbara smiled and passed her one of her shawls before she closed the door, leaving them alone once again.

'Shall we walk?' said Ivy as she shrugged the warm shawl over her bare shoulders.

Without waiting for his reply, or asking where he wanted to go, she marched down the stone steps, onto the gravel drive and turned left. She was heading to the side of the house and to the path through the back garden that would lead us to the cliffs. She hoped the tide would be low. She envisaged them perched on one of the large boulders on the beach, sitting close, the heat of their bodies keeping the cold at bay as they watched the sun disappear behind the sea. Then they would kiss as the moon rose to light the way back to the house. Friends, once again.

Ivy could hear Terence behind her, the crunch of gravel beneath his feet; then his footsteps hard and loud on the stone path through the long garden, turning silent as they reached the soft grass at the bottom.

The wind was wild and fierce there, without the shelter of the house to tame it. She held onto the shawl, gathering it beneath her chin to prevent it from blowing away. Her hair spun around her face like a web. Ordinarily, she would have laughed, but right then, she didn't want to have to battle with something else. She forced it behind her ears and strode on.

After a hundred yards or so, the cliff top came into view. A colony of puffins was gathered at the edge. Her favourite bird. Their bright orange beaks with their perfectly matching feet, like well-dressed ladies at the races in coordinating outfits, always brought a smile to her face.

'Look, puffins,' she said. 'They're so cute, aren't they?'

Terence shrugged. He loved the tiny birds as much as Ivy did. 'They're here every year,' he said.

Ivy chose to ignore him. His petulance was infuriating. His love or hatred of puffins was not what they were here to discuss. As they walked closer to the birds, they scampered into their burrows. Ivy wanted to shout an apology. 'I don't mean to disturb your evening, but I have something important to discuss with this impossible man. We need space away from the house. But don't worry about us, little birds; everything will be fine. You might see us again tomorrow, strolling on the beach hand in hand, our naked feet splashing about in the shallow waves, impervious to the cold of the Atlantic water, as we will be enraptured by each other.'

If she didn't have anything else, she had hope.

'Shall we walk on the beach?' she said. Why wait for tomorrow? Carpe diem.

'In those shoes? Don't be ridiculous,' said Terence. 'You'll break your neck getting down there.'

Ivy looked out to sea. The waves were full of white horses. She bent down, unfastened the clasp of the leather straps around her ankles and kicked off her shoes. He was right, five-inch wedge heels were undeniably conducive to a twisted ankle; there was no doubt about that. The path from the cliff top down to the beach was narrow and steep. Ivy would have to take it slow and watch her footing. The sand was soft and easily displaced underfoot. The only thing holding it together were clumps of long grass. Taking the path at night was asking for trouble.

'The shoes are off,' she said. 'Let's go.'

'What?'

The wind was swirling around her skirt, whipping at her legs. She gathered the material and lifted it above her knee. 'I said let's go.' She raised her voice to be heard over the wind. Whether Terence heard her, she wasn't sure. Behind them, the closely packed pine trees were swaying, their branches clapping a round of applause. In front of them, the waves were throwing themselves onto the shore, like an appreciative audience at their feet.

Ivy flounced past Terence, but he grabbed her arm and pulled her back from the edge of the cliff. She tried to shake him free, but his fingers dug into her flesh.

'You're not going onto the beach,' he said. 'It's too dangerous.'

'I want to,' she shouted.

He released her immediately. She didn't move. Her hair stuck to her lipstick. She waited for him to move it, for his cool fingers to brush her flushed cheek. She had a flashback of the previous summer when she had watched him and Sandra in the garden, as she flirted with him, tossing her hair this way and that. Then, Ivy had expected him to reach out to Sandra and move her hair from her face, but he hadn't. He couldn't have been unmoved by her charms, but he resisted her. That night, he chose Ivy. And every night thereafter, he chose her. But tonight, he didn't want her. His rejection was worse than any pain she had ever felt before.

She flung herself onto the grass next to his feet, and was relieved when he sat beside her. The wind was picking up. A storm was coming. It shivered over her shoulders. Terence neither put his arm around her nor offered her his jacket.

'Darling, tell me what's wrong,' she said. 'I can't bear this animosity any longer.'

He sighed. He rubbed his fingers through his dishevelled hair. Those beautiful, slender fingers that had typed his best-selling books, that had stroked her face, her body with such tenderness. 'I came to see you last week.'

'What do you mean?'

'I saw your performance at The Young Vic.' He sounded impatient, as though Ivy should have known that he was there, and by not noticing him in the audience, she had somehow snubbed him.

'I didn't know,' she said. 'You know I can't see faces in the audience when the lights are on. They are so bright, I can't see a thing.' He didn't reply. 'You told me you were busy. Why didn't you tell me you were coming?'

'I wanted to surprise you.'

He turned to her for a fraction of a second. He looked hurt, but she couldn't understand why. He had been at the opening night - he attended all her opening nights, as she attended all his book signings - and they had been to dinner afterwards and then sat up late into the night, until they drifted off to sleep in each other's arms close to dawn. But he hadn't told her he was coming again.

'I don't understand,' she said. 'Why didn't you come to my dressing room?'

'And interrupt you?' he said with a sudden lightning flash of anger.

'What? You would never interrupt me.' She reached out to touch his knee, but he brushed her off, like he had that morning when she wanted to pull him back to bed. 'What are you doing, Terence? Don't push me away like that.'

'Why not? Isn't that what you want? Haven't you orchestrated this argument so you can end this?' He waved his finger in the space between them, back and forth. 'Then you can go to Allan with your freedom. Well, he can have you. If that's what you want, you can have each other.'

He clambered to his feet. The sun was almost set. The sky had turned from peach to blueberry to damson. It would be dark soon. Although it didn't get properly dark on Holm Island in the summer, not like the inky blackness of a Scottish winter, tonight the sky was so filled with clouds that the moonlight didn't stand a chance of fighting its way through.

Ivy suddenly wanted to go back to the house. She stood beside him. For a moment, she felt unbalanced in the wind. She wanted to hang onto his sleeve, to grab his hand. She wanted to be back at Hollow Pines, in the comfort of the bar, chatting and laughing with their friends while Hugh poured them all a brandy. But she also wanted to get to the bottom of this.

'I don't want Allan,' she said. 'I want you. You're my husband.' She could have told Terence that she had no idea what he was worried about, but she knew about his simmering jealousy towards Allan, who played the part of Stanley in *A Streetcar Named Desire*. She had played Stella, Stanley's long-suffering wife. Terence knew the plot as well as Ivy did. He knew that Stanley and Stella shared a kiss on stage. On the opening night, when he mentioned that the kiss seemed a little too passionate for his liking, Ivy laughed and told him that if that was the case, then she was playing the part exactly how it should be. And so was Allan.

'So what was he doing in your dressing room?' asked Terence. 'Before you lie to me and tell me he wasn't there, don't bother. I know he was with you.'

Ivy was about to deny it. It wasn't that there was anything to deny. She hadn't done anything wrong, but the way he was accusing her filled her with stormy defiance.

She forced herself to stay silent and wait for the accusations.

Then the rain started, suddenly and violently. They were soaked within minutes. Initially, Ivy was annoyed that her hair and makeup were ruined, but then she was glad of it. Terence wasn't a fan of the rain. This would force him to speak. Get this over with. Then they could hurry back inside.

'I saw Denise,' he said. His voice grew louder, competing with the wind. 'She told me you and he were in your dressing room.'

'For a minute, that's all,' shouted Ivy. 'He congratulated me on a run of good performances. Excellent performances, in fact, that's what he called them.' Why she wanted to rub salt in his wounds, she didn't know. He didn't need to hear about another man fawning over her.

Terence nodded.

'What else did the bitch say?' asked Ivy.

'Why are you calling her a bitch?' he asked. 'Because she told me your secret?'

'No, because she's a bitch, that's why,' she said. 'There is no secret. She is making it up. She wanted the part of Stella and…'

'Oh, don't be stupid,' said Terence. 'Are you saying that playing Blanche wasn't good enough for her? That's ridiculous. It's a decent enough part.'

'That's twice you've called me ridiculous. I thought you were a writer. Can't you think of any other insult?' She stabbed her finger at his chest.

'This isn't about me and my writing skills,' he said. 'It's about what you and Allan were up to in your dressing room.'

'Nothing!' she shouted.

'So why did Denise stop me from going in? I had flowers, for God's sake. She told me I was wasting my time and if I didn't want to look foolish, I should go home.'

'But...'

He raised his hand to stop her. 'If I hadn't seen the passion with my own eyes, I wouldn't have believed it.'

'We were acting.' She was inches from his face, shouting above the storm. 'There was nothing between me and Allan. There *is* nothing between me and Allan. Now you're the one being ridiculous. You think I can't be alone in a room with a man without wanting to have sex with him? That's so insulting.'

'That isn't what I...'

She shouted over him. 'You've listened to Denise, someone with an axe to grind, taken what she said, smothered it in surmise and renamed it the truth, and in doing so, you've insulted someone you're meant to be in love with.'

He was silent for a second. Ivy honestly thought the end of the argument had reached them. But no, it had a long way to go. 'I saw you when you left the theatre,' he said. He turned away from her, looking out to the blackness of the sea. It was dark now. She couldn't see his expression, but she knew it would be one of hurt.

A flash of lightning struck the turbulent waves, making her jump. She resisted grabbing his hand.

'You kissed on the steps of the stage door,' he said.

'No. No, we didn't kiss.' She was finding it difficult to control her anger. She grabbed the collar of his jacket and pulled it towards her, forcing him to look at her. 'He kissed me. There is a world of difference. He was saying goodbye. A colleague saying goodbye, that's...'

Terence grabbed her shoulders with each hand and pulled her towards him. He forced a kiss on her lips. His lips were hard and unpleasant. 'Is that how you kiss colleagues goodbye?' he shouted. 'Shouldn't it be like this?'

He planted a kiss on each of her cheeks then, quickly and chastely.

He let her go, and she stumbled backwards over one of her discarded shoes. She lost her balance and landed on the soft grass. Her pride was hurt more than she was. When Terence didn't reach out to help her up, anger enveloped her.

'I'm sick of this.' She had to shout over the clap of thunder. She hadn't had a chance to count between the flash of lightning and the thunder, but it had been a matter of two or three seconds, which meant the centre of the storm was close. 'I'm not going to apologise for being a good actress. I'm not going to stroke your ego because you're too damn insecure.'

She hit him hard in his chest with the palm of her hand. She felt the impact, although it wouldn't have hurt Terence, not physically. But the hurt she saw on his face would haunt her for the rest of her life. Her last unforgettable words to him were so cruel.

## Chapter Fifteen

## Catrina

Catrina tries to put thoughts of the Lucas lookalike out of her mind and concentrate on being present in the moment. The breakfast is delicious, the hotel is luxurious, and she is grateful to be here with her best friends and her new man. It is time she started to appreciate what is right in front of her.

Simone has picked up the hotel spa's large, glossy brochure from a pile on the corner of the reception desk and has opened it on the table between them.

'Look, they do facials, manicures, massages, the lot. What do you think? Or shall we just go to the pool and jacuzzi?' she asks.

The spa was built only a few years ago, the brochure tells them. It isn't attached to the hotel, but is a detached building, just a few hundred metres walk away down a woodland path. It looks like a handmade Swiss chalet, with pine cladding and a steep gabled roof, but with the surprise of a luxurious indoor swimming pool, a sauna, and a couple of aromatherapy steam rooms, together with treatment rooms and a small nail salon. The photographs in the brochure show that the swimming pool is surrounded on three sides by floor-to-ceiling windows. The jacuzzi, large enough to fit six or eight people, is next to the window at the top end of the pool, giving a view into the pine forest beyond. It looks idyllic.

Catrina looks at her short, unpolished nails. Lucas didn't like nail varnish, and he hated acrylic nails with a passion. Maybe an ex-girlfriend had ruby-red talons that she used to scratch his back with, and which left him with PTSD after an acrimonious split. He never explained his reasoning to Catrina. She simply stopped painting her nails when he told her he didn't like them and, over the years, she got used to leaving them natural.

'What do you think, Ryan? Shall I get my nails done?' she asks.

He shrugs and looks at her like she has lost her marbles. 'What are you asking me for?' he says through a mouthful of sausage and baked beans. 'They're your nails. Do what you want with them. You'll look beautiful whatever.'

Troy bursts into laughter. 'Smooth, man,' he says. 'That's the correct answer.'

'I know,' says Ryan. He nudges Troy with his elbow and smiles. 'Get your Brownie points in whenever you can. That's what I've learned.'

Simone leans across the table and clinks her coffee cup with Ryan's. 'Ryan, you're a gentleman,' she says. 'Sometimes. And you certainly know how to turn on the charm when needed.' They both laugh. 'He's right, though,' she says to me. 'Your nails, your choice.'

Simone is aware that Catrina had stopped painting her nails because of Lucas. She is also aware that her friend doesn't wear as much makeup as she used to. Lucas liked women to look more natural. A little bit of mascara was all she needed, he told her. He didn't like heavy eyeliner or too much eyeshadow. He hated foundation, so she got used to smoothing on the tiniest amount with her fingertips. He never noticed, but it made her feel better than having bare skin. She would hide the bottle at the bottom of her makeup bag, so he wouldn't see it.

The first time Simone saw her without her beloved eyeliner, which Catrina had worn religiously every day since school, she thought she had lost it or needed to buy a new one. She offered to lend Catrina hers until she had time to go shopping.

'I'm not getting another one,' she said. 'Lucas likes me like this.' They were at their house, the one she rented with Lucas. Simone was pouring the wine, and Catrina was chopping a salad for lunch. It was a beautiful, sunny day, one of those rare occurrences in England that coincided with a Bank Holiday weekend. Troy and Lucas were already outside, each with a glass of beer in hand, firing up the barbeque. Catrina could see Simone out of the corner of her eye as she sliced tomatoes and threw them into a large bowl with cubes of feta and cucumber, and could see that unanswered questions were on the tip of Simone's tongue.

Before Troy, Simone had dated a guy who had tried to control her, telling her what to wear, who to see, what to say. He hadn't lasted for more than a couple of months. Simone isn't the type to be told what to do. He was history before you could say 'who's next?'

'I know what you're thinking,' said Catrina. 'But this is my idea. Lucas didn't ask me to stop wearing it. He just prefers women with less makeup.'

'Is that so?' said Simone.

'Yes, it is. He isn't the controlling kind. It isn't like that at all.' Catrina was aware that she was beginning to sound defensive.

'Isn't it?' Simone raised her eyebrows, waiting for Catrina to justify why she was doing what she was doing. 'Is this the new you, then? Au naturelle? First, you stopped painting your nails, and now eyeliner is a thing of the past, is it?' She stood in front of Catrina with her hands on her hips.

Catrina almost laughed. But then she remembered this was her Simone was talking to, not a class of misbehaving school children. 'Not necessarily,' she said, trying not to let her indignation show. 'You do things that Troy likes, don't you? Don't tell me you've never put on sexy lingerie for him. I want Lucas to look at me and find me attractive, which just happens to be when I'm wearing less makeup. This is the same kind of thing.'

Simone sucked in air through her teeth, which Catrina knew meant that she had plenty more to say, but was keeping quiet to keep the peace. It wasn't the same kind of thing. They both knew that. Wearing nice clothes on a date because your man will find you attractive in them, and toning down your usual character traits are two different things entirely. But Catrina wasn't in the mood to justify her decision. The truth was that she wasn't sure how she truly felt about it. What she was sure about was that she wanted Lucas to be happy.

She finished the salad and put the bowl in the fridge. They each grabbed a glass of wine and went outside. Nothing more was said about it.

'Okay, I'll have a manicure,' she says now, trying not to flinch at the extortionate price printed in the hotel's brochure.

'Excellent,' says Simone. She puts her arm around Catrina's shoulder, pulls her close, and plants a kiss on her cheek. The gesture brings tears to Catrina's eyes, which she quickly blinks away. They both silently acknowledge that this is a tiny step towards her getting Lucas out of her system and getting back to her old self. One painted fingernail at a time. 'That's sorted then. I'll give them a call and see when they can fit us in. You two boys can amuse yourselves for a couple of hours, can't you?'

They both agree that they have a football match to watch on the giant screen in the bar, a world to put right, and a few different whiskies to try while they do it. Catrina is about to tell Ryan to take it easy with the whisky, particularly as they have another wine tasting session at lunchtime, but she checks herself and decides to leave him to his own devices. He is a grown man, and if he can amuse himself drinking whisky and watching football while she is getting pampered, then there isn't much wrong in her world right now.

By eleven o'clock, she is sitting on a stool at a slim manicure table in a room which smells of rosemary oil, pine trees, and outdoor freshness, while a beautician shapes and polishes her nails. She has chosen a bright, burnished orange gel. Simone is having a back and shoulder massage in the room next door. They have arranged to meet in the pool when they are finished. There are two other nail tables in this section, both occupied, and the room is humming with gentle panpipe music and whispered conversations. This is the most relaxed she has felt for a long time.

The beautician's head is down while she concentrates on painting Catrina's nails. Behind her, through the window, Catrina can see Hollow Pines in the distance. A delivery van with *Greens* painted on the side is parked at the side of the hotel. Pictures of lettuce and broccoli florets confirm that the company is a green grocery. The driver, wearing a white t-shirt with the *Greens* logo emblazoned on the front, is hauling trays of vegetables from the van to the back of the hotel, presumably to the kitchen door.

A taxi pulls up at the front of the hotel, and a man and woman in their twenties climb out and go up the steps into the hotel. She spots Ivy chatting to the taxi driver. It occurs to her then that they probably should have asked her if she wanted to go with them for a swim. She can't imagine what she will be doing all day on her own. She looks like she might be setting off for a walk, with a coat and scarf wrapped tightly around her, but she won't get far before the rain comes. Black clouds are already congregating, and, according to Andrew, it's going to get pretty wild later on.

Catrina takes her hand out from under the LED lamp and admires her new nail polish. It needs another coat before the job is done, but already it makes her smile. When she looks up again, the delivery van and the taxi have gone. She can see Ivy making her way towards the path that leads to the hotel's back garden. She almost bumps into someone as they both reach the corner of the building at the same time. The man laughs, holding his hands up in an apologetic gesture. He is wearing a black t-shirt and black jeans. The hotel uniform. His brass-coloured name badge is attached to the front of his t-shirt, but from this distance, Catrina doesn't have a hope in Hell of reading what it says. She squints to get a better look at him, but he is too far away for her to properly make out his features. He looks like the man she saw in the corridor this morning. Will his badge say *Lucas?* No, of course not. He isn't Lucas. Her mind is playing tricks on her again, like it did this morning. The man in the corridor is no more Lucas than she is. She remembers Ivy telling her that she used to see men who looked like Terence all the time.

But if it isn't Lucas, then why is her heart beating out of her chest? Why does he have the same hair colour? Why is his chest the same shape? She has rested her head on that chest so many times, it is as familiar to her as her own pillow. The way he laughs with Ivy. She wishes she had better eyesight, then she might be able to see the familiar dimple in his left cheek.

*Lucas, is that you?*

'Who's that man, do you know?' she asks the beautician.

The beautician turns around, following Catrina's gaze. 'Michael,' she says, without a beat.

Not Lucas then.

She doesn't ask Catrina why she is asking. Her colleague comes across and asks if she has the bottle of *Purple Passion*. In the hunt for the missing nail varnish, Michael is forgotten. They have moved on.

The question is, has Catrina?

## Chapter Sixteen

## Ivy

Ivy's mind is too active to sit and read, so she gives up and closes her book. She has tried to concentrate, but has been reading the same page multiple times without taking any of it in.

The reception area is busy, and for a while, she enjoys watching the comings and goings of the guests and the staff. People watching is something she can spend ages doing. She and Terence used to do it often. He said it helped him when he was writing. He would listen to snippets of conversations in cafés and bars, and even in the park on their Sunday afternoon walks. He would make mental notes whenever he heard something amusing that he could use in a book at a later date.

*Maybe this is what has made me so tearful today. Emotions and vivid, relentless memories of Terence have bombarded me ever since I landed on Holm Island, like waves crashing on the shore. There is nothing I can do to keep them at bay.*

She needs a change of scene. As she has a couple of hours to spare before lunch, she decides that a walk will do her good, so she takes the lift back to her room to get her coat.

With the bedroom door closed, she allows her tears to fall freely. She hasn't cried about Terence for years, and yet this weekend, she has shed tears a few times. It is no good telling herself time and time again that it was a bad idea to come here. It clearly was, but she is here now, and there is no chance of getting off this island until tomorrow. She has to accept the status quo.

If only she had enough money to hire a helicopter. She would ask Andrew to telephone someone - there must be a pilot somewhere on the mainland - and she could be whisked out of here in a jiffy. But unfortunately, the life of a theatre actress is not as lucrative as people think. Her house in London is paid for, and she has enough spare cash to buy nice clothes and take holidays whenever she likes, and yes, it might be said that she splurges a little too often on soft leather shoes, a colourful Liberty scarf or two, and luxury scented candles, but a helicopter escape is a tad extravagant.

She splashes her face with cold water in the bathroom and gives herself a good talking to. She will feel better when she is in the fresh air. Ignoring the gathering clouds, she wraps herself in her raincoat, adds a warm scarf and makes her way outside.

It is windy, but the air is relatively warm and fragrant, more like the English south coast than a Scottish island. The ferryman must know that there is a storm coming - they very rarely get the weather forecast wrong these days - although for now, the sky is a stunning cerulean blue and the clouds are powder white.

As Ivy makes her way gingerly down the hotel's front steps, she notices a taxi turning into the gates at the bottom of the drive. They arrive at the bottom of the steps at the same time.

'Good morning, Miss Montclaire,' says the driver, as he climbs out of the vehicle. It is the same driver who deposited her here yesterday.

'Oh, good morning,' she says, embarrassed that she doesn't know his name. She was in such a mood yesterday that she never thought to ask. He must think her frightfully rude.

'What do you make of the hotel, then?' he asks. He has that same look in his eye that he had yesterday as he looks up to Hollow Pines - utter adoration. 'It's grand, isn't it?'

'It certainly is,' she says. 'It's a beautiful building.'

A young couple alight from the back seats, say thank you and goodbye to the taxi driver, and skip up the steps to the front door. They have revolved through the glass tube and disappeared into reception before Ivy has time to blink.

'The exuberance of youth,' she says. 'It's nice to see, isn't it?'

'Aye, it is that,' he says. 'I wish I could move that fast up a flight of steps.' He laughs. 'My old knees won't allow it these days.'

'Mine neither,' she says. 'Have you just collected them from the ferry?' She didn't see the couple carrying any luggage, but for a moment, she hopes that the news about the ferry being cancelled might be wrong, and she can go home after all.

'No, they're a local couple,' replies the taxi driver. 'Just dropping them off for lunch. There's some wine tasting thing going on, I believe. I'm coming back for them later this afternoon.'

'Ahh, yes, the wine tasting,' she says. 'I'm here for the very same reason, although I'm not a huge wine drinker.'

'Then booking yourself in for a wine tasting event doesn't seem like the wisest thing to do, in my opinion.'

Ivy laughs. She is used to straight-talking Scots. At least she used to be. The taxi driver is just stating the truth. There is no malice behind his statement. 'You're absolutely right,' she says, 'which is why I was planning to go home a day early but…'

He shakes his head vehemently and sucks in air between his teeth. 'Not today, you won't. The ferry's cancelled today. Big storm on its way, apparently, but don't worry, it should all be clear in time for your departure tomorrow.'

'Well, that's good news,' she says, although it isn't, of course. Not being able to go home today is the worst news. 'I will see you tomorrow, then, as arranged. It was nice to see you.'

'And you, Miss Montclaire. See you tomorrow,' he says. He is wearing the same faded green corduroys that he wore yesterday, although this time he has chosen a red tartan shirt rather than his Aran jumper. It appears to be just as old. A patch of black fabric has been sewn onto the right elbow. Ivy wonders whether the wear and tear is due to him resting his elbow on the car door frame as he drives, or some other activity. She wonders whether being a taxi driver is his only job. Probably not. The island is so small, he surely wouldn't be busy enough to make a living.

When the taxi disappears down the drive, she sets off on her walk, taking her time over the loose gravel at the front of the hotel. A large wooden sign, its legs sticking into the gravel, points the way to the swimming pool and spa, which wasn't here on her last visit back in the seventies. Someone has made and erected other, smaller wooden signs that point the way to various walks. *The Woodland Walk* through the pine forest, *The Wildflower Meadow* off to the left, and *The Beach* at the back of the hotel.

Ivy has walked through the forest many times, hand in hand with Terence. The tree canopies bend to the direction of the wind and create the perfect shade for hot summer days. She wonders if she will be able to find the same tree whose exposed roots provided somewhere for them to sit. Resting their backs against the giant trunk, they laughed once about how drunk Hugh had been the night before, and how he had slipped on a dropped tomato and crashed onto his bottom. He couldn't get up because he was laughing so hard, and nobody offered to help him. The more he struggled, the more hilarious it was. That night, everyone learned what Scottish men wear under their kilts.

For some reason, Ivy discounts the wildflower meadow, probably because most wildflowers - poppies, harebells, and cornflowers - are past their best at this time in late September. She follows the sign for the beach. Not that she needs a sign to show her the way. She could make her way there blindfolded. With her head down, making sure her feet are firmly planted, she almost bumps into a handsome young man on the corner of the building. She presumes he is one of the gardeners. He laughs and apologises as he steps aside to let her pass.

The garden at the back of the hotel is pristine, just as it was when Hugh and Barbara lived here. Sprigs of lavender brush Ivy's coat as she passes, and the smell floats around her. Barbara's old multi-coloured rose garden has been replaced by dozens of blue hydrangea, interspersed with delicate white anemone. No doubt planted by a young, progressive landscape gardener with a particular cooling theme in mind. The overall effect is calming and peaceful, but Ivy wonders what Barbara thinks. She loved her roses and would spend hours fussing around them, picking off a leaf here, a bud there, to keep them at their best for as long as possible. Perhaps roses are considered old-fashioned these days. Then it occurs to Ivy that the rose garden was here fifty years ago. It is unlikely that anything Barbara planted would still be alive. She keeps forgetting how long ago everything was.

Eventually, she reaches the bottom of the flagstone path that runs through the garden. Cultivation quietly yields to the wild, as the garden gives way to the open grass that leads to the cliff. There is no boundary to the grounds of Hollow Pines, just a gentle surrender from order to untamed growth. She keeps walking, aware that her feet are taking her towards the cliff, and although she doesn't want to see it again, and she knows she shouldn't venture too far away from the hotel, she is somehow unable to stop them. She should go back. The rain can come at any minute. The wind is picking up. She should have a walking stick with her. There is an umbrella stand full of them next to the reception desk, with a sign saying *Help Yourself*. She contemplates doing a U-turn, but she knows that once she is back at the hotel, she will want to stay there. This is her only chance to get to the cliff, to make her peace with Terence.

'Keep going, Ivy,' she whispers to herself. 'You can do it.'

One step in front of the other will take her to the place of Terence's death. Is she ready to see it again? Is she ready to face what happened that night? She decides it is best not to think about it. This trip is something she needs to do. Old age is upon her; before it's too late, she needs to make her peace with what happened to Terence. She can't live under a cloud of guilt any longer.

After a few minutes' walk, the cliff comes into view. Ivy can see the beach down below and the white horses of the waves as they race to shore, just like they did on that night. She continues to the edge of the steep path that leads down to the sand. It doesn't look any different, as though the past fifty years haven't happened, and it is still 1976. Except that Terence isn't here, and neither are the puffins. Their breeding season is over now. They will be wintering at sea now. Their absence stabs at her heart, unexpectedly. She feels bereft. She has never been to Hollow Pines so late in the year. The cliff devoid of puffins seems unnaturally empty, like walking through a school long after the children have gone home.

*I will close my eyes for a moment and send a silent message to Terence. My darling, I hope you can forgive me. You know I have loved you my whole life. You know I am desperately sorry for that night. I would do anything to have you here with me right now.*

A seagull screeches overhead. Ivy opens her eyes and watches it. Buffeted by the growing wind, it seems to be calling out to her to help it land. Then it is joined by another one, and another one, and the three of them turn and fly out to sea, swept away on the breeze. She abandons her message to Terence. Now that it has been interrupted, she doesn't know what else to say. Over the years, she has said everything that she needed to say. She has apologised to him a thousand times in her head. He must know how sorry she is, and when they meet again in the afterlife – if there is such a thing - they can talk about it. She has faith that she will be able to tell him one day. She has never been the religious type and is not particularly au fait with the Bible, except for the stories she was taught at school, but in recent years, the thought of seeing Terence again, whether that be in Heaven or whatever you want to call it, has kept her going.

She looks down onto the beach. A small, wooden rowing boat is bobbing in the rough sea, dangerously close to the rocky shore. There is nobody aboard. She looks around, but she is alone. The owner of the vessel is nowhere to be seen. She wonders whether it is owned by the hotel for the guests to use, or more likely, a local fisherman who is trying to avoid paying any fees to moor it properly at the harbour. False economy in such weather. A few more crashes against the rocks will be the end of it. Splinters of wood will be all that remain. Then she sees the end of a couple of paddleboards, abandoned, tucked away behind one of the large rocks. The turn in the weather probably forced their owners inside.

Another stab of a painful memory hits her. A snatched conversation between her and Terence one day at the beach. Sinking her toes into the sand as the icy waves splashed over her ankles. She told him how she used to play with her little sister on Newquay beach as a child. Terence was quiet for a moment. He gripped her hand, gave it a squeeze.

'We can bring our children here one day,' he said. 'Would you like that?'

He didn't need an answer. He knew she wanted that more than anything in the world.

The rain comes suddenly now, although not entirely unexpectedly, bringing with it a sudden drop in temperature. Ivy leaves her memories on the beach and makes her way back to the hotel, head down, the collar of her coat held tightly together around her neck, as much as her old fingers will allow. Her head feels like it's in a vice. Her spine screams at her. She desperately needs to get back, to lie down, to take her painkillers, and watch mindless television.

Somehow, if she can, she needs to block the horrible memories of the most traumatic night of her life. They have tormented her for long enough.

## Chapter Seventeen

## Catrina

After a few lengths of the pool, Catrina and Simone decide they have had enough exercise and sit on the edge of the pool, dangling their feet in the cool water. Catrina tries not to keep looking out of the window to catch a glimpse of the man the beautician said is called Michael. She wants to tell Simone about him, but what would she say? That she saw the man from the corridor this morning, and from a distance, he seems to have the same smile as Lucas? As the words form in her mind, they sound ridiculous. Simone will tell her that she is being daft. She will repeat what she said this morning in her room, that all white men his age look alike, with their cropped hair, going a bit thin on top. Growing stubble to compensate for their lack of hair. Catrina just needs to convince herself that it's not him. She should be trying to avoid the man called Michael, not seeking him out. She has a handsome man waiting for her in the hotel bar. He is the one she should be seeking out.

'Are you okay?' asks Simone.

'I'm having a lovely time,' says Catrina, with the brightest smile she can manage. 'As birthdays go, this isn't bad, is it? Are you enjoying yourself?'

'I love this place,' says Simone. 'We should come back in the winter, when there's snow everywhere. It will be heaven.'

Catrina laughs. 'Have you looked out of the window? It seems like winter already. It seems like they don't bother with autumn around here. They simply skip it and go straight for cold.'

The wind has gathered strength and is hurling the raindrops against the windows, like children throwing pebbles from the beach. Each one lands with a sharp tap that echoes around the pool room.

Simone's eyes sparkle as a huge grin spreads across her face. 'Maybe we shouldn't bother getting dried. We should run back to the hotel in our swimwear,' she says.

'That's like your wild swimming idea,' says Catrina. 'One that I will take on board, and then swiftly dismiss as preposterous.'

'Spoil sport,' laughs Simone. 'We'll do it next time, though. You can't get away with it twice.'

'Sure, whatever you say.'

'Seriously, though, I am pleased to see that you and Ryan seem to be getting along well,' says Simone. 'How would you rate your first trip with him, out of five?'

'It's a solid four,' says Catrina.

'Four, eh? Room for improvement, then. What does he need to do to raise his game?'

'I'm quite happy with a four out of five. I can't expect perfection, can I?'

'Nonsense,' says Simone. 'Why would you settle when you can have perfection?'

It's a rhetorical question, which they both sit with for a while. They have had dozens of conversations about men and relationships over the years. Simone's bar is set at a much higher level than Catrina's, who used to worry that nobody would ever match up to the perfect man Simone had in her mind. But Troy seems pretty close. He adores

Simone and will do anything to make her happy. It really is a joy to see them together.

'Ryan isn't Lucas, I know,' says Simone, 'but he's a good man. And he's more handsome, in my humble opinion.' She laughs to show that Catrina shouldn't take offence on Lucas's behalf. 'You do like him, don't you?' she says.

'Yes, yes, of course I do. Do you?'

'Yes, I think he's great, but I'm not the one dating him, am I?'

'No, that's true. Honestly, he's lovely,' says Catrina.

'But?' Simone knows when she is not telling her everything.

'Oh, it's nothing. We're fine now. I got a bit pissed off with him last night, if I'm honest. It was something and nothing, and everything is sorted now.'

'What did he do? Tell me,' she says.

'He got drunk.' Catrina shrugs, knowing that Ryan didn't do anything wrong, and she was the one being unreasonable last night, particularly given the fact that they had all been drinking too much.

'And?'

'That's it. I know, I know. But it annoyed me last night when he wanted to go out on the porch. I know it has a canopy, but even so, it was pouring down and freezing cold, and he wouldn't take no for an answer.'

Simone laughs. 'Yes, I remember him trying to drag you outside. They have a basket of rolled-up blankets by the door. Have you seen them? You could have taken one of those.'

'Yes, I know. I just didn't want to go. Blanket or no blanket,' says Catrina. 'I can see the funny side now, but last night I didn't. I was probably tired after all the travelling, and I over-reacted.'

'We all had a little too much. Didn't you? I saw you

necking the wine at dinner. Ryan wasn't the only one. So what's the issue?'

'I don't know.'

'Well, I know,' says Simone. She nods at Catrina with a knowing smile, like she has a secret. Her raised eyebrows indicate she is about to give one of her sanctimonious speeches. Simone is a wonderful teacher (she works at the same school where Lucas worked, and Catrina has her to thank for introducing them), and she will make the best mother one day, but she should keep her preaching for the children. Catrina doesn't say so, of course, because she doesn't want to hurt her feelings. Whatever Simone is about to say will be said with love. It always is.

'Go on,' says Catrina, reluctantly. 'I know you won't be satisfied until you tell me how much I'm self-sabotaging.'

Simone reaches into the pool, cups the water with her hand, and throws it in Catrina's direction. She has always been hopeless at sport, so she receives the brunt of the splash herself, which breaks any growing tension and makes them giggle.

'Well, you know I'm not one to preach,' she says, with more than a little sarcasm. 'Seriously, though, Ryan is a great guy. He's intelligent, he's handsome, he has a great job. I worry that you won't know how good he is until you have pushed him away.'

'Like that song, you don't know what you've got until it's gone,' says Catrina.

'Exactly,' says Simone, pointing a forefinger at her, as though she has hit the nail right on the head.

'I know.'

This time last year, a month before Lucas went missing, the four of them had dinner in The Ivy in Manchester. Simone and Troy love The Ivy and even have their favourite table, on the middle floor, tucked away in a corner next to the bar, which she asked for on that night. Simone paid the bill, a tradition the two women have been following on their birthdays for over a decade. When it is someone's birthday, they get to choose the restaurant, but they have to pay. Many people would do the opposite, and the birthday girl would get a free meal, but it seems to work for them.

It was a Friday night, two days before Simone's birthday. The table was booked for eight-thirty, and it was approaching nine before their first course came. Catrina could tell Lucas wasn't happy about that. He didn't like to eat so late, but Simone wanted some time after work to get herself dressed up. Catrina didn't argue with her. It was her birthday, so she got to choose what time they ate.

'You know I've got the race the following morning?' Lucas had said when Catrina told him the arrangements. 'And I've got to drive all the way to Liverpool, so it will mean an early start.'

'Yes, I know,' she said. 'But it's Simone's birthday. It isn't as though she chose the date just to piss you off.' She didn't often speak back to him like that, but it grated on her nerves the way he called them 'races'. He was a good runner, and he liked to do half marathons and 10k runs whenever he could, but calling them races was a bit much. He wasn't likely to win or even come in the top ten.

'I'm aware of that,' he said. 'But, it can't be a late night, and I won't be drinking.'

'Okay,' she said. 'Let's see how it goes, shall we? Simone might not want a late night anyway, because she's got a family party the next day.'

As it happened, it was a late night, and the later it became, the more agitated Lucas became. Catrina could tell that with every passing minute, he was seeing it as a minute less in bed. He liked to get a full eight hours before a *race*. He turned down the Champagne, covering his glass with his hand and making a point of telling the waitress that he needed to be 'fresh' in the morning. 'I'm doing a half-marathon,' he explained to her, as though she gave a toss. It was only when Catrina gave him a stern look that he relented and said he would have a mouthful to raise a toast to the birthday girl. He was nothing if not polite.

Catrina felt like he had ruined the night. He was moody. He was constantly checking his phone to see the time and sighing when another round of drinks was ordered. Catrina was so annoyed with him that they didn't speak all the way home. She was glad that he was up and out of the house at the crack of dawn the following day. She pretended to be still asleep while he clattered about the bedroom getting ready, grunting with every hamstring stretch, even though he would need to stretch again after the drive to Liverpool. When he began rubbing his nipples with cream to stop them from chafing, Catrina had to bite hard on her tongue to stop herself from screaming at him to get out of the house and leave her to sleep.

'Do you remember this time last year?' says Catrina, splashing her feet in the cool water of the pool. 'Your birthday meal in The Ivy.'

'How could I forget?' says Simone. 'It took me all day to get over that hangover. I thought I'd have to cancel my family meal.' She laughs. 'Troy kept me topped up with water and paracetamol all day to keep my headache under control. Great night, though, wasn't it?'

'Yes, our birthday meals always are,' says Catrina. She doesn't tell her how Lucas had spoiled it. 'I'm looking forward to tonight.'

'Yes, me too.' Simone lifts her feet out of the water and examines her neatly painted toes. 'We should do something like this for your birthday. You know, a full day somewhere in a spa. Manicures, pedicures, that kind of thing, or another weekend away, rather than just a meal.'

'I don't think the budget will allow for it this month,' says Catrina. 'You know my birthday is only ten days away.

'Yes, okay, maybe not. That's what you get for being the youngest. I can't help it if my birthday comes first and we spend all our money on it. We'll do something special, though, won't we? With Ryan and Troy?'

Catrina nods and smiles. Tears have trapped the words at the back of her throat.

'I know it's your first without Lucas, but it's going to be okay. You're going to be okay,' says Simone, throwing her arm around her friend's shoulder and pulling her close.

'Come on, let's swim,' says Catrina. She needs a distraction; otherwise, she might cry. 'We can't tell the boys that all we have done is sit on the side of the pool and talk.' She jumps off the side, into the water, and Simone follows her.

Half an hour later, on the walk back to the hotel, Catrina is in a much better mood. Despite only doing a few lengths of the pool and at a pace slower than an old turtle, she has managed to build up an appetite. Troy and Ryan are waiting for them in the bar. They seem to have enjoyed their morning. Catrina can hear them laughing as she walks through reception. When she sees Ryan's face break into a huge smile at the sight of her, her heart warms to him. She isn't wearing any makeup, and her hair is dripping down her back, but he still kisses her tenderly, and the way he looks at her tells her he has missed her. If Lucas were here, he would want to know how many lengths they had done and would instruct them both on the proper way to stretch afterwards. All the fun would have been sucked out of the swim.

'How much time do we have before lunch?' asks Catrina.

'They serve until two, I think,' says Ryan. 'We've got plenty of time, why?'

'Can you give me five minutes? I want to run upstairs, drop off my bag, and hang my swimsuit in the bathroom to dry.'

'Sure,' he says. 'We will wait here.'

'Simone, are you coming up?' she says. 'I'd like to borrow your eyeliner, if that's alright? It is about time I started wearing it again.'

'Alright? Girl, you can *have* my eyeliner with pleasure. Ryan, have you seen this beautiful lady's nails?' She holds up Catrina's hand for him to see. Ryan takes hold of it and kisses her fingertips.

'Gorgeous,' he says.

I'm back, thinks Catrina.

## Chapter Eighteen

## Ivy

Ivy staggers into the hotel reception as Catrina, Simone, and their gentleman friends are coming out of the bar, on their way to the dining room. Ivy is desperate to sit down. She has been out far too long. She shouldn't have walked so far. The last few yards through the hotel's grounds seemed to take an eternity. The long path through what used to be the rose garden went on and on forever. She kept her head down, trying to ignore the cold, biting rain driving into her face, and trundled on, cursing her old legs for not being able to go any faster. Now, she is thoroughly soaked. Her feet squelch in her shoes, and rain drips from the bottom of her raincoat onto the floor.

'Ivy, how lovely to see you,' says Catrina. 'Are you having lunch? We're just on our way in. Would you like to join us?'

'Oh, you should come and try the wine,' says Simone. 'We are having Spanish wines today; a white Rioja, would you believe? I've never heard of one of those. I always thought Rioja was a red wine.'

Ivy remembers Hugh's impressive wine cellar and the Rioja Blanco he had imported by the case after his trip to Valencia in 1971, where he and Barbara had fallen in love with it. They had ordered a bottle most nights in a side-street taverna that someone in the hotel told them was the best in town - off the beaten track, as yet undiscovered by the tourists, but kept busy with the locals.

Hugh pressed a couple of bottles into Terence's hand that summer, telling him to pack them carefully in tightly rolled clothes in his suitcase. When they got home, it was weeks before they opened the first bottle. They were waiting for a special occasion. Hugh had revered the wine so much that it seemed a waste to open and drink it on an ordinary day. So they saved it for Ivy's birthday and drank it in the garden, slouching in old blue and white striped deckchairs which they had discovered in the shed, left by the previous tenants of the ground-floor flat. They ate Dover sole dripping in lemon butter and a green salad from the greengrocer in Fulham, and discussed the plot of the book Terence was working on. It remains one of Ivy's favourite birthdays.

'Ivy, are you alright?' asks Catrina. 'You look a little pale.'

'I think I have overdone it on my walk, that's all,' she says. 'I went a little too far. The mind is willing, but the flesh is weak, I'm afraid, when you get to my age.'

'You need to come and sit down and have some food, come on.' Catrina reaches for her arm, but Ivy shrugs her off.

'No, really, I'm not hungry, I just want to lie down.'

She wants to get to the lift, but they are blocking the way. All of them staring at her. Both of the women then look at each other for a second. A look passes between them. They are probably thinking of the frailty of their grandmothers. Ivy wants to tell them that she is fitter than the normal eighty-year-old, don't they know. She walks down into the centre of Beckenham most days, she swims every Thursday afternoon, and honestly, there is no need to fuss. But she can't summon the energy for explanations. The light in here is too much. She covers her eyes with her hand. That chandelier, beautiful back in the day, when a prism of colour danced around the floor during one of Barbara's soirees, is unnecessary during the day. It seems to be adding heat to an already hot room. It is stifling in here.

She tugs at her scarf to release her neck from its stranglehold, but the material fights against her, gripping her tightly. She can't breathe.

'Is everything okay?'

She doesn't know who asks the question. Catrina's face morphs into Simone's. Why are they moving around so?

'Can we get a chair over here?'

Someone is shouting. Ivy can see the man's mouth moving – is it Ryan, or Troy? - but the words are faint, as though he has left his voice in another room and is waiting for it to catch him up.

Suddenly, just as her legs give way, she is pushed into a chair which someone has very kindly placed at the back of her knees just in time. Strong hands are on her shoulders. Catrina is crouching in front of her, her eyes wide with concern.

'Ivy, Ivy, are you okay? Can I have some water, please?' She flaps her hands in front of Ivy's face, causing the slightest of welcome breezes.

Andrew runs from behind the reception desk and disappears from view. He seems to be moving in slow motion, as though running through invisible treacle. After what seems an age, he reappears and shoves a glass of iced water into Catrina's hand. She holds it to Ivy's mouth and orders her to drink.

*I should probably be taking my pills now, but I'm not sure of the time. I might as well take them, while I've got a drink, but I don't know where they are and can't seem to find the words to ask*

*Catrina to check my pockets. Never mind. I can take them later, back in my room.*

She sips the cold water. The blurred faces around her slowly sharpen back into focus, as though she has been looking at them through the viewfinder of an old SLR camera, her fingers trembling on the focus ring, twisting the lens left and right until they are clear once again.

'I thought you were going to faint there, Miss Montclaire,' says Andrew. 'How are you feeling now? Any better?'

She nods and smiles. For now, the energy for speech eludes her.

'She probably needs to eat something, doesn't she?' Catrina asks. She is studying Ivy's face and stroking her hand, but the question isn't directed at Ivy, so she doesn't feel the need to reply. 'Did she have any breakfast? We didn't see her in the dining room this morning, did we? Do you know what time she went in?'

'She didn't eat breakfast, as far as I know,' says Andrew. 'I brought her some coffee and biscuits, and she sat over there for a while before she went outside. Do you feel up to having some lunch, Miss Montclaire?'

Ivy shakes her head. 'Not really, dear, but thank you.'

'I'm glad you're back with us,' says Catrina. She stands, bends down to her, and kisses her cheek.

Ivy finds the unexpected sign of affection touching. The young people these days seem to kiss much more than Ivy's generation. Even the young men kiss and hug their friends, which is something Terence and Hugh would never have done. A firm handshake was the closest they got to physical touch. Ivy has seen young people in coffee shops and outside bars, groups of friends of both sexes kissing each other on both cheeks, Continental style. It warms her heart to see the old shackles of convention finally being cast aside.

'I think you might have fainted for a moment,' says Andrew. 'I'm going to call the doctor, if that's alright. Let her take a look at you.'

'No, no, please,' she protests. 'It's a simple blood sugar issue, that's all.'

'Are you diabetic?' he asks.

'No, but I haven't eaten yet today. I'm a silly old woman for not looking after myself properly, that's all.'

She assures Catrina and her friends that she will be fine and that they should go and enjoy themselves. She asks Andrew to escort her to the library, which he does gallantly. She doesn't want to be alone, and the warm and welcoming space of the library will be perfect for a restful couple of hours. He tells her that he will get a sandwich made for her, and makes her promise to eat it. No arguments. He says he will also send in a pot of tea, and she must take it with plenty of sugar. She tells him sugar is one of her vices, which seems to please him. He tells her he will add some of those delicious shortbread triangles to her tray. If she doesn't manage to eat them all, she can take them back to her room and have them later.

The library is quiet. Only one woman with a small child on her knee occupies the chair next to the French windows at the back of the hotel. Ivy directs Andrew to the same chair she sat in last night when she was chatting with Catrina. The table between the two chairs is directly underneath the small window, offering perfect, natural light for reading. Ivy eases herself into the chair, whilst Andrew holds her by the elbow. The room spins for a moment before it slows and eventually settles back to normality. She makes a mental note to see the practice nurse when she gets back to London. She can't make a show of herself like that again. As lovely as it is to get some attention - she can't remember the last time someone showed enough concern to make sure she was eating properly - Catrina and her friends are on their holidays, and they don't want to be concerned about someone they don't know. Ivy is not their problem, nor does she wish to be.

She only has one more night here. All she has to do is take care of herself, eat properly, and drink plenty of water. She must be well enough to go home tomorrow. The last thing she needs is to be taken into hospital. She doesn't want to have to spend weeks on end on this island. That would be simply dreadful.

Andrew passes her a non-fiction book about Antarctica and assures her he will be back soon with her sandwiches and tea.

The library is so peaceful, the silence punctuated only by the whispers of the mother and son at the back of the room and the ticking of a wall clock. Reading always makes Ivy's eyes tired, and she is about to doze off, her eyes closed, when she hears her name. It is so quiet, for a moment, she thinks she has misheard it.

'Ivy,' says the voice again. There is something so comforting and familiar about the local Scottish accent.

Ivy opens her eyes.

'Hello, Ivy. I heard you ordered some sandwiches. I thought I would bring them for you. I hope you don't mind.'

'Barbara,' says Ivy. 'Is that really you?'

## Chapter Nineteen

## Catrina

Lunch was an authentically made prawn and chorizo paella with lots of salad on the side, and slices of warm garlic bread. It was served with a cool and crisp white Rioja, which Catrina is definitely going to buy and take home. Dessert was crema Catalana - a rich custard flavoured with cinnamon and lemon, topped with caramelised sugar. With dessert, they were given a sweet red wine from the Basque Country, but it reminded her too much of her nanna's sherry which is dusted off every Christmas, so she passed hers to Simone. After all that, she is now feeling as full as an egg.

As everyone finishes their drinks at the table, Catrina can't help thinking of Ivy. As she watched her being led to the library by Andrew, she looked like she had shrunk in the rain. She seemed suddenly older. Andrew had linked her arm in his, and she was leaning on him like someone who no longer trusted her legs to remember how to walk.

'I hope Ivy is going to be okay,' says Simone, as though reading Catrina's mind.

'She was very pale, wasn't she?' says Catrina. She remembers the previous night in the library, the pain etched on Ivy's face when she pushed herself out of the chair. 'I'll check on her later. Maybe she will feel better when she has had a rest and something to eat. I'd like to have another look in the library. I can sit with her for a while if she is still in there.'

'Yes, good shout,' says Simone. 'Right, well, it's my birthday still, so what do you fancy doing, Troy?'

'You,' says Troy. He laughs and kisses the side of Simone's neck, causing her to squeal.

'Stop it, you sex pest,' she says. She pushes him away with one hand while simultaneously holding onto his shirt with the other.

'I haven't given Simone my birthday present yet,' says Troy. 'So we'll see you later, okay?'

'But you gave me...'

'Shhh, I've got you another present,' says Troy. They both giggle, their eyes fixed on each other, as though they are already alone.

Catrina's heart jumps a little with a mixture of jealousy and love for them both. She was where they are now with Lucas - sure of him, sure of their love, sure of their future - but she no longer has that. Things are different with Ryan. He is handsome and funny, but their relationship is still so new, not quite so sure.

She looks at him across the dining table. He is laughing at Troy and Simone. He looks handsome when he smiles, showing the dimples on his cheeks, which he told her he used to get teased about at school until his mum had told him how dimples were made.

'How are they made?' asked Catrina, thinking there would be some interesting, biological explanation. At the time, they were sitting side by side on her sofa, the remnants of a Chinese takeaway scattered around them like wrapping paper on Christmas morning.

'Well,' said Ryan. 'Remember that my mum told me this,

so it is her hypothesis, and there isn't any proof that it's true.'

'Go on,' said Catrina.

'When God has made all the children and he is ready to send them down to earth,' said Ryan, 'he lines them all up on the cloud. Then he goes along the line to check that they have all met his exacting standards.' Catrina began to giggle. 'It's true, it's true,' he said. 'Anyway, He goes along the line and when he sees a child who's ready, he pokes them in their tummy and says, "You're ready." That's why everyone has a belly button.' Ryan lifted his t-shirt and pointed to his own belly button. 'See.' He pulled his t-shirt down quickly. 'No, you can't touch it, not yet anyway.' The way he smiled, his eyes crinkling at the edges with mischief, made Catrina want to do exactly that.

'Get on with your story,' she laughed.

'So God goes along the line saying, "You're ready, you're ready, you're ready," and when he gets to someone who is particularly cute...'

'Someone like you, for example,' said Catrina.

'Yes, exactly,' said Ryan. 'He then gets that child's face between his thumb and forefinger and says, "And you're bloody gorgeous," which causes the dimples.'

He burst into childlike laughter at his own joke, which made Catrina giggle even more. She picked up a cushion and beat his chest with it until he grabbed it from her and threw it on the floor amongst the empty takeaway cartons. He pushed her onto her back on the sofa and lay on top of her. For a moment, she thought he was going to be romantic and gaze into her eyes and tell her that she was *bloody gorgeous* too, but he blew a raspberry on her neck, like you would with a baby, and they both laughed until their stomachs hurt.

Moments later, as he led her upstairs to the bedroom,

she struggled to remember a time when Lucas had made her laugh so much. Then immediately felt guilty for allowing Lucas into her thoughts as she was on her way to bed with another man.

Now, as she considers Ryan, she isn't sure whether it is the fact that she is wearing eyeliner, or the fact that her nails are freshly polished with glossy nail varnish, or the fact that her stomach is full of delicious food and wine, but she has a sense of complete happiness. Ryan is good for her, she decides. Maybe now is the right time to finally let go of Lucas and forget him.

She quickly swallows down her jealousy at Simone and Troy's closeness and grabs Ryan's hand. 'Well, I was going to suggest getting a coffee and taking it to the library, maybe playing a board game, but if you two have better things to do, go ahead.' She laughs and waves a hand in their faces, as though they are already dismissed.

'Lovely as a board game sounds...' says Simone. She gets up and pushes the chair neatly underneath the table.

Catrina takes that as their cue to leave, and everyone makes their way out of the dining room.

'Come on, before you change your mind,' says Troy, as he tugs Simone towards the stairs, too impatient to wait for the return of the lift. 'We'll see you later.'

'In about five minutes, mate,' says Ryan, laughing.

'Hey, don't judge every man by your own low standards,' says Troy.

'It's nice that you and Troy are getting along,' says Catrina when they have disappeared up the stairs.

'He's a great bloke,' says Ryan. 'I really like him.'

'I'm glad. It's important to me that you like my friends.'

'Of course,' he says. 'I mean, if you and I are in it for the long haul, then...'

He leaves the sentence open, like a question hanging

without an answer. Catrina knows he's waiting for reassurance. If they had the same conversation this time yesterday, when they had just arrived at the hotel, she wouldn't have been so sure. Now, after remembering how difficult Lucas was sometimes and after Simone reminding her what a wonderful man Ryan is, she is beginning to feel better about where their relationship is going.

'I'm definitely in it for the long haul,' she says. 'If you are.'

Ryan pulls Catrina to face him, lifts her chin with his forefinger, and kisses her softly on the lips.

'Hey, get a room, you two.' It's Andrew. He is standing by a potted palm next to the reception desk, trying to frown, but failing. His eyes are giving him away. 'This is a respectable hotel, you know.'

'I do apologise, dear Sir,' says Ryan, suddenly channelling an aristocratic English duke with a monocle. 'But you see, I have this terrible dilemma.' He gestures vaguely around him as though addressing his peers in a Mayfair gentlemen's club. 'She's just so beautiful, I am unable to resist her charms.'

'Oh bugger off, you silly sod,' says Catrina, punching him playfully on the arm.

'I can see the predicament you are in,' says Andrew, nodding solemnly. 'You're a hopeless case. There is no saving you from yourself.'

Catrina pulls Ryan towards the bar, where they order two cappuccinos. The bar is quite busy - the rain, which began as a persistent drizzle, is now bordering on torrential, so has halted any outside activities. There is an older couple at one of the tables, about the same age as Catrina's parents. They are old enough to have been married twenty-odd years, but the way the man is leaning on his elbows across the table and grasping the woman's hand, and the way she is playing with one of her earrings with her other hand, Catrina concludes that they haven't known each other for long. Their relationship is still in its early stages. This might be the first time they have been away together. They are giving each other far too much eye contact for a couple that has been together for decades. As they wait for their coffees to be made, Catrina puts her arm around Ryan's waist and leans her head onto his shoulder.

'That could be us in another twenty years,' she says.

'I hope so,' says Ryan, kissing her cheek.

When the coffees are ready, Ryan carries them into the library, which, surprisingly, is almost as busy as the bar. Catrina spots Ivy chatting to another woman of a similar age. She waves, but Ivy doesn't see her. Her conversation seems quite intense, private even, and Catrina gets the feeling she shouldn't interrupt.

She finds a table for two at the back of the room near the French doors, which is perfect. She sinks into a leather Chesterfield armchair with well-worn seat cushions. A woollen blanket, the colour of wisteria surrounding a cottage front door, is draped over one of the arms. She unfolds it and covers her legs.

'Here you are, my darling.' Ryan puts a steaming hot cappuccino on the table in front of her. 'Are you okay sitting so close to the window? Are you cold?'

'No, I'm fine, thank you. This blanket will keep me warm,' says Catrina. 'This is a nice place to sit. I like listening to the sound of the rain on the windows.'

It is drumming on all the windows in the room, like a hundred impatient fingers tapping on the glass. Catrina finds the sound soothing and mesmeric.

Next to them is a young family - mum, dad, a baby a few months old, and a toddler. The dad is leaning back in his chair, an ankle crossed onto the opposite knee. He is scrolling through his phone with no cares in the world. The mum looks frazzled. She is breastfeeding the baby, a delicate shawl thrown over one shoulder, which covers her exposed breast and the top half of the baby. Their toddler, a cute little boy with bright red hair, pale skin, and freckles, dressed in jeans and a Celtic United football top, is bored. There is a half-finished jigsaw of Peppa Pig on the table. The little boy begins to whine and tug at his mother's shawl. She snatches it back before he pulls it off. At the rebuke, the little boy cries and throws himself on the floor. Catrina can see that the mother is about to cry herself and sends her a sympathetic smile. The dad is oblivious to the goings on around him. Whatever is on his phone is capturing his attention. The mum looks towards the window, no doubt pleading with the rain to stop so that her child can play outside. But the rain continues.

The man's phone rings, and he jabs at the screen before holding it to his ear. He listens to the voice on the phone for a few seconds, then rests his head on the back of his chair, looking up to the ceiling, a pained expression on his face. He closes his eyes. He takes a deep breath and blows the air out in a quick, angry burst like a fire-breathing dragon roused from its lair. He gesticulates to his wife and walks off towards the door, his shoulders rigid.

'I wonder who he's talking to,' whispers Catrina, leaning closer to Ryan.

'He doesn't seem very happy, does he?' whispers Ryan. 'Go on, have a guess. What do you think his conversation is about?'

'I think someone has booked him to do a magic show, but he can't do it because he can't find his rabbit and top hat.'

Ryan laughs. 'I think he's a fisherman,' he says. 'The hotel chef wants him to go fishing because they don't have enough cod for tonight, and he's refusing to go because of the storm.'

'Don't fishermen have a ruddy red face and whiskers?' says Catrina.

'Not always,' says Ryan.

'Yes, they do. They are never clean-shaven, like him. They have beards. Nobody has time to shave when you have to get up at the crack of dawn to catch fish.'

'You're thinking of pirates,' says Ryan.

'No, he's not a pirate because he isn't wearing a striped jumper. And where's his parrot?'

'Good point,' says Ryan.

'Have you seen a pirate?' The couple's little boy has wandered away from his mum and is looking up at Ryan with an expectant look on his face.

'Yes, I think I might have done,' says Ryan. 'We were just wondering where his parrot was. Have you seen it anywhere?'

The little boy's eyes widen in delight. 'A parrot? Is it here? Mummy, that man's got a parrot.' He runs back to his mum, telling her the story. She laughs and ruffles his hair.

'I'm going to see if there are any books about pirates over here,' says Ryan. He gets up from the table and begins to walk to the bookcase where the children's books are displayed. 'Would you like to come with me, if that's okay with your mum?' he says to the little boy.

'Thank you, that would be great,' says the little boy's mum, giving Ryan a grateful smile.

Catrina is shocked to see that Ryan is so good with the little boy. She would have expected Lucas to be good with children, as he was a teacher, but if he were here, he would be tutting and sighing and demanding they take their coffees into the bar where they were less likely to be *disturbed* by raucous kids.

Catrina finishes her coffee. Ryan is sitting comfortably on the floor, reading a story to the little boy from a large picture book with a colourful elephant on the front cover, so she wanders over to the adult fiction section on the opposite wall. The books are arranged in alphabetical order. The bookcase nearest to their table is filled with books whose authors' surnames begin with N, all the way through to P. On the top shelf, she notices a book with *Terence Nightingale* stamped on the spine. *The Swirling Sea Mist.* This is the one Ivy told her he finished here, when the place used to be a house. She glances over to Ivy, who is still busy talking. A plate of sandwiches sits on her knee, although she doesn't seem to have eaten many, as it is still piled high.

Catrina takes the book back to her table.

# Chapter Twenty

# Ivy

Barbara places the tray onto the low coffee table between the two chairs. There is a plate of triangular, crustless sandwiches – some smoked salmon and cream cheese, and some egg mayonnaise - together with a plate of shortbread biscuits, a teapot, a small jug of milk, and two delicate cups and saucers.

'I asked for an extra cup,' says Barbara. 'I didn't think you would mind me joining you.'

'Of course not,' says Ivy. She pushes herself to her feet. They are facing each other across the table, like a couple of aristocrats about to duel at dawn, pistols drawn, someone's fate already decided. Ivy is unsure of the next move.

'Come here, you old fool,' says Barbara. She opens her arms the way she used to when Ivy and Terence arrived at Hollow Pines for their summer break, tired after a long journey and ready for a drink. She appears to be warm and welcoming, like she was back then, but Ivy finds herself hesitating for a moment. Is Barbara truly pleased to see her after all this time, after everything that has happened, or is she merely playing the part of the gracious hostess? The part she can play so well. She must have some acting skills. She once told Ivy she had dreamed of being on the stage when she was young, and she envied her career. She would have followed her dream, but she loved Scotland too much to ever leave it. She said she couldn't bear to live in London. She would hate to feel hemmed in and to have to live with so many neighbours. She wanted to see fields and hills around her, not houses and office blocks. 'There are too many people,' she said. 'That's the top and bottom of it.' Even when Hugh travelled to London for work, she didn't accompany him. 'Someone has to keep the home fires burning,' she said.

Ivy goes to her; she can't help herself, and they wrap their arms around each other. It feels immediately comforting. Ivy wants to cry again, although she doesn't. There has been enough of that this weekend. She admonishes herself, silently. How could she ever have doubted Barbara's affection? She isn't a particularly adroit actress; she has never had any formal training. She is Barbara. Her good friend. Her lost friend. This affection is real.

'How are you?' says Ivy, pulling away.

'Aye, I'm well, thank you,' says Barbara. Her Scottish accent is as strong as ever, and Ivy is immediately transported back to the seventies. Her voice sounds so familiar, as though she heard it only yesterday. 'Here, sit yourself down.' She leads Ivy by the arm back to the chair and fusses the cushions out of the way. 'There now, are you comfortable? Andrew tells me you had a bit of a turn. Would you like to put your feet up? I can put one of the cushions on the table to act as a footstool.'

Ivy shakes her head. 'I'm almost eighty, Barbara,' she says. 'Having a turn is a regular occurrence. Nothing to worry about.'

Barbara laughs. 'Aye, I know what you mean. Do you remember when *a turn* used to mean someone who came to sing for you at parties or weddings? Now it means fainting fits followed by doctors' appointments and concerned telephone calls.'

Ivy laughs properly for the first time this weekend. For the first time in ages, in fact. Barbara hasn't lost her sense of humour. She could always make her laugh. She watches as Barbara pours the tea - she hasn't asked Ivy how she takes hers - a splash of milk and a teaspoon of sugar, how she has always had it.

'You remembered,' says Ivy, as Barbara passes her a cup.

'Of course,' says Barbara. 'I have never forgotten you.'

'Thank you,' says Ivy. *Thank you for the tea. Thank you for not forgetting me. Thank you for being here.*

They sit facing each other, sipping their tea in silence. There is so much Ivy wants to talk about, about Terence and what happened that weekend, in particular, but she is afraid that the chasm between them is too wide for anything other than small talk. Deep conversations, like rough paths through the Highlands, are something to be avoided by old women. They can be treacherous and will invariably end in pain. She cannot bear any more of that.

'How's Hugh?' she asks.

'He passed away a couple of years ago, I'm afraid,' says Barbara. The expression on her face doesn't alter, like she has seen too much in her life to react to something as inconsequential as her husband's death. It occurs to Ivy that, although Barbara may have followed the ups and downs of her life via newspapers, Ivy doesn't know anything about Barbara's life. She has no idea whether she has been happy or whether she has suffered miserably, whether she has had good health, or bad.

'I'm so sorry, I didn't know.' She kicks herself for not making enquiries before she came on the trip. It wouldn't have been difficult to find out. She is not so stupid that she can't use a computer. She may have been able to find her on social media. She was afraid to, if truth be told. She didn't want to read about either of their deaths. Neither did she want to read that both of them were still alive and well. Having had a close and loving marriage for over fifty years, when her relationship ended so long ago would have been a kick to the stomach that Ivy was not strong enough to bear. Ignorance is indeed blissful.

'I wrote to you, Ivy,' says Barbara. The statement is said without any chastisement, rather simply as a reminder. 'Why didn't you ever come back? You know you would have been more than welcome here.' She smiles kindly, and Ivy knows her statement is true. She would have been welcome.

Shame floods her face, which she is sure Barbara can see. 'It was rude of me not to reply,' she says. 'I'm sorry, I just, I don't know, it felt easier to have a fresh start. Coming back here would have been so painful after what happened. I simply couldn't face it. The long journey up from London without Terence, and then having to sleep in a room on my own, it was too much.'

'I understand that, of course,' says Barbara. 'The first time, yes, it would have been awful without your husband by your side. But then, after that, it would have been easier. You may have found it a comfort to be here. Hugh and I missed you over the years. The summers didn't seem as lively after that.'

Ivy doesn't reply. What can she say? Barbara's last sentence irritates her slightly. How can she say that the summers at Hollow Pines weren't as lively? As though Ivy could be blamed for Hugh and Barbara not being able to throw a successful party. Ivy's summers weren't as lively, either. Now she feels she is being held responsible for Hugh and Barbara's happiness, as well as her own.

Barbara doesn't know how Ivy has berated herself for

Terence's death for fifty years. The weight of the guilt she has carried around has been almost unbearable. She should never have left him out there on the cliff, alone, and angry, at the mercy of the malevolent wind and rain. She should have insisted that they return to the house together, where they would have been safe and dry. While she was getting warm that night, wrapped in a towel with a drink in her hand, her darling Terence lay on the beach, his body broken by his fall.

She was told that his death would have been instantaneous. He wouldn't have felt any pain. But how does she know that is true? She always suspected that the doctor was being kind to her and hiding the truth. Terence could have lain on the ground for hours, his face and body being pounded by the rain as his life slowly slipped away, one tortured breath at a time. She has never forgiven herself for that. She will never be able to. Returning to Holm Island, the place where Terence died, and continuing to party with Hugh and Barbara was out of the question. Ivy didn't deserve such happiness. She couldn't have enjoyed herself without Terence. All she deserved was solitude.

'I never wanted to lose contact with you,' says Barbara. 'I wrote to you a number of times, but then I read in the paper that you had relocated to New York for a while, and I didn't have your new address.'

Ivy nods. 'I fancied my chances on Broadway,' she says. 'It made sense to move there. I've never been a fan of long-distance air travel. I couldn't bear to keep going backwards and forwards over the Atlantic, so I gave up the London flat and bought myself a place in New York. I rented a house in Soho.'

'That must have been nice,' says Barbara. 'I could have come to see you.'

'It was tiny, really. New York has always been more

expensive than London...'

'But I should have come,' says Barbara. 'We were young. I could have slept on the sofa, or on the floor, for goodness sake. We could have had the best time.'

'But, Barbara...'

'I should have been more persistent. I'm sorry for that.'

'It was my fault,' says Ivy. 'I didn't send you my address.' She blinks away tears that are threatening to fall and concentrates on sipping her tea.

'I didn't need your home address,' says Barbara. 'I should have written to you at the theatre. They would have passed on any letters, wouldn't they? I'm sorry I didn't.'

Ivy sits on the edge of her chair now and places her teacup on the table. 'You have nothing to be sorry for,' she says. 'What are you talking about? None of it was your fault. I chose to distance myself, and I didn't really consider your feelings at all. I am the one who should be sorry.'

Time has etched lines onto Barbara's face. Her blonde hair is now mostly white, her blue eyes are paler, but that mischievous glint is still there, and traces of beauty remain.

'Well, serendipity has brought us together now,' she says. 'Better late than never, don't they say?'

Ivy smiles. 'Yes, indeed it has,' says Ivy, remembering the day she sought shelter in the travel agent's. The day that led to this.

Ivy passes Barbara a sandwich, and they chat about the wine weekend as they eat. Ivy tells her how much she is enjoying the food and the small amounts of wine she allows herself. She relays the story of how she came to book the trip on that rainy day in Beckenham. They laugh when Ivy tells Barbara how the young travel agent didn't bat an eye when she gave her name. Ivy Montclaire doesn't mean anything to young people these days. Then they talk about how well the hotel is doing under Andrew's excellent guidance, followed by banal things like the Scottish weather and what films they have seen lately, and what books they have read.

The most important topic, the weekend of Terence's death, is avoided by them both.

## Chapter Twenty-One

## Ivy – September 1976

When the letter from Barbara arrived, Ivy was at home having breakfast - cold, thinly sliced and lightly done toast with marmalade. She heard the sound of the letterbox and opened the letter at the kitchen table, to read whilst she ate. She wasn't surprised to find that the sender was Barbara. She had written to her a couple of times already. Both of the previous letters had been placed back in their envelopes and stored in the bureau in the living room.

Barbara's letter was inviting Ivy to share Christmas with her and Hugh. She wanted to pin her down before anyone else invited her. It was only a couple of months after Terence's death, and Ivy was finding it difficult to plan the next day, never mind so far into the future.

*My dearest Ivy,*

*Social calendars can so quickly become full, so I thought I would send you this quick note before anyone else invites you. December at Hollow Pines can be so beautiful, especially if it snows, which I hope it will, and we would love you to join us for Christmas. You can stay for a week, or just a few days, but the longer the better, in my view. We would both love to see you.*

*The house is beautiful in the winter. Hugh loves to chop the wood to keep the fires burning. While he is doing that, we can settle in front of the fires with a bottle of wine and chat to our hearts' content. I have already mixed the fruit for the Christmas cake. I plan to make it next week, so there is plenty of time to feed it with brandy. You need to come and help us eat it, otherwise we will be ploughing our way through it until spring.*

*We are not planning to invite anyone else. Hugh and I discussed it, and decided you would probably prefer not to be surrounded by lots of people. Let's make it a quiet one, just the three of us. No raucous parties, I promise.*

*If you would like to stay for the week, which you are more than welcome to, on Hogmanay we will all go to bed before midnight and then wake bright and early, have a big Scottish breakfast, and have a rousing New Year's Day walk in the hills. We could take a flask of coffee and try to spot some deer. How does that sound? We have often heard the stags roaring during the rutting season, but have never been able to see them close up. Let's see if we can, shall we?*

*With lots of love,*
*Barbara x*
*PS: Please write back. I have enclosed a stamped address envelope in case you don't have any lying around.*

A rush of unreasonable anger coursed through Ivy as she held the letter in her hand. It was preposterous to think that she needed to make plans for Christmas and New Year already. As though she would be just as popular without Terence. As though people would be clamouring to ensure her attendance over the festive season. As though a grieving widow is a cherished party guest. What nonsense.

The fact that Barbara had enclosed a stamped addressed envelope for Ivy's response infuriated her further. Did Barbara think she wasn't a fully functioning adult who couldn't get herself to the Post Office and buy a stamp? Clearly, she did. Didn't she know Ivy had stamps in her bureau, together with a stack of envelopes, and note paper somewhere, too? No, Barbara didn't know that, because she had never been to her house. She had never been to London. She didn't appreciate that even if she didn't have stamps and envelopes *lying around*, this was London, not a Scottish island, and items of convenience could be bought at the corner shop. London was too crowded for Barbara. Too noisy. It was always them, Terence and Ivy, who had to trek to the back of beyond, hour after hour on trains and ferries, to keep the friendship alive. Well, not anymore.

Ivy screwed the letter into a tight ball, together with the stamped addressed envelope, and threw them both in the bin, along with her uneaten toast.

She simmered all morning until she decided to walk to the corner shop to get herself something for dinner. She hadn't been out for days, and the cupboards were all but bare. She put on a long cardigan and a pair of boots and opened the front door.

A group of half a dozen photographers was waiting outside the flat. They rushed towards her, firing questions like bullets. So fast and furious, she didn't have time to process what they were saying before another one hit. Bang. Bang. Bang.

A cacophony of noise. Cameras flashed. Voices shouted. Men in raincoats.

She strode ahead of them, head down, ignoring them as much as she could. She took shelter in the shop for half an hour, waiting for them to get bored and pack away their cameras and notebooks. But she had forgotten how tenacious reporters and photographers can be – goodness knows why, as Hugh and Terence were exactly the same. Eventually, the shopkeeper, a fiesty EastEnder named Helen, said, 'Right, I've had enough of those bastards. Let's get rid of them.'

She marched out of the back of the shop, through her living quarters - a tiny room with a three-seater sofa pushed up against one wall and a teak dining table surrounded by four wooden chairs in the middle in front of a coal fire - and through the back kitchen, and out into the tiny garden where a hose pipe lay curled like a sleeping king cobra. Ivy watched as Helen screwed one end of the hosepipe to the outside tap and instructed Ivy to turn it on when she gave the order. She ran back through the house and into the shop, dragging the hosepipe with her.

'Right, Ivy, turn it on,' she shouted from the shop.

Ivy turned the rusting tap, which was attached to the back wall of the house. The gush of cold water began to fill the pipe, which slowly expanded and straightened.

'Come on,' shouted Helen. 'You'll have to lead them into my trap. I can't do it by myself.'

Ivy ran through the house, back to the shop at the front. Helen, holding the hosepipe with one hand, shoved Ivy towards the door with the other.

'Now, pull it open,' she commanded.

The bell over the door jangled furiously. As the mob rushed forward, Helen turned the hosepipe towards them, soaking their suits and cameras, as Ivy hid behind her. Swear words and vicious threats were exchanged on both sides, but everyone knew Helen's husband, and she made it clear what would happen to anyone who bothered Ivy again.

'Go and turn the water off, will you?' said Helen.

Ivy ran outside and turned the tap, as Helen allowed the hosepipe to empty into the street. The mob retreated.

Ivy was offered a cup of tea - or something stronger - but she wanted to get back home, to the relative safety and security of her own place.

'Thank you so much, Helen,' she said. 'You're an

absolute lifesaver. I don't know what I would have done without you.'

'You're welcome, Mrs Nightingale,' said Helen, passing Ivy her bag of shopping. She always used Ivy's married name, even though she told her not to.

Much as Ivy appreciated Helen's assistance, her heart raced with anxiety all the way home. She fully expected dripping wet, angry men to be gathered at her front door. She rehearsed her speech as she walked, ready to give them the story they wanted so they would leave her alone, once and for all. But as she approached, she could see that the road was empty, apart from a couple of toddlers racing up and down on their three-wheeled bikes. She opened the door quickly and bolted it behind her.

For dinner, she warmed a tin of tomato soup and threw in chunks of brown bread, which she chased around the bowl with a spoon until they grew soggy. She had no appetite. She sat at the kitchen table, staring into the bowl until the soup grew cold, then threw it down the sink. She washed the bowl and left it upside down on the draining board on top of a pile of others that had been there for days; a ceramic construction of a domed basilica that nobody would ever visit.

## Chapter Twenty-Two

## Catrina

As it is the last night of the wine-tasting event, the hotel is going all out to impress the guests with tonight's dinner. The meal is French-themed and is accompanied by the best Champagne Catrina has ever had, and a deliciously cold Sauvignon Blanc. The first course was a choice of oysters with garlic, parsley, and Cognac butter, or a warm goat's cheese salad sprinkled with walnuts. Catrina ordered the oysters, and Ryan ordered the salad, so they could share. The main course was poulet à l'estragon - chicken in a creamy tarragon sauce - with tiny roast potatoes. Everything was delicious, but the fizzy champagne and rich food are now starting to give Catrina indigestion.

'Before the dessert comes, I'm going to nip upstairs to see if I have any indigestion tablets,' she says. 'I think I've got some in my shoulder bag.'

'Okay, my love,' says Ryan.

As she is leaving the dining room, the waiter appears at their table to top up their glasses. She hears Ryan asking him to top up hers with more wine. He's such a thoughtful person. Lucas would have held his hand over the top of the glass and poured her some water instead, whilst telling everyone she had had her daily quota of alcohol units and any more would be irresponsible and detrimental to her long-term health.

She decides to take the stairs back to the room. She is wearing flat shoes and is only going up three floors. She begins the climb slowly – she is not particularly fit, now that her running regime has lapsed, and doesn't want to return to dinner with a flushed face and a sweat. She reaches the second-floor landing, and is just about to begin the last flight of stairs when she hears a heavy thud of footsteps and almost collides with a man running down the stairs from the top floor. He is carrying a pile of neatly folded white bath towels, which obscures his view somewhat.

'Shit,' he says. He comes to a sudden stop, then backs up a couple of steps, so that he is now towering over her. 'Shit,' he says again. He clutches the tower of towels to his chest like they are made from spun gold, and he is about to be robbed.

His eyes meet Catrina's, and they stare at each other for a few minutes, neither of them wanting to speak first. The black jeans and black t-shirt - the hotel's staff uniform - suit his warm skin tone and deep brown eyes. His hair is still cropped close to his head, but is very slightly longer than the last time she saw him. He has the remains of a summer tan. He used to look so handsome in black. Catrina remembers buying him a new black shirt for her brother's wedding, the wedding he never attended, because she knew he would look good in it. It was hanging in his wardrobe for a long time before she took it to the charity shop.

'Lucas. What the hell,' she says eventually. She is glued to the spot, not knowing what else to say. She has so much to say. Yet nothing. Her eyes frantically search his face. Her heart races, pounding against her ribcage like a trapped bear in a circus cage. She feels suddenly light-headed. Hot and cold simultaneously. The staircase in front of her seems to ebb and flow, like those in the House of Fun at the fairground. Except that there is nothing fun about this.

So she is right, after all. Lucas is the man with the name badge that says *Michael*. She has seen men who look similar to him many times before, as Ivy has also seen men who look similar to Terence, but when she saw him, her instinct told her that this time it was different. Even when she told Simone this morning that she thought she had seen Lucas, and Simone tried to assure her she was being silly, Catrina knew Simone was wrong, and she was right. Then, when she saw him laughing with Ivy in the garden, even from the distance of the spa chalet, she knew it was him. In the past, deep down, she knew the other men weren't him; she just wanted them to be. But this time, something had been telling her that she wasn't wrong, even though she still can't believe he is here in front of her, within touching distance. She stares at his chest, at the name badge with the wrong name. Michael.

'Cat,' he says. His voice sounds so familiar, as though she had heard it only yesterday. She has heard him whisper her name a thousand times. He always called her Cat; he's the only one who does. Never Catrina. She never thought she would hear him say it ever again. 'I'm sorry, I...'

She flies at him, arms flailing in front of her. She wants to hit him, to punch him, to scratch his eyes out. She manages to land a couple of punches to the side of his head before he grabs her wrists and holds them tight. The towels now lie on the floor, scattered like bricks in the remnants of a demolished building.

'Get off me!' she shouts.

He releases her immediately.

'I can explain,' he says.

She steps away and sinks to the floor, her back to the wall behind her. She is suddenly exhausted, like she hasn't been able to fully relax for the past eleven months. The torrent of tears comes quickly. She is angry with herself for borrowing Simone's eyeliner. Now she will have rivulets of black running down her cheeks. She swipes them away with the back of her hand. This isn't how she envisaged she would look if she ever saw him again. She wanted to remain calm and serene, and look groomed and beautiful, as though she had just walked out of an expensive hair salon. She wanted that *look what you've been missing* air about her. She wanted him to look at her, pine for her, desire her.

He kneels in front of her and reaches for her hands. She snatches them away. He looks rejected. He moves to sit beside her, leaning against the wall between two bedroom doors. After a moment, she turns to look at him. He is studying the carpet, head down, picking at tiny threads in the tartan, running his fingers along the white line in the pattern. He looks at her. There are tears in his eyes.

'I'm sorry,' he says. He slips his left arm behind her back, and she sinks her head onto his shoulder. She moves one arm behind his back, and the other one reaches for his neck. Before she can process any more thoughts, they are clinging to each other like survivors of a sunken ship with no hope of rescue.

'Why did you do it, Lucas? Why did you leave me?' She is sobbing now.

She thinks for a moment about how she will face Ryan again. How can she return to the dining room, her eyes swollen with tears? But she can't contemplate that right now. First, she needs to speak to Lucas. She needs to find out why he disappeared in the way he did.

'I never wanted to hurt you,' he says.

She pulls away from him and wipes her tears. He leans over and strokes her cheek with his thumb. She wants to close her eyes and relax her head into the palm of his hand. She wants to kiss him and hold him, and lead him to her room so they can spend the night together, like they used to. She wants to talk until sunrise, find out where he has been, what he has been doing. She wants her old Lucas back. But then she realises he isn't her old Lucas. Her old Lucas, the man she used to know, would never have left her. He loved her and would never have done anything to hurt her. She doesn't know this man. His familiar face is the face of a stranger.

'You do believe me, don't you?' he says. 'I didn't mean to hurt you.'

'There are always choices in life,' she says. 'You made the choice to leave me and, yes, you did hurt me.'

He reaches over and kisses her cheek. His lips search for hers, and for a moment, she relents and kisses him before she pushes him away.

'I can explain, but not now,' he says.

'Don't do that, Lucas.' She scrambles to her feet. 'You've got some huge explaining to do. Talk to me. Now.'

'I'm meant to be working,' he says. He stands and begins to gather the dropped towels. 'I need to put these in the housekeeping trolley for the morning staff.'

'Fuck the housekeeping trolley,' she says. 'Are you serious? I'm not letting you out of my sight until you explain what's going on. I might never see you again. How do I know you're not going to run off?'

She pushes herself to her feet and stands, legs wide apart, in the narrow corridor, as though she has the strength to prevent him from passing her if he wants to go.

'I won't be going anywhere,' he says. 'I promise.'

'Do your parents know?' she asks him. It has just

occurred to her how relieved his mother will be to know where he is. She can stop blaming Catrina for pushing him away. He can finally tell her that she didn't push him anywhere. He ran of his own accord.

'Know that I'm here?' he asks.

'Yes, of course, what else do you think I'm talking about?' she snaps. She is getting angry now. She has carried grief around on her shoulders for months and months. You would think she would feel instant relief, now that she has found him, but she doesn't. The weight feels heavier. She now has the added burden of how to deal with his parents. If Lucas doesn't come back to England, if he doesn't want to tell his parents where he is, if he wants to stay hidden, how does she deal with that? Does she tell them, or trust him to do it? She doesn't know. She doesn't want to have to deal with it.

'No, they don't know,' he says.

'Why not?' Her voice is shrill and loud. 'Have you any idea what they have been through? Any idea at all?'

'Yes, I...'

'No, don't you dare tell me you can understand. I know what you're about to say. I can read you, Lucas. Don't forget how long I've known you.'

'I know, I know.' He looks up and down the corridor, as though searching for eavesdroppers. 'My darling Cat, you don't understand how wonderful it is to see you.'

He steps towards her, but she pushes him back with both hands on his chest. 'Don't change the subject, Lucas. Tell me what's going on.'

'I'm in witness protection. You can't tell anyone that you've seen me.'

'Are you serious?'

'Yes, I'm serious,' he says. 'God, I've missed you. I still love you, Cat.'

How long has she waited to hear those words? She looks into his eyes, searching for sincerity. She isn't sure whether she can see it or not. Confusion is clouding her judgement.

'Why don't you believe me?' He frowns at her, suddenly angry. Two deep lines appear between his eyebrows.

She has missed his face so much, but she hasn't missed this side of him. The side that is quick to anger. Too quick. 'Why are you shouting at me, Lucas? I didn't say I didn't believe you. Don't get angry. Aren't I the one who's meant to be angry?'

'I know, I know. Sorry. I've gone through hell over the past year. Do you know that?' He is standing close to her. She can see stubble on his chin and the deep brown of his eyes, which seem darker in the dim corridor.

She nods. 'Of course, you have. It must have been awful. Tell me what happened.'

'I witnessed a murder.'

'When?'

'At Tom's stag do.'

'What? Tom's stag do? No, you didn't.'

'Yes, I did. It was a few streets away from the hotel. Everyone had gone to bed, but I couldn't sleep. I went outside to get some air. There was a fight and a bloke was kicked to death. It was horrific. Two men were on him. He lay on the floor, curled up like a baby, with his hands over his head, and he was begging them to stop. He was crying, but they just carried on. I swear I heard his ribs crack.'

'Oh my God, that's awful,' says Catrina.

'Yes, I saw their faces, clear as day.'

'So, you told the police?'

'Yes, they were there within a few minutes and...'

'Hang on, hang on, Tom never said anything to me about this.'

'He didn't know about it. I was taken away really

quickly. I barely had time to talk to you. I didn't see Tom after that.'

'But, wouldn't it have been on the news, the telly or the radio?'

Lucas shrugs. 'What do you want me to say, Cat? There are murders every few minutes. They can't put them all on the news. There are other things to talk about, you know.'

'I know, but...'

'You think I'm making this up? Okay, okay, yes, that's right, there was no murder. There were no police. I just decided to leave the love of my life, leave the job I loved, and all my family, and come up here to the arse end of nowhere to work as a hotel skivvy. Is that alright? Is that what you want me to say? Is it?'

'Of course not, I'm sorry. My head's all over the place, that's all.'

'The times I wanted to pick up the phone, to hear your voice. I have texted you hundreds of times, and deleted them again,' he says. 'It isn't allowed. You know I never would have left you unless I had to.' He puts the towels on the bottom stair, and pulls her into a hug. She can feel his breath on her neck. He feels so familiar, so right. Her soul has missed him. They were never meant to be separated. They were meant to be together forever. She finds his lips and kisses him again, this time long and slow.

The ping of the lift bell forces them apart. Lucas pushes her away. The lift door opens, and a middle-aged woman steps out, her room card already in her hand. If she thinks it is odd to see a staff member and a guest chatting in the corridor at this time of the evening, she doesn't show it.

'It's turned dreich out there,' she says. She has a strong Scottish accent. She nods to the tall, narrow window over the stairs, which is being pelted with rain.

'Oh yes, it's bad, isn't it?' says Catrina. 'Been raining

most of the day.'

'It's a bit more than rain now,' she says. 'The wind's howling through reception. They need to do something about the gap underneath that revolving door.' She lowers her voice. 'I don't like to admit it, but I'm still a smoker, and I popped outside for a quick ciggie and nearly got blown off my feet. It's no wonder today's ferry was cancelled.'

'Oh, I didn't know that,' says Catrina.

'Aye, it's high tide, you see. They won't run in strong winds and high tides. It's not safe. It's a lethal combination.'

'Well, I must get on,' says Lucas. 'It was nice to chat to you.' He picks up the towels.

As he passes, she whispers. 'I'll meet you later, in the back garden, by those glass doors in the library. Eleven o'clock.'

He doesn't reply. She watches his back as he disappears down the stairs, unsure whether she will ever see him again.

## Chapter Twenty-Three

## Ivy

When Barbara asked Ivy to join her and her family for dinner at the hotel, for a moment, Ivy considered declining, but she couldn't think of a single reason why she could. The fact that she didn't relish the idea of sitting at a table with her in the same dining room they used to party in fifty years ago, which now seems empty and devoid of life without Terence and Hugh, seemed churlish. So here she is.

Barbara's son, Andrew's father, is at a golf tournament in Aberdeen for the weekend, so, fortunately, Ivy doesn't have to sit across the table from someone who would remind her of Hugh even more than Andrew does. Barbara's daughter-in-law, Mhairi, is keeping the conversation alive with constant questions about Ivy's career. How did she learn all those lines? Was she ever nervous? Which character was her favourite? Did she ever fall in love with a leading man, or anyone else in the theatre company? The easy answer to that question is no. Ivy never allowed herself to fall in love again. Nobody could match up to Terence, but the truth is, Ivy didn't think she deserved to be loved. She still thinks the same.

'I bet many of them fell in love with you, though,' says Mhairi. 'You were stunning in your prime.'

'She's stunning now,' says Barbara, with a wink.

'Of course, she is,' says Mhairi. 'But you know what I mean. You must have had men eating out of your hands your whole life.'

Ivy is spared any further talk of her love life by the appearance of the sommelier, who tops up their glasses with a delicious Sauvignon Blanc. She shouldn't mix wine with painkillers, but tonight she is ignoring the medical advice and allowing herself a small glass. Her nerves are still jangling after the sudden appearance of Barbara in the library. She is glad they have finally spoken after all these years, and they have promised to keep in touch after this weekend, but even so, it was a shock to see her, a shock which Ivy is still reeling from.

'The seventies was a very different place,' says Barbara. 'Men were more forthright, I've got to say. If they were interested, there was no ambiguity. They made it very clear.'

'They certainly did,' says Ivy. 'They could be quite the nuisance sometimes.'

A crack of lightning lights up the dark sky outside the dining room, as though someone has flipped a switch and turned the night off, replacing it, temporarily, with the white glare of midday. A rumble of thunder follows within a couple of seconds. The centre of the storm is close. The hotel's lights flicker. A murmur passes through the dining room; the guests' concerns and worries drift between the tables like thick fog rising from the river. Eating has stopped for a moment as the guests focus on the lashing rain on the dark windows. Gradually, the clatter of knives and forks on porcelain resumes.

Ivy's mind is a blizzard of emotion. She has no control over it, any more than she has control over the weather. Barbara, Mhairi, and Andrew are chatting, but she is not paying attention. Their conversations are dimmed by memories she is forced to confront. Another bright flash of lightning and rumble of thunder drags her back to the past, like an unwilling passenger being forced on a journey they don't want to undertake. Back to 1976, to the last time she was with Terence. To a thunderstorm just like this one. Hot, violent, and frightening. She can't stop thinking about him and their last encounter.

How she wishes her last conversation with Terence could have been different. Why did their argument need to be so pointless? Why did they need to argue over another man, an inconsequential man, at that? Ivy didn't have any feelings for Allan, and he didn't have any feelings for her. There was nothing whatsoever between them. She can't believe that Terence ever thought so. That horrible cow, Denise, planted the seed of doubt in his mind out of pure jealousy. She had never liked Ivy, ever since Ivy was given the role of Stella, which Denise was convinced was hers.

Ivy should have tried harder to make Terence feel more secure. She could have done more that night to explain that she and Allan were friends, that's all. Allan wasn't like other men. He wasn't lascivious or suggestive. He never made a pass at Ivy - or any woman - or made her feel uncomfortable in any way. In fact, Ivy had a secret suspicion that he was gay. It wouldn't have surprised her if he'd confessed that he had a boyfriend. In the seventies, only the brave came out of the closet and lived their life the way they should have done. Many men pretended to be straight when they weren't. They married a close friend and pretended to love her. Many of them had children. The outside world would never have known how unhappy they were behind closed doors. Ivy was sure Allan was one of those men, pretending to be interested in women purely to protect his reputation.

She should have explained this properly to Terence instead of getting defensive and shouting when she had nothing to be defensive about.

That night in her dressing room, the final night of *A Streetcar Named Desire*, when Terence assumed that she wanted to be alone with Allan, they were doing nothing except talking about how well the shows had gone over the previous weeks. Each night had been a success. Ivy was drinking coffee and offered to make Allan one, only a cheap instant coffee with powdered milk, but it was palatable. But Allan said he was tired and wanted to get home. She suspected at the time that he had someone special waiting for him, although she didn't pry.

It shocked her when Terence said he had seen passion between them on stage, which he perceived to be real. He wouldn't believe that they were acting. She had never known him to be jealous before then. She had kissed many men on stage, as part of the performance, and Terence hadn't batted an eyelid. He knew it didn't mean anything. She was his and only his.

A few years before that, when she was playing the leading part in a dramatic play called *The River Knows*, a drama set in the criminal underworld of London, in which she played the part of a woman who found herself lying to the police to cover up a murder carried out by her son, someone left a single red rose on the corner of the stage every night for a week, with a handwritten card. Each night, the card said the same thing, *'For the fabulous Miss Montclaire, with love from an admirer, x.'*

They had done the final bow on the opening night. The curtain had closed. The theatre lights were up, and the audience was beginning to leave.

'Miss Montclaire, this is for you.' The young ice cream seller, a pretty girl who was working in various theatres while she studied drama, had skipped up the steps at the side of the stage and had found Ivy behind the curtain. Terence, as a famous author and Ivy's fiancé, as he was at the time, was receiving as much attention as the actors. Pats on the back, a shaking of hands, kisses to the cheek. Compliments were thrown around like confetti. They landed pleasantly, bringing joy and smiles to everyone. Supposedly, that was why a single red rose wasn't troublesome. Terence was too busy dealing with his own admiration following the success of his third book. In any event, Ivy hadn't seen the man who had left it and hadn't had any personal contact with him, so Terence could easily dismiss any jealous thoughts as insignificant the moment they raised their ugly head. After all, he was the one who was taking her home. He was the one due to marry her in the autumn. He was the one who was photographed next to her as we exited the stage door. His name was printed next to hers in the newspaper the following morning. Terence Nightingale and Ivy Montclaire. The glamorous couple. One name was rarely said without the other.

With the next lightning strike, which occurs just a minute or so after the first one, the lights flicker off, then on again. Then they go off, and stay off. Not just here in the dining room, but in the reception hall, too. People around the room scramble in their bags and pockets for mobile phones. Soon, the place is half-lit by tiny phone torches and the single candle in the middle of each table. The waiting staff bustle about, taking more candles out of drawers and dotting them around the room. One of them dashes into the reception hall, his hand gripping four slim candles and a box of matches.

Andrew immediately rises from the table. 'Ladies and gentlemen, if I can have your attention for just a moment.' The murmur dies down while everyone listens. 'This kind of thing isn't unheard of on Holm Island. As you know, we do tend to get the brunt of the weather before it hits the mainland. If you can bear with us for a few minutes, the generator should kick in soon. Please continue to enjoy yourselves. It shouldn't be too long before we can get around to making you all some coffee. In the meantime, get that wine down your necks. Cheers, everyone.' He takes his half-empty wine glass from the table and holds it high in the air.

Everyone shouts cheers and takes a sip of wine, as though they are toasting a happy couple at a country wedding rather than an impromptu visit from a disruptive storm. Ivy takes her angina spray from her handbag and squirts it underneath her tongue. As though returning to Hollow Pines wasn't bad enough, they now have to experience a storm, too. This is too much.

Lovely as it has been to see Barbara again, she really shouldn't have come back. She should have been firmer with the travel agent and insisted on a trip to Italy instead.

## Chapter Twenty-Four

## Catrina

'Where have you been, babe?' asks Ryan as Catrina returns to the dining room. 'You've been gone ages. I thought you'd fallen asleep.'

'Sorry, I should have messaged you,' she says. She is trying to be upbeat and perky, but knows she isn't coming across in that way. She would love to be more like Ivy - talented actresses would be able to lie their way out of any situation, she would imagine. It must be a very useful skill to have sometimes. 'My mum phoned. I got carried away talking, just telling her what a lovely time we're all having.'

'I told you something like that would have happened,' says Beth-Ann. The travel writer has positioned herself between Troy and Ryan and is watching Catrina intensely. 'Women can chat for ages without realising how long they have been, especially when they talk on the phone.'

Catrina silently thanks this woman she has only known for a day. Hopefully, Ryan believes her. She looks across the table at Simone, who is concentrating on eating her dessert and doesn't catch her eye. Catrina wonders what Simone would say if she knew what had just happened. She wouldn't believe that Catrina had just been speaking to Lucas, and that the man she spotted this morning is really him.

Ryan kisses Catrina on the cheek and rubs her thigh. 'Everything okay?' he asks.

'Yes, why?' Her voice comes out much higher than she meant it to. Pretending to be normal is the most difficult thing to do when things are so far away from normal. Stay calm, stay calm, she tells herself.

'Your eyes look red, that's all,' he says. Catrina can see genuine love and concern in Ryan's eyes. 'You've not been crying, have you?'

'Of course not,' she says. 'Why would you think that?' She picks up her dessert spoon and pushes profiteroles around her plate. Usually one of her favourite desserts, she doesn't have the stomach now for the rich, flaky pastry, cream, and chocolate sauce. The smallest bite is likely to make her throw up.

Ryan shrugs and takes a sip of his wine. He can tell she is lying to him. Catrina can feel him watching her, and she takes hold of his hand underneath the table and squeezes it. She has no idea how she will find the words to tell him that Lucas is back in her life. What this means for her and Ryan, she can't begin to think about. She can feel the tears beginning to well again. Mortified, they slip down her face before she is able to stop them. Ryan brushes one away with the back of his hand. The tenderness tugs at her heart like the memory of their first kiss, and his warm breath on her neck the first time he said he loved her, as they lay in bed that Sunday morning, the waft of bacon in the oven drifting up the stairs.

She reaches over and kisses him. Not a quick peck on the lips, but a full-on snog, right there at the table. It seems the only way to distract him. After a half-second hesitation, he begins to kiss her back, urgently and passionately.

'Go on, girl,' shouts Simone from across the table.

Catrina can hear her and Beth-Ann laughing, followed

by the clinking of glasses. She pulls away, unsure of where to look. She has never done anything like that before, especially not at a table with friends watching.

'That's how you keep your man,' says Troy, pointing a finger at Simone. 'You need to do that to me more often.'

Catrina feels a balled napkin land on her cheek. Simone has thrown it from the other side of the table. 'Enough now, girl. You're giving him ideas.'

She forces herself to laugh when all she wants to do is crawl under the table and bawl her eyes out.

'Are you crying?' asks Troy. 'Jeez, man, I've heard of women crying with passion, but if you can get her in that state with a simple kiss, what are you like in bed? I need to know your secret.'

'Troy, stop!' says Simone. 'Catrina, give me that napkin back, I need to throw it at him now.'

Simone is laughing, but Catrina can see she wants to talk. She has seen the tears, too. She knows when her friend is not being herself.

'I've had way too much to drink,' says Catrina, trying to add a slur to her words. She pushes her dessert plate into the middle of the table. 'Alcohol makes me emotional, you know that.'

They don't know that, because it doesn't. Ryan has never before seen her cry when drunk, and neither have Simone and Troy, but she seems to have got away with it.

A sudden flash of lightning diverts attention away from her. It is followed by the biggest clap of thunder Catrina has ever heard. It makes her jump. She screams when the lights flicker, which makes everyone laugh. She is thankful to be mocked for being skittish, rather than being quizzed for crying. She is relieved when the conversation moves on to talk of the weather and how changeable it is in Scotland.

With the next lightning strike, the lights go out.

'It's a good job we have already eaten,' says Beth-Ann. 'The poor kitchen staff will be in a tizzy. The dishwasher won't be working with the electricity out.'

She takes a notebook from her bag and scribbles something in it with an expensive-looking pen. Catrina hopes she isn't judging the staff harshly for how they cope with the power cut. She feels sorry for the young ones. They have had a long day and will want to get home without this added inconvenience causing them more work. But she doesn't challenge her, fearing that the slightest confrontation will cause more tears.

Andrew jumps from his seat and explains that the lights should be back on soon when the generator kicks in. He toasts the storm, which makes people laugh, and the wine waiters rush from table to table, filling glasses.

'I meant to ask you, Catrina,' says Beth-Ann, 'who was that man you were talking to on the stairs earlier?'

Catrina can feel the blood drain from her face. She is glad to be sitting down, as her legs feel as weak as a kitten's. 'I don't know what you mean,' she says. 'When?'

'When you went to your room before,' says Beth-Ann. 'You were talking to someone.'

Catrina shakes her head vehemently. 'No, you must be mistaken. It wasn't me.'

'I don't think so.' Beth-Ann looks to Simone for confirmation, as though Simone were there. 'If it wasn't you, it was someone with your hairstyle and that same black dress. Are you sure it wasn't you? On the second-floor landing?'

The lilt in her voice makes it sound like a question, rather than an accusation. But Catrina can tell from the look on her face that Beth-Ann is sure she isn't mistaken.

'Ahh, well, that's the issue with wearing a little black dress. Everyone has one, don't they? You only have to look around the room,' she says, trying to sound convincing.

'I could have sworn it was you, though. I popped back to get my notebook, and I wanted to say hello, but you looked pretty intense, the two of you.'

Catrina wants to scream, *Oh my God. Stop it, woman. Why are you interrogating me?* But she plasters a smile on her face. 'Like I said, it wasn't me. Our room is on the third floor, not the second,' she says decisively. 'I jumped in the lift and went straight to it.'

She has never been so grateful for a power cut. Ryan's head is swinging from side to side, right and then left, then right again, like a spectator at a nail-biting tennis match, watching Catrina and Beth-Ann as they speak. Catrina prays that, because of the dim lights, he won't be able to tell how much she is sweating.

'Time for a comfort break,' says Simone. 'Catrina, can you come with me? I don't want to go into the toilets on my own in the dark.'

They both take their phones, the torches illuminating the way out of the dining room, across the reception hall, and into the ladies' bathroom.

'What was that about?' asks Simone, as soon as the door closes behind them.

Catrina glances around to check they are alone. She pushes the door to one of the cubicles, checking that it is empty. Thankfully, there is nobody else here. 'It's Lucas,' she says. 'I bumped into him on the stairs. I told you it was him I saw this morning in the corridor.'

'What? Are you kidding?' Simone's eyes are wide with surprise.

'No, I'm not kidding. It was him. I spoke to him,' she says.

'You actually spoke to him? You didn't just see his lookalike from a distance?'

'No, I actually spoke to him.'

'What the fuck,' says Simone. She rests her hands on the enamel sink, as though steadying herself for more revelations.

'I know,' says Catrina. 'It's a shock, isn't it?'

'You're telling me,' says Simone. 'What's he doing here? Where the hell has he been all this time?'

'He's in police protection. He witnessed a murder when he was in London.' Catrina smiles, hoping that Simone will be relieved knowing that Lucas had no choice in the matter, that he was whisked away from her and his family for his own safety.

'Whose murder?' asks Simone.

'I don't know, some bloke,' says Catrina. 'They kicked him to death. Some gang war, I presume. He said the people involved are nasty, hence the police protection thing.'

'Bullshit.' Simone's anger is sudden, fierce, and completely unexpected.

'What? Of course it isn't bullshit, what do you mean?'

'I don't believe him,' she says. Simone has heard hundreds of stories from teenagers over the years – the dog has eaten my homework, that kind of thing – which has left her with a sharper-than-average lie detector.

'Why?' asks Catrina.

'I don't know, it just doesn't sound right. Don't look at me like that. I know it's dark, but I can see that frown of yours. Shake it off, lady, you can't direct your anger at me. I'm just telling you what I think.'

'I'm not angry at you,' says Catrina.

'Tell your face that, and keep your voice down,' says Simone. 'Do you want Ryan to be any more suspicious? He knows something is wrong.'

'Do you think he does?' Catrina wonders what the

conversation was about at the table in her absence.

'Seriously? You have to ask that question? You go upstairs for a minute, come down in tears, all your eyeliner has disappeared, then Mrs Gob Almighty back there tells him you were talking intensely with someone on the landing. Getting up close and personal with a man. You don't have to be an idiot to put two and two together and make five.'

'But I said that wasn't me.'

'He isn't stupid, Catrina. Don't make him out to be. I'm not saying he will have guessed you were talking to Lucas, but it is clear you were talking to someone. He probably thinks you bumped into an ex, whoever that might be. He'll be waiting for you to tell him about it.'

'I don't know what to say,' she says. The truth is, she hasn't thought of what to say to Ryan. 'I'm a little shocked at your response, I've got to be honest.'

'Are you?' Simone looks hurt. 'I'm just telling you how I see it. Lucas hasn't given you a second thought for nearly a year…'

'That's not true.' Catrina's voice is loud now, as her anger grows.

'Yes, it is,' says Simone, matching her volume. 'If he had, he would have got in touch. And now he gives you some cock and bull story about witness protection. Well, I think he's lying to you, that's my view.'

Catrina and Simone aren't the kind of friends who argue. Even in their young days when they liked the same boy, they never let anything come between them. The boy was cast aside in favour of their friendship. Catrina doesn't want to argue with Simone about Lucas, but she doesn't understand why she isn't jumping for joy that he has been found. She tells her that's what she's thinking.

'But he was never missing, was he?' says Simone. 'He

just didn't want to be found. There's a subtle difference, can't you see?'

Catrina shakes her head. 'Not really.'

'Oh, Catrina, take off your rose coloured specs for goodness sake. I don't believe he couldn't have sent you a message, police protection or not. Even if he didn't want to use his phone or email, he could have posted a letter, or sent it by bloody pigeon carrier, anything to let you know he was alive and well. He's a selfish prick. You're better off with Ryan. Lucas was never good enough for you.'

With that, she walks out and leaves Catrina in the dark.

Simone's words ring in her ears on the way back to the table. She shouldn't have told her about Lucas's witness protection. He told her not to. She wants to cry again. Her emotions are all over the place; she doesn't know whether it's Saturday or July.

If only she hadn't seen Lucas. If only they had gone to Barcelona instead of here. Then she would never have bumped into him.

She loves Lucas, but was beginning to get her old self back, and now he is back, he has turned her world upside down, so much so that she feels dizzy.

## Chapter Twenty-Five

## Ivy

The hotel's generator restores light to the dining room within minutes, although to Ivy it feels as though it has been much longer. Neither she nor Barbara has a phone, and as Andrew is busy directing his staff and has taken his phone with him, their table has been lit only by a single candle and the tiny torch from Mhairi's phone. Barbara seems to be taking the whole incident in her stride and is regaling stories about how many times they have relied on the generator over the years when they lived at Hollow Pines.

'Winter storms are vicious on the west coast,' she says. 'When we lived here, the power lines were blown down with such regularity that we got to know the engineers quite well. It felt like I was forever making them warm drinks while they sorted things out. Once, one of them was here so long that he went home at the end of the day with a meat pie. You never stayed in the winter, did you?' she asks Ivy.

Her question pulls Ivy back to the present day, away from Terence. 'No, I turned into a southern softie in the end,' she says. 'I'm not sure I had the disposition to cope with such cold as a Scottish winter.' Ivy ignores the look

Barbara gives her, telling herself that she is imagining the resentment she can see on her face.

*Barbara won't still harbour a grudge towards me for ignoring her offer to spend Christmas and New Year with them in 1976, will she? Surely not. Barbara isn't like that. Is she? The Barbara I knew wasn't like that, but I hardly know this older version of her.*

'I bet you spent winters in the south of France, or the Italian Riviera, didn't you?' asks Mhairi. 'Being wined and dined by handsome Mediterranean men, escaping the worst of the British weather.'

Ivy laughs politely. Mhairi isn't expecting her to deny it, so she doesn't. She allows Mhairi to keep the fantasy of how she thinks an actress's life is lived. There is no need to explain how she kept herself busy purely to keep the loneliness at bay; taking one job after another, as hours and hours spent learning lines didn't leave much time for thinking, which was exactly what she was aiming for at the time, reasoning that if she filled her days with other people's words, she wouldn't have to re-live hers and Terence's. Those horrible words that passed between them that night, like poison running through a pounding vein.

'I don't know how you coped with being famous,' says Barbara. 'Those bloody awful photographers snapping at you day after day, year after year, just to get a story.'

'They did it to everyone,' says Ivy.

'They still do,' says Mhairi. 'Look at how many photos are splashed across social media these days. It isn't just newspapers; now it's online, too.'

The newspaper gossip columns ran dozens of stories about Ivy's love life throughout the years. She wants to ask Barbara how many she saw. She wants to tell her that they weren't true. Although, Barbara must have seen the photo of Ivy leaving a New York restaurant with a Hollywood actor twice her age in the early eighties. That story ran for months. He had given up his film career and was concentrating on the stage, as a lot of them did in the autumn years of their career. The two of them spent months on Broadway together. The papers on both sides of the Atlantic assumed they were dating. Neither of them denied it. It suited him to be seen with his arm around a woman. Another gay man living a lie. They had become close friends, and Ivy was happy to do him the favour.

'It shouldn't be allowed,' says Barbara. 'It's intrusive, and they don't seem to care how much damage they cause, do they?'

'Did you ever read the story about me and a mystery man in Italy?' she asks Barbara.

'The year after Terence died? Yes, I remember that,' says Barbara. 'I wondered who he was and where you had met him.'

'It wasn't true, you know,' says Ivy. 'I wasn't having a love affair. The mystery man was my cousin, David.'

'You don't need to explain anything,' says Barbara. A wave of her hand dismisses Ivy's concerns. 'You were entitled to fall in love again. Your life didn't need to come to a grinding halt because we lost poor Terence.'

The way she says *we* makes Ivy's heart contract. They lost him, too. Ivy sometimes forgets that other people were devastated by Terence's death, almost as much as she was. Hugh would have missed his dear friend dreadfully over the years, especially during the summer.

'How old were you when Terence died, if you don't mind me asking?' says Mhairi.

'Thirty-one,' Ivy tells her.

'Oh, you poor thing, you...'

Ivy holds up her hand. She doesn't want to hear that it was okay for her to move on with another man because she was so young. It wasn't okay, and she never did move on. If she had, it would have meant leaving Terence on his own in the past, and he didn't deserve that.

She turns to face Barbara. 'I never moved on,' she says. 'After Terence, I never dated anyone. All those photographs you saw and stories you may have read, they weren't true. I had male friends, plenty of them in fact, and we spent time together, going to fancy restaurants and a nightclub or two, but I never loved anyone else.' She can see tears glistening in Barbara's eyes, reflecting the flame from the candle that hasn't yet burned down. 'David's wife had died of cancer the previous year. I was meant to be on holiday with her, not David. She had talked about going to Italy for ages, and I said I would take her one day, so I bought her the holiday for her fortieth birthday. Their son had just left home, and you know that saying, life begins at forty? Well, I wanted to treat her to a holiday I knew she couldn't afford. But then she began to feel unwell.'

'Oh, that's awful,' says Mhairi.

'Yes, it was. She never made it to the holiday, unfortunately. Her unexpected death within six weeks of her diagnosis shook our whole family to the core. As the date for the holiday grew closer, I wasn't sure whether to mention it to David. I was prepared to cover the bill and let it go, but then David asked if I still wanted to go and whether I would consider taking him. He said that a week in Lido di Jesolo would do him good, and Lynette would have wanted us to go. So I arranged for the name on the tickets to be changed and the two of us went.'

'Followed by the paparazzi, I presume,' says Barbara.

'Yes. Two days into the holiday, the headline *Beachside Romance? Author's Wife and Mystery Man Heat Things Up Abroad* glared at me from the front page of an English newspaper. David said Lynette would have laughed and told me not to waste my time and energy putting them right, but I was furious. I had every intention of writing to them when I got home and forcing them to publish a rebuttal, but I didn't.'

'You shouldn't need to explain yourself,' says Mhairi. 'It's nobody's business, is it?'

'No,' says Ivy. 'But referring to me as *The Author's Wife* was a stab to the heart, let me tell you. I spoke to Terence's parents immediately, and told them it wasn't true, so that was the important thing. Although they wouldn't have minded. They didn't want me to spend the rest of my life on my own.'

'I'm sure they didn't,' says Barbara. 'I can't believe you did. You deserved to fall in love again.'

*No, I didn't. She is wrong. Having love is the last thing I deserved after what happened that night.*

'I hope you sued that horrible newspaper,' says Mhairi.

Ivy shakes her head. 'I spoke to my agent that night from my hotel room, and he said, "Darling, the only thing worse than being in the newspaper is not being in the newspaper. Let them print their salacious stories. While your name is on the tip of everyone's tongue, the jobs will keep flooding in."'

He was right. Ivy had more offers than she had time to fulfil. The years sped by, and although she still pined for Terence, she managed to cope by keeping her work diary full to the brim. She learned to live with the hole in her life that should have been filled with the love of a husband and children.

She shrugs. 'I'm sorry, Barbara, I should have told you the stories weren't true.'

'You should not,' says Barbara, vehemently. 'I was happy to think of you enjoying yourself. I didn't want you to be alone.' She reaches across the table and grasps Ivy's hand tightly. 'We had some good times here, didn't we?'

'Yes, the best,' Ivy assures her. 'I used to love coming here.'

'I am so glad that Hugh and Terence got chatting that day in London and became pals. If they hadn't, we would never have met, would we? Thank goodness for The Beatles, eh?'

Barbara tells Mhairi the story of Hugh and Terence meeting at the rooftop concert in London. Afterwards, Ivy gets the feeling Barbara is waiting for her to tell her how sorry she is for not keeping in touch, for not responding to her letters. They were good friends, but only for such a short time. They could have been friends for the rest of their lives, but Ivy's actions prevented that. It would be easy for Ivy to tell Barbara that she regrets what she did, but at the time, she did what she felt was right for her sanity. Hollow Pines was Barbara's home, and it was the place she loved more than anywhere else. But for Ivy, it was a place filled with horrific sadness and despair, and it was best avoided.

'Darling, are you all right?' asks Barbara.

'Yes, thank you, I'm fine,' says Ivy. 'Just that thinking and talking of Terence makes me incredibly sad.'

Her eyes flick to the window and the rain, like ghostly handwriting, tracing grief-stricken words on the glass.

'I know,' says Barbara. 'I think of him every time it rains, too. I'm sorry.'

Ivy doesn't ask what she is sorry about. She knows what she means. Barbara is sorry they didn't do more that night. She is sorry everyone was so drunk that they didn't notice Terence hadn't returned. She is sorry everyone went to bed without giving him another thought.

Barbara repeatedly told Ivy afterwards how she blamed herself for not finding him sooner, even though it was Ivy who blamed herself for leading him out there, to the clifftop. When his body was eventually found, crumpled and broken on the rocks on the beach, Barbara was the one who told the police it was her fault. She knew something was going on between Ivy and Terence, an argument brewing, when she saw them on the porch. She told the police sergeant how she had offered Ivy her shawl so they could stay out longer to discuss things, so she wouldn't be cold. She should have dragged the pair of them back inside, she said. Knowing the storm was coming, she should have insisted that they take their argument into the library, where it was warm and dry, not to the edge of a dangerous clifftop, which would inevitably lead to tragedy. As though anyone would have known what would happen. Hindsight is an invaluable tool that nobody has.

At the time, Ivy couldn't bear to hear Barbara's apology. Her grief didn't allow her to remember who Barbara truly was - an empath, a kind and gentle person who loved Ivy with the ferocity of a twin sister. Instead, it twisted Ivy's thoughts, self-preservation kicking in, probably. Hate was easier to deal with than remorse. Barbara's apology came across as narcissistic and egotistical. This tragedy wasn't hers; it was Ivy's. The fault wasn't hers; it was Ivy's. Ivy couldn't allow Barbara to take it from her. It was easier for Ivy to hate Barbara and distance herself from her than be reminded of how she had failed Terence.

If Ivy had visited Holm Island again, the pain would be waiting for her; an unwelcome roommate. A bully.

So she chose to stay away. Until now.

## Chapter Twenty-Six

## Catrina

Ryan, Simone, and Troy are sampling different whiskies in the bar when Catrina makes her escape just before eleven o'clock. She has tried not to be distracted since they left the dining room and settled in the bar. There is a large round clock, black with silver Roman numerals and silver hands, hanging on the wall behind the bar. Apart from surreptitiously checking the time every five minutes, she has tried to give Ryan her full and undivided attention, but the thought of speaking to Lucas again is consuming her. She would have liked to have messaged him to ask him to meet her later, sometime after midnight, when Ryan would be asleep, but Lucas's old phone was left in the hotel room in London the night he disappeared. Catrina has no way of contacting him. In any event, even if she knew his number, she wouldn't be able to get through to him. The wi-fi is down because of the storm, and a 4G signal doesn't seem to exist around here, storm or no storm.

As the clock fingers finally make their way to eleven, she tells Ryan she will be back in a few minutes. She explains that if she doesn't return the library book now, she will forget in the morning. It's a special edition of Terence Nightingale's book, so she doesn't want it to be lost. A sober Ryan would have told her not to be so stupid. The cleaning staff will find the book in the room and take it back

## The Author's Wife

to the library. It isn't a problem. Books are surely left all over the hotel. But the tipsy Ryan isn't thinking it through. He doesn't question her. He lands a kiss on her cheek and tells her to hurry back. As she begins to walk away, he pats her bottom and tells her he can't wait to get her into bed later. She feels so guilty for lying to him.

Simone is chatting to Beth-Ann, Andrew, and Andrew's mother. Catrina quickly makes her escape while her back is turned. Hopefully, Simone won't notice that her friend has gone.

Catrina doesn't plan to be away for long. She will make arrangements to chat to Lucas properly when they are home. She will get his new telephone number. She will tell him to speak to his parents. Then they can meet somewhere next week, somewhere private where they won't be seen. They can talk about their future, and whether or not they might have one.

The library is in darkness. Catrina finds the light switch on the wall and flicks it down, but nothing happens. She tries again, but still nothing happens. It seems that the generator isn't wired up to all of the rooms in the hotel. Maybe it only reaches some rooms, such as the reception area, dining room, bar, and bedrooms - the ones that need emergency electricity. The library is clearly not important. This doesn't help her. With the door closed, the library is so dark that she can hardly see where the furniture is. Using her phone torch, she fumbles her way to the French doors at the back of the room, which lead to the garden. She tries one of the handles and is relieved to discover it isn't locked. She opens the door and, standing on the threshold, looking out into the garden, waits for Lucas to arrive.

The minutes tick by. He still isn't here. She is about to leave when someone comes in. She can hear footsteps behind her.

*Finally. He must have misheard me, and he has come to the library, rather than the garden next to the library. I can't imagine what has kept him, but it doesn't matter now. Maybe, with the electricity going out, he got roped in to help.*

Her heart beats out of her chest with a mixture of anxiety and pure excitement.

But it isn't him.

It's Simone.

'What are you doing here in the dark?' she says.

There is accusation in her voice. What she means is, why aren't you with Ryan? Catrina is aware that Ryan is going to get suspicious if she keeps leaving him for spurious reasons. She doesn't need Simone telling her.

'Shhh, shut the door,' says Catrina, waving her arms frantically at the light that floods in from the reception. 'I don't want Ryan to see me.'

'He told me you were here, so, I don't know what you mean. Why can't he see you?'

'I told him I was returning a library book,' she says. 'I didn't want to lie to him. Well, no more than necessary, anyway. I thought it was safe to tell him where I was going, in case he saw me coming in here. He is never going to follow me while he has a drink to keep him occupied.'

The door closes. Simone walks to the French door and pulls it closed, shutting out the cold night air and lashing rain. She sits in one of the old-fashioned armchairs and indicates that Catrina should sit down, too, in the one opposite. Simone puts her phone upside down on the low table between them, the torchlight illuminating Catrina's face from below, like someone about to be tortured and interrogated.

'But you're not returning a library book. You're standing by an open door in the dark. What's going on?' says Simone, with the air of an experienced teacher who won't take any nonsense from a recalcitrant teenager.

'I'm waiting for Lucas.'

'You've got to be kidding,' she says.

'No,' shouts Catrina. Her nerves are so frayed that the slightest wrong word and a disapproving raised eyebrow from Simone sends her plummeting, like she has been teetering on the edge of a cliff all evening. 'Why would I be kidding? He was my fiancé, and we have things to talk about.'

'Let me hold your hand while I say this…'

'Don't you dare,' says Catrina.

Simone sits back in her chair, her chin raised, her eyes cold. She looks ready for a fight. She doesn't know that her opponent is already wounded and that the blow she is about to deliver isn't fair.

'Don't dare what?' she says.

'That horrible patronising phrase *Let me hold your hand while I say this*. You're not doing a TikTok video, Simone. This is me, your best friend. Don't talk to me like that.'

Simone takes a deep breath and nods. 'You're right,' she says. 'That was shitty. I've had too much to drink to have a grown-up conversation.'

'It doesn't mean you need to start out like we're in the playground.'

'Touche,' she says. 'Let's start over.'

Catrina glances at the French door, but it's so dark outside that she can't see a thing. She can't tell whether Lucas is outside or not. She looks at her phone. It is now 11:08. She can't leave Ryan in the bar much longer. It was a mistake to tell him she was coming to the library. He could so easily come and find her. Her assumption that he would be happy to stay with Troy is misguided. After leaving the table for almost half an hour earlier in the evening, this is getting beyond ridiculous. Ryan will start asking questions that she is not ready to answer. 'He said he would be here at eleven,' she says.

'I mean, given that he was always a stickler for time keeping, I'd say that he isn't coming. How long are you prepared to wait?' asks Simone.

*Forever?* 'I don't know,' says Catrina. 'Maybe just a few more minutes. If I don't see him tonight, I don't know when I'll ever see him again. He didn't tell me where he is staying. I can't go home tomorrow without speaking to him, can I?'

Simone doesn't reply immediately. Catrina can see she is carefully choosing her words, and loves her for that. Simone believes in tough love, but she also believes in treating people with care, consideration, and grace. Right now, she is giving Catrina all of those things.

'What were you going to say to me before?' asks Catrina. 'When you said you would hold my hand while you said it. Tell me.'

'Really?' says Simone. 'Can you take it?'

'Yes.'

'And you promise not to shout and take your frustration out on me?' Simone smiles. Catrina can see a glimmer of her best friend behind the scary façade. The woman who always has her back and always will have.

'I promise.'

'I would need to see Lucas and look him in the eye to determine whether or not he is lying,' she says. 'But at first glance, well, what you told me earlier, it just doesn't add up.'

'Go on,' says Catrina.

'So, he said there was a murder in London, and he's a witness, right? Hear me out,' says Simone. 'I don't expect all the murders to be on the news. It's a big city, millions of people, blah, blah. But let's say this is some kind of gang war killing…'

'He didn't say gang war, I just assumed that.'

'Okay, so it's either gang-related, or it's a victim who was in the wrong place at the wrong time. He looked at some people the wrong way, and they decided to beat the shit out of him. Whichever. The perpetrators are bad enough guys that the police decide Lucas has to be taken into protective custody, yes?'

'Yes, that's what he said.'

'Well, did the police decide that on the night of the murder?' she asks.

'I don't follow,' says Catrina.

'You spoke to him in the early hours of the morning, didn't you? He said that he was sorry and he wasn't coming back. That doesn't sound like someone about to be taken into police protection. It's all too soon. He wouldn't have even given a witness statement to the police at that stage. The murder had only just happened.'

'I don't know what time it happened. It could have been hours before he rang me.'

Simone sighs heavily. She leans forward, resting her elbows on her knees. 'Now I really do want to hold your hand while I say this.' She gives a little laugh to let Catrina know she isn't being purposefully cruel, well, not a hundred percent. 'At that point, when you called him and he supposedly knew he was going into police protection, but he couldn't tell you, no, I'm sorry, I'm not having it. He couldn't have identified the murderer or murderers by then. It all happened too quickly. He would have had to give details to the police, they would check CCTV, speak to other people. It would take a while.' She leans back, letting her words sink in. 'Do you see? He's lying.'

Catrina blinks tears away. Her eyes are already swollen. She can't cry again. She has to be strong. 'I get what you're saying, but…'

'But what?'

'Lucas isn't a liar. He's a straight, up and down, what you see is what you get kind of guy. Why would he lie to me about this? If he wanted to run away, leave me, leave his family, all of that, why wouldn't he just do it?'

'But that's exactly what he did,' says Simone. 'Do you see?'

Catrina takes a deep breath. 'You're right,' she says. 'I feel like a fool.'

'You're not a fool,' says Simone. 'You're a woman in love. We are all taken in by the romantic fantasy given to us, aren't we?'

Catrina's head flops back onto the high back of the chair. She has lost the strength to hold it up. 'You think he never really loved me, don't you?'

Simone shrugs. But the tiny nod of her head belies what she is truly thinking. A tiny, almost imperceptible move, as though she doesn't want to be the one to break the truth. She must have seen it all along. This conversation must be a relief to her. She no longer has to listen to Catrina telling her how fabulous Lucas was and how great their relationship was. She can speak her truth now.

'If he truly loved you, you would be with him in police protection, wouldn't you?' she says, with an air of smug satisfaction.

Catrina doesn't respond. She is too tired for all these lies.

'I don't really know how it works, but I'd imagine that if it were Troy…'

'Yes, I know – he wouldn't go without you.'

'No, he wouldn't. And I wouldn't go without him.'

'So, what happens now?'

'Come here,' Simone jumps up. She pulls Catrina to her feet and into her arms. Catrina rests her head on Simone's shoulders. 'Nothing happens now,' she says. 'We carry on as normal, and you forget about him. He doesn't deserve any more of your time, does he?'

## Chapter Twenty-Seven

## Ivy – July 1976

Ivy shouted at Terence, on what would be his final night, over the noise of the wind and the sea behind him. His hurt, angry face as she shoved her palm into his chest would continue to haunt her for years afterwards.

'I'm sick of this. I'm not going to apologise for being a good actress. I'm not going to stroke your ego because you're too damn insecure.'

The moment she got back to Hollow Pines and pushed open the front door, she wanted to take her words back. She was immediately filled with regret, as though the warmth and comfort of the house shook her to her senses, like a wise, old aunt offering silent, knowing reassurance and quiet disapproval. But bravado and pride had always played their parts in her and Terence's relationship, expertly and without hesitation.

'Ivy, where on earth have you been?' asked Barbara, suddenly appearing in the Great Hall with a towel for her soaked hair.

'Your shawl,' said Ivy. 'I'm so sorry it's wet. I hope it isn't ruined.'

'My dear, it's an old cotton thing, not one of those silk ones that you adorn yourself with.' She took it from Ivy's shoulders and threw it to the floor, as if to prove how unimportant a garment it was. 'Come on now, dry those tears and tell me all about it. Where's Terence?'

She looked over Ivy's shoulder to where Terence should have been standing. The door was open to the elements. Within moments, the doormat was as soaked as Ivy's shoes as rain hurtled in. The crystals of the chandelier rattled in the wind. Barbara peered out. By now, it was almost pitch dark. The usual half-dark of the summer was smothered by the storm clouds. Ivy had barely been able to find her way back. If the path hadn't been so familiar, she could easily have been lost.

'I left him stewing,' she said. 'He can stay out there all night for all I care.'

'You don't mean that,' said Barbara. She was right; Ivy didn't mean that. Barbara had never known her and Terence to argue, and she must have known how hurt Ivy was. They didn't have one of those tempestuous relationships that artistic people often had. Theirs was gentle and loving, quiet and unassuming. 'Whatever you have quarrelled about, it will all sort itself out. These things always do. You know he loves you.'

Ivy nodded. 'He accused me of having an affair.'

'No! He knows you better than that. How could he?' said Barbara, her eyes wide with disbelief.

'Well, as good as,' said Ivy. 'He was very cross. He said I kissed Allan too passionately on stage.'

'On the stage? But you were acting,' said Barbara.

Ivy laughed mirthlessly. 'That's exactly what I said.'

'Well, it won't do him any harm,' said Barbara. 'It will keep him on his toes if he thinks other men want you. Let's get you a drink.'

She led Ivy into the bar, where Hugh pushed a martini into her shaking hands. Then another, and then another. When she woke the following morning, Terence wasn't by her side. She was cold without his body to keep her warm. She turned over and reached for the glass of water and headache tablets that were always on the bedside table. After taking two tablets with a couple of mouthfuls of water, she lay back on her pillow. She barely remembered getting to bed. Her dress was lying in a heap on the floor next to her shoes. Where on earth was Terence?

She dressed quickly and went downstairs. When she saw Barbara in the dining room, she told her that she didn't know where Terence was. She hadn't seen him since last night. Barbara said that he had probably slept in another bedroom. She said that men tend to hold onto anger and sulk, and continue with petty arguments longer than women do. She told her not to worry.

'Jealousy only grows from love,' she said. 'We will find him and you will be reconciled in no time.' She then asked the waiter to pour Ivy some coffee and to bring some fresh toast. Ivy didn't have the stomach for her usual scrambled eggs.

As more and more of the gang arrived for breakfast, they were quizzed about whether they had seen Terence. But nobody had, either the previous night or that morning. Ivy was beginning to panic, a feeling that was shared by Barbara.

All the bedrooms were searched, but he was nowhere to be seen. When it became clear that he wasn't in the house, Hugh gathered a search party and went to look for him. Ivy and Barbara were told to wait in the house, in case he came back. Ivy told Hugh that the last place she had seen him was on the cliff top, so they went there first. The storm had cleared, and the sky was once again blue, although the chill of the previous evening was still in the air.

Within fifteen minutes, one of the young kitchen staff was sent back to the house with the message that Terence had been found. The boy's stricken face told Ivy it wasn't good news. He was pale, his hands shaking, as though he had been hiking in the Himalayas and his energy had been sapped by the cold. Hugh and two of his friends were waiting with Terence's body on the beach, Ivy found out later. The boy had been sent back with instructions to telephone the police and the coast guard. He wasn't meant to tell Ivy anything else, but she grabbed his shoulders and shook him until the terrible words tumbled out.

'He's dead,' he said, his eyes wide with the horror of the situation.

'Where is he?' Barbara cried.

'On the beach.'

Tears ran down the boy's face. Ivy pushed him aside and ran outside barefoot. She ran through the garden, down the stone path past Barbara's beautiful roses, whose scent trickled out, faint and reluctant, as though they were too sorrowful and weary to bother fragrancing the air that day. At the end of the garden, her speeding feet hit the grass and carried her towards the clifftop. She could hear faraway voices mixing with the crashing waves. For a moment, she imagined the boy was wrong and it was Terence she could hear chatting to Hugh and the other men, but as soon as she reached the top of the cliff and peered down the steep path to the beach, she could see his body on the rocks, his limbs broken and twisted.

Later, the policeman asked her if there was anything bothering Terence, whether he was of sound mind. He had his pencil poised and ready, waiting to conclude the case with one word - *suicide*. No, absolutely not. He would never have done this on purpose, Ivy told him. Never. It must have been an accident. The policeman wanted to know why Terence hadn't followed her back to the house, particularly as the weather had taken a turn for the worse, but she couldn't answer that question. If she hadn't been famous and attractive, there may have been a risk that she would have spent the night in the police cells, accused of pushing her husband over the cliff edge.

The newspapers would have had a field day: *Best-Selling Author Killed in Crime of Passion. Author's Wife Arrested.*

But attractive women have a way of beguiling young men, and the policeman was indeed beguiled by the famous actress before him. He didn't doubt for a second that this was nothing but a terrible accident. He gave everyone a lecture about never being outside in the evening without a torch and never going too close to the cliff edge, as though lightning could indeed strike twice and this unfortunate death could happen again to any of them if they didn't take sufficient care.

In the afternoon, Barbara took Ivy upstairs and tucked her into bed. A glass of warm whisky and lemon was placed on the bedside table. She said dinner would be served at 7pm but Ivy told her not to come for her. She wanted to be left alone.

She closed her eyes and tried to sleep, but all she could see was the look of pain on Terence's face as she hit his chest and shouted at him. She remembered Barbara telling the policeman that he hadn't followed her back to the house because he probably needed space to calm down.

'They so rarely argued, you see,' she said. 'I can imagine him choosing to sit outside on the wet grass rather than inside in the comfort of Hollow Pines, until he felt his heart rate gradually return to normal and his anger dissipate. When he was ready, he would have scrambled to his feet and then returned to the party.'

Except that he didn't.

'Yes, yes,' agreed the policeman. 'By then, his clothes would have been soaked, and it would have been dark. He must have been disoriented and walked too close to the edge of the cliff. On dark nights around here, you can't see your hand in front of your face.'

Everyone agreed that must have been what happened.

After hours of lying on the bed, Ivy couldn't take any more. She threw the blanket off, pushed her feet into her shoes, and crept down the stairs. Everyone was in the dining room. Nobody saw her leave the house.

She chose to kill herself at a specific spot on the road, just after the bend, where a speeding car wouldn't be able to avoid hitting her. She believed she had been the cause of Terence's death, and there was no doubt about it, she didn't deserve to live a moment longer. If she hadn't been so angry, if she hadn't stormed off and left him, if she hadn't slapped him, he would still be alive. He would have returned to the house safe and sound. If she hadn't pushed him away from her, if she hadn't jabbed her finger in his chest, he would still be alive. He wouldn't have lost his footing and fallen to his death. They would have kissed and made up, and all would be well.

She reached the road and knelt in the middle, bending forward into child's pose, her hands clasped across the back of her head as her forehead and knees pushed into the road. The tiny stones dug into her young skin while the rain battered her back. She bore the pain as a penance while she waited for an inevitable impact.

After a few minutes, she heard a car approaching and waited for it to propel her from this life into the next. When the car stopped just inches from her body, she burst into tears. That wasn't supposed to happen. She was meant to be dead. She was meant to be with Terence. She didn't want to live without him. She didn't want to be a widow. She wanted to be a wife.

The driver clambered out of his car. Ivy turned her head

to see his black leather shoes illuminated by the headlamps of his car. Expensive-looking, hardly worn.

'What the bloody hell...' he shouted over the noise of the car engine and the horizontal whipping rain. He grabbed her elbow and pulled her to my feet. 'Are you okay?' he asked.

Ivy stared at him. She wanted to tell him that he shouldn't have stopped. She didn't want him to stop. Why hadn't he run over her? She wanted to tell him that, no, of course, she wasn't okay. Normal people don't lie in the road waiting to be run over.

'What are you doing? I nearly killed you.'

She shrugged and shook her head simultaneously. She couldn't find the words to express her jumble of emotions.

'Where do you live?' he said.

She managed to tell him she was staying at Hollow Pines. He pushed her into the front seat of his car and took her back.

As Barbara tucked her into bed for the second time that day, Ivy told her she didn't want to live without Terence. She told her it was her fault that he was dead. Barbara placed her finger over Ivy's mouth and told her not to speak. Ivy never got to explain that she could have been kinder. She could have defused the argument with a kiss. Terence could never resist her, not really. She knew it was going dark. She should have grabbed his hand and insisted that they return to the house together. Friends and lovers once again.

If she had, who knows what kind of life they would have lived together.

She may have been pregnant before the end of the year. They were settled as a married couple in London, where they could have had two or three children. Both of them wanted to be parents. She might have given up the stage for a while. Terence was bringing in plenty of money. He might have gone on to write a dozen more best-selling books.

They would have been happy. Ivy would have been a wife and a mother, not the lonely, single woman she ended up being.

How different her life would have been if it weren't for that single moment in time.

# Chapter Twenty-Eight

## Catrina

Catrina has slept periodically. She is relieved when Sunday morning finally comes around. She flicks on the television, but there is no signal. She checks her phone. No wi-fi, still. She makes herself a coffee, has a shower, and takes her time drying her hair, by which time the sun is beginning to rise.

She can't spend another minute alone in her hotel room without Ryan. She hasn't seen him since their terrible argument last night, when she told him she had seen Lucas and had arranged to meet him in the library. She thought that honesty was the best policy, but it seems that isn't always the case. She was overwhelmed and more than a little tipsy and wasn't thinking straight. She has ruined everything. In an attempt to do the right thing, she didn't leave out any details. She told a wide-eyed Ryan about how she had bumped into Lucas on the staircase, what he had told her about being in witness protection, and even about their kiss. Ryan's eyes filled with tears as he listened. Immediately contrite and kicking herself for opening her big mouth, Catrina clung to the sleeve of his shirt and told him it hadn't meant anything. It was a moment of madness. No, a moment of nostalgia, that's all it was. But it was him, Ryan, that she wanted. She was over Lucas and never wanted to see him again. Simone had made her realise that he was lying about being in police protection. Not that that was why she didn't want him, no, no, she was over him, despite that. She was rambling, her words tripping over each other in their hurried attempt to appease Ryan and bring an end to the misery she had caused by her stupid thoughtlessness.

But Ryan was no longer listening. He shook her off as though she were an annoying puppy and marched away, out of their room, shouting that she better not follow him. Despite his wish to be left alone, Catrina followed him. She ran down the stairs and searched for him in the bar and in the library, even in the darkened dining room, but couldn't find him anywhere. When she went back upstairs, she expected him to be in their room, having calmed down after a few minutes on his own, but he wasn't there either. She tried to ring his phone, but either he had no signal or he had turned it off. It went straight to voicemail.

Now, she needs to be with people. She needs to hear different voices, other than the ones in her head, panic-inducing thoughts, running wild, telling her that she has ruined everything between them. In the middle of the night, as she lay on one side of the king-sized bed, the expanse of Ryan's side cold and empty, she told herself she would be able to fix it. But no amount of deep breathing and visualising calm scenes of nature helped. She sat cross-legged on the bed, eyes closed, and tried her best to meditate and relax in order to get herself back to sleep. She repeated the mantra *Ryan loves me, Ryan loves me, Ryan loves me.* But her brain, like a fourteen-year-old being taught Latin under the premise that, in the real world, it really does help to be able to conjugate verbs that nobody has used for two thousand years, refused to believe it. Instead of gentle summer breezes in wildflower meadows, all she could visualise was thunder and lightning in a sinister forest. It was more Hansel and Gretel than The Sound of Music. There was no fresh mountain air, twirling skirts, and beautiful singing. Just a sinister feeling of doom.

With the wi-fi still not working, she scribbles a note on the hotel's notepaper and shoves it under Simone's bedroom door, telling her she will meet her downstairs in the dining room. She tells her that Ryan won't be joining them for breakfast, as they have fallen out. She doesn't add that the reason for the falling out is Lucas, but Simone will put two and two together.

Andrew is behind the reception desk.

'Morning, Andrew,' she says. 'I'm a bit embarrassed telling you this, but Ryan and I had a terrible argument last night, and he didn't come to bed. I don't suppose you know where he is, do you? Did he book another room?'

Andrew leans his elbows on the desk, a concerned look on his face. They are so close, Catrina can almost see herself reflected in his eyes. She can see why Simone was attracted to him. He looks more handsome than he did a few days ago, more rugged with a day's stubble on his chin and with his bed-head hair, the colour of toffee-apples, more natural looking without the gel to tame it. She wants to reach out and touch it. The thought makes her blush. She is missing Ryan, that's all it is. She is not attracted to this man. Not one iota. She just needs a hug.

'Yes, he did, but I'm sorry I can't tell you which room he is in,' says Andrew.

'Really? So, he is here then?' says Catrina.

Andrew straightens up, and she is glad of the space created between them. 'Yes, he asked for another room. I'm sorry I can't give you further details. Ahh, here are your friends.'

It's Simone and Troy. Both are dressed in jeans, trainers, and matching navy blue Ralph Lauren cotton jumpers.

## The Author's Wife

'You look nice, both of you,' says Catrina, giving them both a hug.

Simone looks down at her jumper. 'I was saving this, our matching outfits, for our trip home,' she says. 'I know we're not likely to be going today, but what the hell, I have been looking forward to us wearing them.'

'I am being optimistic that the ferry might be operating,' says Catrina. 'I know how bloody freezing it was travelling over, so you're right to wear something warm.'

'Despite the torrential downpour we're still having, the weather is set to calm down later today,' says Andrew. 'You might be lucky, but you might not. I'll give the ferryman a ring later and let you know what he says. You're all welcome to stay here for an extra night, though, if it's not running. Nobody is due to check in until Wednesday. No extra charge.'

'Thank you, Andrew, that's kind,' says Troy.

Catrina buries her head in Simone's shoulder and lets out the tears she has been holding onto all morning. Simone strokes her hair and tells her everything will be fine.

'I told him I kissed Lucas,' whispers Catrina, not wanting Troy to hear her.

'It's fine, it will be fine,' says Simone. 'Ryan will come round. He loves you.'

Catrina wants to believe her, but also knows that it isn't necessarily the case. He is a proud man.

'Come on, let's get some breakfast,' says Troy, clearly uncomfortable with the outpouring of emotion.

Catrina isn't in the mood for breakfast, but the cup of strong black coffee is extremely welcome. She needs something to keep her alert throughout the day, after her night of broken sleep. She is dreading the end of breakfast when Simone and Troy tell her they want some time to themselves, like they did yesterday after lunch. She doesn't want to be alone. She wants to be with Ryan.

Then suddenly, like a welcome lighthouse beam cutting through fog, her phone pings with an incoming message. Then another.

'The wi-fi must be back on,' she says. 'I've got messages.' She reaches into the bottom of her handbag, which is on the floor between her feet. She pulls out her phone, expecting messages from Ryan, telling her he loves her and that he is ready to talk.

'Is it Ryan?' asks Simone.

'No, I don't know. It's an unknown number,' she says, clicking on the first message.

*Hope you're ok.*

She reads the second message.

*Meet me today at 11. On the beach. Come alone.*

Well, it clearly isn't Ryan. It can only be one other person. Lucas.

She drops the phone into her bag. Sweat begins to pour down her back and under her arms. She grabs the breakfast menu and fans herself frantically. 'Is the heating on in this place?' she says. 'It's stifling in here.'

'What's wrong?' says Simone.

'Nothing, I'm hot, that's all. They haven't opened any of the windows, have they?'

'It's not hot,' says Simone. She is frowning at Catrina, waiting for her to tell her who the messages are from. 'Look, I've got a vest under this jumper and I'm not hot.' She lifts the front of her jumper to show her cream coloured vest, as though what she said was ever in doubt. 'It's like winter out there.'

She nods to the windows. Outside, the rain has eased a little, but the wind is still as ferocious as ever. Fallen leaves are being whipped from the ground, swirling like young ballerinas being drilled by a relentless teacher who won't let them rest. Round and round and round. There is nobody about outside, unlike yesterday when the front of the hotel was busy with guests coming and going. Now it is deserted, as everyone shelters inside.

'So?' says Simone.

'So what?' says Catrina, pretending she doesn't know exactly what Simone means.

'Who were your messages from?'

'Oh, nobody,' she says.

Quick as a flash, Simone reaches under the table and grabs Catrina's bag. Before Catrina can stop her, she has retrieved her phone, opened it, and read the messages. She throws the bag back on the floor, but keeps the phone in her hand, clutching it tightly to her chest, with the screen facing towards her, any further messages hidden from view. 'You're not going,' she says, decisively. She sits back and folds her arms, willing Catrina to defy her.

'Who made you my keeper?' says Catrina. They sound like bickering children. The minute the words are out, Catrina wants to reach out and grab them back before they reach her friend's ears. Simone is trying to protect her; she is looking out for her emotional welfare.

'Does someone want to tell me what's going on?' asks Troy.

Simone slides the phone across the table towards him. He picks it up and reads the messages. Catrina then manages to snatch the phone back and cling to it before Simone confiscates it again.

'It said *meet me on the beach*,' says Troy. 'Who are you meeting on the beach? I don't understand.' When Catrina doesn't answer immediately, he says, 'No! You're not having an affair, are you? Is that why you and Ryan argued?'

'No, of course not,' says Catrina. She turns to Simone.

'Have you not told him?'

Simone shakes her head and looks a little sheepish. 'No,' she says.

'Well, can you tell me now?' says Troy. 'This is starting to piss me off. I didn't think we had secrets. What's going on?'

'We don't have secrets,' says Simone. 'I would have told you, but, oh, I don't know. Maybe I was hoping it wasn't true.'

'You were hoping it wasn't true? Are you serious?' says Catrina. The woman at the next table spins around, but when Catrina glares at her, she turns back to her breakfast, although it is clear by the tilt of her head that she is still listening. 'Why wouldn't you want it to be true?' Catrina whispers. 'You know how devastated I have been. How could you say that?'

'I know you've been devastated, but you were also so unhappy with him,' says Simone. 'That's why.'

'For God's sake,' says Troy. 'Someone let me into the loop.' He looks angry.

Yesterday, Catrina didn't ask Simone not to tell Troy about Lucas. When she told her she had seen him, she presumed she would tell Troy. She wouldn't expect Simone to keep a secret from her husband, especially not one as huge as this.

'I've seen Lucas in the hotel,' says Catrina. 'I told Simone last night, and then I told Ryan when we got back to our room. We had a huge argument, and he stormed off. He didn't come to bed last night.'

'Are you kidding me?' Troy's coffee cup slips from his fingers. It clatters on the saucer, spurting hot black coffee over the tablecloth. The coffee bleeds into the white fabric like an ink blob in a confession statement. Catrina grabs her napkin and begins to mop up the spillage, but it's futile. The cloth is stained. The damage is already done. 'You've seen Lucas?' Troy's expression is a mixture of disbelief and confusion. He turns to his wife. 'Why didn't you tell me, babe?'

Simone starts to cry, which makes Catrina want to cry. 'I'm sorry,' she says. 'I wanted to ignore it. Maybe deep down I was hoping he would disappear again.' She shrugs. 'I know it's not what you'd expect me to say, Catrina. But in all honesty, after the initial heartbreak, you've been much happier with Ryan than you ever were with Lucas. Some days, you were so miserable. I don't think you realised how bad things were, because you argued so often, it had become normal. I didn't want Lucas coming back into your life and spoiling what you have with Ryan.' She turns to Troy. 'I thought that if I told you, you would go all out and start searching for him and bring him back into the fold.'

'Not if you didn't want me to, babe,' says Troy. His voice is tender and quiet, filled with love, which pulls at Catrina's heartstrings.

'Sorry, Catrina. I've not been a great friend, but I was protecting your best interests. Can you see?'

'Of course,' says Catrina. She offers Simone the wet napkin, and Simone laughs at the absurdity of wiping her face with a coffee-soaked cloth, which makes Catrina smile, too.

Catrina has never been more confused in her life. She doesn't want to entertain the thought that it would have been better if they had gone somewhere else for the weekend, and she had never bumped into Lucas. How can she think that? His parents will be over the moon to know that he is alive and well. But now she might have ruined things between her and Ryan. She realises that she loves Ryan. There is no doubt about that, and she doesn't want to hurt him. He is the one she wants to spend the rest of her life with. She just needs to put things right.

Her mind flashes with past arguments between her and Lucas, like a slideshow of bad holiday snaps. The time when they ignored each other at Simone's sister's engagement party because they had argued over something trivial on the way there. The time when they had a shouting match in their back garden, in front of Simone and Troy, because he accused her of drinking too much. He said one bottle of wine was more than enough for one person, and anything more than that was giving him *red flag vibes*. A cloud of hostility had hung over the garden for the rest of the afternoon. The time when she was dancing with Troy's brother at a wedding, when Lucas had marched onto the dance floor and dragged her away in a jealous rage. The crowd had parted like Moses in the Red Sea as they watched the two of them leave the room.

Then there were countless other times when Simone had listened to Catrina moaning about him. Things he had said, things he had done, things he had accused her of. Now that she thinks about it, Simone is right. Catrina wasn't as happy with Lucas as she thought she was. They were comfortable. They had been together a long time. They were at the age when most of their peer group were engaged or married - some had children already – which put pressure on them to do the same.

It is clear to her now that if Lucas hadn't disappeared, they would never have made it down the aisle. If their relationship hadn't fizzled out, she would have ended it.

Simone has finally held the mirror to Catrina's relationship and allowed her to see the truth.

'Are you going to meet him?' asks Simone.

'No,' says Catrina decisively.

## Chapter Twenty-Nine

## Ivy

Today is Sunday. The day Ivy is meant to be going home. She never looked forward to the long journey back to London, even when she was young, and had Terence to chat to. But this weekend, from the moment she stepped foot off the ferry, she has been looking forward to getting back on it today and escaping from Holm Island and the past that has haunted her for fifty years. However, Fate, the little witch that she is, has other ideas. Nobody is going home today, unless a miracle happens and the storm suddenly dies.

Ivy climbs out of bed, pulls back the curtains and sighs. There is no sign of a miracle. The wind doesn't seem to have abated at all. It is as fierce as it was last night. The pine forest is swaying rhythmically, this way and that way, the trees like choreographed synchronised swimmers moving to a fast pulsing beat of music. The last of the delicate summer flowers that border the hotel's long, curved driveway are cowering from the battering they are receiving from the rain. Some of them are already dead. Soaked petals are strewn across the lawn and the gravel, like fallen soldiers.

Never mind. There is nothing she can do about factors

beyond her control. This morning, she has arranged to meet Mhairi and Barbara in the library after breakfast, and she is determined to enjoy herself.

'We can read books, drink tea, and chat to our hearts' content,' said Barbara last night. 'Unless you'd like to go for a swim, or anything? I can't think of anything else we can do in this dreadful weather.'

'Oh goodness,' said Ivy. 'I absolutely do not want to do anything tiring. This trip has sapped me of enough of my energy, I'm afraid. A chat and a read in the library sounds perfect.'

After a breakfast of porridge with honey and banana that she asked to be delivered to her room, Ivy gets dressed and takes the lift down to the ground floor. As she stands in the Great Hall, she can see that the library, whose door has been propped open by a stuffed highland cow doorstop, is busy. There are at least a dozen people milling around choosing books. Some are already seated, glasses on, heads down, with their book open before them. Before her friends arrive, she tasks herself with sourcing some good books for them to choose from. She runs her fingers over the spines of the books in the fiction area, her head on one side as she reads the titles. She pulls one out, a brightly coloured Caroline James book about some friends on a Caribbean cruise, which she thinks Barbara might like. She is engrossed in reading the blurb on the back of the book when Catrina comes in.

'That's a good one,' says Catrina, pointing to the book. 'I read it on holiday last year.'

'Good morning, Catrina,' says Ivy. She hugs the book to her chest. 'In that case, I will take it on your recommendation and will read it myself.' She tucks it under her arm.

She tells Catrina that she would like two more books for

Mhairi and Barbara, two friends of hers. She explains that Barbara is Andrew's grandmother and Mhairi is his mother, who is married to Barbara's son. They spend the next few minutes scanning the shelves for ones they might like. For Barbara, she chooses a book about a woman in Cornwall who inherits a London cafe from an old, distant relative she didn't know she had, and decides to make the move to the capital to run it. Barbara always used to tell her she wouldn't be able to bear the crowds and the noise of London, especially after spending the summer at Hollow Pines, so she might like to read about the protagonist's journey. As she doesn't know Mhairi that well, Ivy chooses a Philippa Gregory book about Henry VIII, deciding that everyone is fascinated by him and his many wives, so she can't go wrong with that choice.

As they peruse the shelves, Catrina tells Ivy that her friends, Simone and Troy, have had a 'slight disagreement' at breakfast, so she has left them to talk it out, adding that she didn't want to go back to her room alone, and she isn't sure where Ryan is, so she came into the library instead.

'It isn't anything serious, is it?' asks Ivy. 'It seems a shame to fall out when they are here for a birthday celebration.'

'They will be fine. Have you got time to sit for a while?' asks Catrina.

Ivy gets the impression that Catrina wants to talk, not only about her two bickering friends, but also about herself. 'Of course, dear,' she says. 'Barbara and Mhairi aren't here yet, and if they arrive soon, it doesn't matter. We can still talk. They're not going anywhere in this weather.'

They both look out of the window, where it is still lashing down, although with a little less ferocity than the previous night. They find a small table snuggled between the fiction and the non-fiction bookcases. On either side of the table, there is just enough room for two surprisingly comfortable tub chairs. Ivy sinks her aching back into the feather cushion on the chair.

'I love this tartan,' says Catrina, placing her cushion on her knee and stroking the fabric. 'It's all over the hotel, isn't it? There's a blanket in our room with the same design, and the carpets upstairs.'

'Yes, it's beautiful,' says Ivy. 'It's called MacDonald, Lord of the Isles. Hugh's family tartan.'

'Hugh?'

'My friend who used to own the hotel. Barbara's husband.'

'Oh yes, I remember you saying, Hugh and Barbara. You and your husband used to come here and stay with them, didn't you? Terence.'

'Yes, Terence.' Ivy runs her finger over the embossed title of one of the books on her knee, *The Other Boleyn Girl*.

'They made that into a film, didn't they?' says Catrina.

'Oh really? I haven't seen it, I'm afraid. I've read the book, though. It's very good.' Ivy would like to steer the conversation away from Terence and talk about anything else, and the tragedy of the Boleyn family seems as good a subject as any. She is carrying too much emotion, and fears it might spill out if she talks about herself and Terence. 'It was tragic what the Boleyn men did to those women, practically sold them to the king, didn't they?' she says.

Catrina nods. 'Yes, sad, isn't it? Imagine having to marry someone you don't really love, or worse, *not* being able to marry someone you really love.'

'Well, you didn't get to marry the love of your life, did you?'

Catrina shakes her head. 'No, I didn't.'

'Lucas, isn't it, the name of your missing fiancé?'

Catrina gives a sardonic laugh. 'Yes, that's right. Except

that he isn't missing anymore. Remember me telling you that I saw someone in the hotel who looked just like him?'

'Yes, I do remember, and I said it used to happen to me when I first lost Terence.'

'Well, it turns out it was him.' She pauses dramatically, waiting for what she has just told Ivy to sink in.

'Whatever do you mean? That the man you thought was Lucas was actually him?'

'Yes.'

'Are you sure? Have you spoken to him? I mean, have you seen him close up?' asks Ivy.

'Yes, I saw him last night. I popped back to the room for something, and we literally bumped into each other on the stairwell.'

'Goodness,' says Ivy. 'I can't imagine what a shock that would have been for you. Well, for you both.' The look on Catrina's face tells Ivy that seeing her lost fiancé didn't quite turn out the way she had probably expected it to. She isn't smiling, and she doesn't seem happy. 'Do you want to talk about it?'

'I would love to,' says Catrina. 'Simone isn't being particularly supportive. That's what the disagreement at breakfast has been about. I told her last night that I had seen Lucas, but she didn't tell Troy. He was Lucas's friend; they were quite close, so I assumed she would tell him, but she didn't.' Catrina takes a deep breath and looks so incredibly sad that Ivy wants to give her a hug. 'According to Simone, it would have been better if Lucas had never turned up. I think she thinks I'm going to dump Ryan and go running back to him. She said I didn't seem happy with Lucas when we were together, and that I'm much happier now.'

'People often have the wrong impression of a relationship when looking at it from the outside,' says Ivy. 'It is like seeing it through bevelled glass. They only have a distorted view. Your view is the only one that matters. Ask yourself, is your view clear enough to enable you to make a decision between the two men?'

Catrina looks down at the cushion, her fingers still busy working their way up and down the stripes in the tartan. '

'What is your heart telling you?' asks Ivy.

'That I want to be with Ryan,' says Catrina. 'I was happy with Lucas, or at least I thought I was, but all I keep remembering are the arguments we used to have. I'm beginning to wonder if Simone is right, and that I was never as happy as I thought I was.'

'Only you can know that, deep down,' says Ivy. 'People usually remember the good things about a person when they're gone, so the fact that you are remembering the arguments means...' She pauses for a moment, unsure whether she should continue. She has only known this young woman for such a short time, but she decides to continue. After all, Catrina is the one who said she wanted to talk. 'I'm sorry if you think I am speaking out of turn, but if you are remembering lots of arguments, then it means, well, your friend might be right. At least you know he's alive and well, but let him be part of your past and move on. It doesn't mean that your future is necessarily with Ryan. It just means that it isn't with Lucas.'

Catrina nods, but doesn't reply for a moment. With her head down, she examines her nails. Ivy looks across the room to the French doors. The delicate lavender bushes are being battered by the wind, which whistles around the hotel and in through the gap under the doors. The sound smothers the soft conversations in the library. Ivy wonders whether Catrina likes the design of the garden now, with its modern simplicity. Or whether she would have loved Barbara's roses. It's a shame that such a beautiful flower is seen as old-fashioned and often overlooked in a modern garden.

'Has the rain stopped?' asks Catrina, who has her back to the garden. 'I can't hear it thrumming against the window.'

'No,' says Ivy. 'It isn't quite as bad, and it is still very windy, but it looks like the worst of the storm might be over.'

'Excellent news,' says Catrina.

'I wonder when we will be able to go home,' says Ivy. 'Andrew told me that the tide is receding and the forecast is for the weather to be calm tomorrow, so we might not be able to leave today, but I don't know about you, I will be catching the nine o'clock ferry in the morning, come what may.'

'You know, it's ironic, but when we first arrived at the hotel on Friday, I remember thinking how Lucas would love it here. He loves hotels like this, all dark wood and leather furniture.' Catrina strokes the arm of the chair. 'I knew he would love this tartan everywhere. One of his grandmothers is Scottish, and he used to have holidays in Scotland quite a bit when he was a kid. I felt a bit sad, you know, thinking he was missing out on this wonderful place, and yet he hasn't missed out at all, has he? He has been here for months. I had no clue.'

'He's been here for months?' says Ivy. 'I am shocked. How on earth can he afford that? It's not a cheap place, is it? It must be costing him a small fortune.'

'No, no, he's not a guest. He's been working here. He has given them a false name. Michael. He's some kind of handyman, a Jack of all trades. I suppose all hotels need someone like that.'

'Oh, I see. Did he tell you why he decided to leave his old life?' asks Ivy. 'Because he didn't just leave you, did he? He left his friends and family, too.'

Catrina nods. 'He said he witnessed a murder and was taken into witness protection.'

'Really?' says Ivy. 'The poor thing. And poor you, of course, but you have to admire him, don't you? I mean, not everyone would do their civic duty in that way.'

'Do you not think?'

'Not at all,' says Ivy. 'I don't think I would be able to do it. He has given up his whole life to make sure that a murderer is put away behind bars. It's quite admirable.'

'The thing is, Simone thinks he's lying.'

Catrina explains the timeline and Simone's hypothesis that Lucas's story doesn't add up, because the murderer wouldn't have been apprehended and identified within an hour or so of the murder. It doesn't make sense.

'I see what Simone means,' says Ivy. 'That does all seem rather rushed. Maybe you can speak to Lucas and ask him to explain in more detail how it all happened.'

'Yes, I think I will,' says Catrina. 'He messaged me this morning and asked me to meet him at the beach at eleven o'clock.'

'Oh, that's wonderful,' says Ivy. 'So you will be able to get to the bottom of it, after all.'

Catrina looks at her phone. 'Well, I must go,' she says. 'It is almost eleven. Hopefully, I will see you later.' She gathers her handbag, gets up, and says goodbye.

'I hope you get all the answers you are looking for when you get to speak to him,' says Ivy. 'Then you can put it behind you. I'm sure the two of you have been through the mill enough.'

'Thank you,' says Catrina. 'Oh, I forgot to tell you. I picked up Terence's book yesterday, *The Swirling Sea Mist*. I haven't got around to reading any of it yet, but it sounds good. He was a talented writer, wasn't he?'

Ivy's heart flips in her chest at the mention of Terence's

best-selling book. The last one he ever wrote. The one he discussed with her as she put her makeup on before dinner in this very house. The one he was most anxious about. The one he never felt was *quite right*, but in fact was his most famous and most loved book by his loyal fans.

'Oh, Ivy, I'm so sorry,' says Catrina. 'I shouldn't have said anything. I've upset you now…'

'No, don't be silly,' says Ivy. She swipes at a stray tear with her finger. 'That book holds a special place in my heart, that's all. The mere mention of its name brings back a flood of memories. Good ones, though, so don't worry.'

Catrina bends and kisses Ivy's cheek. 'I would love to hear more about Terence,' she says. 'I will see you this afternoon and will tell you how my chat with Lucas goes, and if you'd like to talk about Terence, I'm all ears.'

When she has gone, Ivy rests her head against the back of the chair and closes her eyes for a second. Her mind begins to wander to Terence, as it has so often done this weekend. Being in the place where they had so much fun, and also where they were last together, it is inevitable that he will be at the forefront of her mind.

She can't help thinking how fortunate Catrina is to be able to speak to Lucas again. What Ivy wouldn't give to come face to face with Terence on the stairwell at Hollow Pines, or anywhere else for that matter. She would give her last penny to see him one more time. If he had gone missing in 1976 and then reappeared, she would be angry with him for causing her to cry and worry about him year after year, but she would fall into his arms and welcome him back to her life. They could pick up where they left off. All talk of infidelities would be forgotten. There would be no lingering jealousy over an on-stage kiss with a colleague. Allan who? they would say. They would laugh about Terence's silly insecurity back then, and Ivy would tell him how much she loved him. She would assure him that she wasn't ever unfaithful. Why would she look at another man when she had everything she ever wished for right here? Her handsome Terence. The love of her life. He was the one who would turn heads when he entered a room, not Ivy.

But she knows that will never happen.

## Chapter Thirty

## Catrina

The problem of how to slip away from Simone and Troy isn't a problem that Catrina needs to worry about. The pair of them haven't come out of their room since breakfast.

*If they can't be bothered to check in on me and see if I'm okay when they know I've had a huge argument with Ryan, then I can't be bothered to let them know that I have changed my mind about meeting Lucas.*

Catrina is wearing trainers, so she skips down the front steps of the hotel, turns left onto the gravel path, and jogs through the back garden, despite the continuing rain making the path extremely wet and slippery. She smiles to herself at the irony. Lucas has been out of her life for eleven months, and now that he's back, she finds herself jogging again. But this time it is for her, not him. Simply because she doesn't want Simone or Troy to see her and demand her return. She is not running because Lucas has demanded it.

She is a few minutes early. By the time she gets to the clifftop, it is still only ten to eleven. Despite the rain, she would rather wait on the empty beach than risk bumping into Simone and Troy in the hotel and them stopping her from coming out. After her conversation with Ivy, she has decided that she needs to see Lucas. He needs to give her some answers, and she won't be satisfied until she hears them. Then she can go and find Ryan, knowing that her conscience is clear and that all loose ends with Lucas have been tied.

The hotel brochure says that the path down to the beach is steep. They are not wrong. But there is plenty of long grass to hold onto. Catrina swallows her anxiety about falling and makes her way down, one tentative step at a time. She doesn't want to risk a twisted ankle.

After a few hair-raising minutes, she makes it onto the beach. It feels more like November than September, and she is thankful for her warm coat. She pulls the hood over her head and turns her back to the wind as whirlwinds of sand fly into her face. She has to squeeze her eyes almost shut to save them from the painful grains.

The sea is only a few metres away from the cliff. It hurls itself onto the shore and rushes out again, as though it has made a mistake and entered the wrong room at a party. Catrina isn't sure whether the tide is on its way out or on its way in, and can't remember what Ivy told her. Maybe she should have checked. Did Ivy say it was on its way out? Her phone is in her jeans pocket, but she can't be bothered checking. She is here now, so it isn't as though knowing will influence her decision. In any case, she doesn't have a phone signal, and the hotel's unpredictable wi-fi is unlikely to stretch this far.

She finds a rock to sit on and waits for Lucas, for the second time this weekend. There are sharp rocks and boulders scattered up the beach as far as the eye can see, like coins thrown into a fountain. She picks up a small one and throws it back into the sea. Should she make a wish? She decides not to. There are so many things she could wish for, she can't decide which one is the most important. Ryan springs to mind, but she pushes the thought away. She can't think about him right now.

'I didn't think you'd come.'

Catrina turns to see Lucas scrambling down the path. He looks handsome. He is no longer wearing the hotel's uniform, but a black The North Face jacket over a white button-down shirt, dark blue jeans, and brown ankle boots. Catrina doesn't recognise any of his clothes. Her heart aches with the thought of him shopping without her. He hates shopping. She always had to drag him into Manchester when he needed anything, with the promise of lunch and a pint of beer afterwards. She is momentarily discombobulated. He looks good, but she doesn't want to find him handsome. She doesn't want to fall for his charms. She is here to confront him. She is here for answers.

'Well, here I am,' she says. 'Why wouldn't I come? I want to hear your explanations.'

She gets to her feet as he approaches. He lunges for her, arms open wide, causing her to step back. 'Whoa. What are you doing? We're not kissing. We're not teenagers, Lucas, having a little rendezvous on the beach away from the grown-ups.'

'No, no, I know that,' he says.

He is stumbling over his words. Now he is the one who is discombobulated. One-nil to Catrina. The point scoring – small victory that it is - gives her a little rush of confidence. She can do this. She doesn't need to let him walk all over her. Not anymore. She is much stronger now. He may have got one over on her when they were together, on more than one occasion, but she will never let that happen again. She is not the same woman she used to be. He doesn't know who he is dealing with. He doesn't know the person she has become. She is ten times stronger now than when she was with him. Having spent a few months with Ryan, she has finally realised how she should be treated – like an equal.

'Shall we sit down?' he asks, pointing to a large round

boulder a few metres away, big enough for two people if they sit close enough together.

'I'd rather stand,' she says.

'What is this?' he asks. He waves his hand up and down in front of her, disparagingly. His eyes take her in, from top to toe.

She is wearing jeans and a pale blue raincoat, the colour of forget-me-nots, but underneath her vest top shows just the right amount of cleavage, and she has left the top two buttons of her coat unfastened, so he can see what he has been missing. She is pleased with her appearance, despite her sleepless night. Plenty of highlighter hides the dark shadows under her eyes, the result of a night of tossing and turning. Expertly applied eyeliner and waterproof mascara have given her a 'looking good, but in a natural way' look. Her hair is tied in a high ponytail, which looks much more casual than curls dancing around her shoulders. She tugs at her hood, which is threatening to blow off, and pulls her ponytail over her shoulder, running her hair through her fingers. Maybe she should have worn it down, after all. He used to like her hair tied up, and she doesn't want him to think for one moment that she has tied it up to suit him.

'I don't know what you mean,' she says, waiting for him to ask why she is dressed as though she is going out somewhere. She is only in jeans, but it is clear that she has made an effort with her hair and makeup. She will tell him that this is how she chooses to dress every day now. Gone are the days of no makeup and no nail varnish. She dresses like this for her, and nobody else.

'The attitude,' he says, with a snarl. 'You were all over me last night, and now you're all standoffish. Are you playing hard to get? Because, if you are, it's not working. It's a bit late for games, Cat.'

Okay, so he hasn't commented on her appearance,

which leaves her more than a little disappointed, but that doesn't mean he hasn't noticed. He is a man, after all.

He is frowning. Anger is playing with the edges of his mouth, turning it into a childish pout. It has narrowed his brown eyes to dark slits. His nostrils flare like a bull at Las Ventas about to charge at the matador's red cape.

'I'm not here to play games,' says Catrina. 'I just want to know why you lied to me about being in witness protection.'

He laughs. He doesn't sound like the Lucas she knows, or used to know. Who is this stranger? Michael, now, clearly. He has morphed into someone else by changing his name. Or is it that he has always been like this – cruel and deceitful - but Catrina failed to notice?

'How long did it take you to work it out?' He laughs again. An evil sound like a James Bond villain. A parody of himself.

'It's obvious. I'm not as stupid as you think,' she says. 'It wouldn't have happened as quickly as you said. You should have done better with your lie.'

'Look, okay, you've found me out. Lock me up.'

He raises his hands in surrender. He is mocking her. He steps towards her. She can smell coffee on his breath. She has the urge to slap his face, but restrains herself.

For eleven months, Catrina has struggled to come to terms with what Lucas did. She has been grieving for the man she thought loved her. But now, the truth hits her with the power of a steam train. It is clear that he only loves himself. He is a classic narcissist who doesn't give a damn about anyone else's feelings. He disappeared, not because he was being a good citizen and helping the police to put a nasty criminal behind bars by giving evidence against him, but simply because he wanted to. For reasons known only to himself, he wanted to leave the life he had and start afresh.

He doesn't care how much hurt he left behind. He doesn't care that she has grieved for him, and that his parents have been bereft and hurt. Who is this man standing before her?

It no longer matters who he is. What Lucas doesn't know is that Catrina has had time to start afresh, too. She, too, is a different person. She has Ryan now, and she has plans and dreams for her future. A future that doesn't include Lucas.

For a second, she considers telling him of her plan to open her own coffee shop. She has had her eye on an empty shop premises just down the road from where she lives. An inheritance from her grandad will enable her to put down a deposit, pay a few months' rent, kit the place out with a fancy Italian coffee machine, enough chairs and tables for thirty people, buy some stock, and still have plenty of cash left over for cute crockery and little additions, such as cushions and blankets for some outside tables. She has an appointment to view the premises next week. But why should Lucas know about that? He isn't part of her life anymore. He doesn't deserve to know anything about her. He doesn't even know that her grandad has passed away.

'Cat?'

She looks up at him. His face is neutral. She used to be able to read him so well, but now she doesn't know what he is thinking. 'What?' she says.

'I'm sorry,' he says.

She doesn't believe him. There are no signs of contrition on his face. No downcast eyes or a blush of shame.

'Yes, you said that last night. The thing is, you don't seem very sorry.'

'I am,' he says. 'I don't know why I did it. I know you want answers, but I'm not sure I have any. I was bored, I suppose. I wanted an adventure.'

He lowers himself onto a nearby rock. It has a sharp edge. Catrina can see it digging into his leg. He's not comfortable, but he is too stubborn to move.

He laughs suddenly. 'I suppose I should have had a year out after university, like those rich kids who go travelling around the world. Maybe some time in Thailand and Australia would have left me feeling more settled.' He kicks at the sand with one of his new boots. She wants to ask him where he bought them. They're nice. She would have picked them out for him if they had been shopping together. 'I am sorry, though.'

'It's too late,' she says. 'I don't care. I thought I did, but I don't.' She raises her hand when she sees his mouth open. 'I don't want to hear any more from you. I can't believe a word that comes out of your mouth, so you might as well close it. All the best, Lucas.' She begins to walk away, then calls back over her shoulder. 'I'll tell your parents that I've seen you, but I would be grateful if you don't contact me again. Goodbye.'

# Chapter Thirty-One

# Ivy

Barbara and Mhairi arrive at the library together. Mhairi holds out a small plate in front of her, piled high with shortbread, custard creams, and ginger biscuits as though carrying St. Edward's Crown on a velvet cushion at the Procession of the Regalia. Barbara follows with a tray of teacups and the biggest teapot Ivy has ever seen. Enough to keep them going for a couple of hours.

'We have a good selection of biscuits here,' says Mhairi. 'These will keep the wolf from the door until lunch.' She deposits the plate on the table and pulls up another chair.

'And I have found us all a good book each,' says Ivy. 'We can swap and change if you like, but I thought you might like this one, Mhairi.' She hands Mhairi the Philippa Gregory book. 'It's about Henry VIII and Anne Boleyn's sister, and their goings-on. This one is for you, Barbara.'

'The cover looks nice,' says Barbara, as she takes the book. 'Let me get my reading glasses on. *The London Cafe.*'

She reads the blurb on the back. Ivy can't help smiling as Barbara grimaces. 'I know you're not a fan of the city, so I thought you should read about how wonderful it is,' says Ivy. 'Then you might like to come and visit me in London.'

Barbara's head snaps up. She pulls her glasses down to

the edge of her nose and peers over the lenses. 'Can I really?'

'Yes, of course. I would love you to. I live in Beckenham now. It's quite leafy, not like London at all really. It has a lovely park, so you can pretend we are in the countryside. The high street is only a five-minute walk away, even at my slow walking pace, so we can go out for a morning coffee or a nice sandwich for lunch. It has lots of delightful places to eat. And my place has three bedrooms and two bathrooms, so it will be lovely to share it with someone. I don't get many visitors these days.'

'That sounds amazing,' she says. 'I would like that very much, thank you.'

'It's very swish,' says Ivy, unable to prevent her smile from spreading when she thinks about home. 'Not like mine and Terence's first place. That was no bigger than the proverbial shoe box. I've come up in the world since then.'

Barbara laughs and clasps the book to her chest, as though it were a treasured gift. 'I will look forward to it,' she says. 'Sooner rather than later, I hope? Let's not let so many years go by without seeing each other, shall we?'

Ivy laughs. 'I don't think either of us has another fifty years to waste, do we? You too, Mhairi,' she says. She is aware that Mhairi, busying herself with the tea making, has been clattering the spoon against the teacups and giving the teapot an extra, unnecessary stir, so she can pretend she didn't hear the invitation that only went Barbara's way. Now, she is watching Ivy intently. 'You, too, are very welcome to come to London and stay. You should come together.'

'Oh my goodness, are you sure? But we've only just met.' Mhairi's eyes, which are gleaming with excitement, belie her protestations.

'Well, we shall get to know each other, shan't we? November is a lovely time to visit London, if you're not too busy with Christmas preparations. The shops are beautifully decorated, and Christmas music plays everywhere. It's the best atmosphere in the world. Especially when it goes dark and the fairy lights are switched on outside all the shops.'

'Can we visit Harrods and Fortnum and Masons?' asks Mhairi.

'Absolutely. Although I have to say, Fenwick on Bond Street is my favourite department store. But we can visit them all.'

Mhairi knocks her knuckles together. If she were five years old, she would be bouncing on the spot and clapping her hands, but adult inhibitions are holding her back. Her joy is infectious, and Ivy immediately feels better. Maybe she was meant to come on this weekend away, after all. Yes, she could be sitting in an elegant pavement café by the side of Lake Garda, but she would never have reconnected with Barbara if she'd done that.

'Right, that's sorted then,' says Ivy. 'I'll see what shows are on and we can book the weekend around what you fancy seeing. I shall sort the tickets out. Andrew told me you're a fan of theatre.'

'Yes, I am, thank you,' says Mhairi. 'I can't wait.'

Ivy has never shown this side of her to Barbara, the grown-up side. They were both so young when they knew each other. Adults, yes, but with so much to learn and so much growth yet to endure. Ivy will look forward to showing her what she has achieved over the years. As she takes her cup of tea from Mhairi and listens to her and Barbara planning their weekend in London and what sights they would like to see – yes, a tour bus is an absolute necessity, and we must go to the Tower of London, and also spend a little time in Covent Garden and Leicester Square - she can't help feeling a smidgen of pride. Some might say it's a sin, and Ivy has never before allowed herself to get carried away by what she has achieved, but what the heck. She isn't religious anyway, so she won't suffer God's wrath if she is not considered to be one of his children in the first place. She allows herself a little pride.

The well-known *rocking chair test*, which people use as a barometer of a life well-lived, comes to her mind. Technically, she isn't in a rocking chair; she is settled in an extremely comfortable chair in a beautiful hotel on an island in Scotland, but it is as good a time as any to look back on her life and ask herself whether she would have done things differently. Of course, she would. There is no question about that. She wouldn't have lost her temper with her darling Terence that night; that is one thing she is certain about. She didn't mean to be so cruel and has regretted what she said every minute of every day since. She hopes he knows that, wherever he is up there in the universe.

A friend once told her that when your time is up, your time is up. She was trying to make Ivy feel less guilty, telling her that nothing she could have done would have changed the events that were predestined for Terence. But Ivy has never believed that. Terence's death could have been avoided. The wind was stronger that night than they had ever experienced before. They both struggled to stand upright as they bellowed at each other. Ivy should never have left him alone. The cliff edge must have been so close, only inches away from his feet. By the time it went dark, he would never have seen it. She should have made sure that he went back to Hollow Pines with her.

Nobody can convince her that he was predestined to die that night. She could have prevented it.

If Terence had lost his balance away from the cliff, he would have simply fallen onto his bottom, as she had earlier when she tripped over the shoe she had kicked off. He would have picked himself up and returned to the house covered in mud, which everyone would have laughed about. If Ivy were still with him when he fell, they would have laughed together. She might have thrown herself on top of him, and they would have ended up kissing.

On another day, at another time, the clifftop would have been a romantic setting. It was never supposed to be the stage for a death. Ivy and Terence were the stars of a love story. They were never meant to play the leading roles in a tragedy, although Ivy played her role extremely well.

'Darling, what's the matter?'

She is snapped back to the present day. Her tea is almost cold. She has no idea how much time has passed.

Barbara is standing over her with a tissue in her hand. 'Here, wipe your eyes,' says Barbara, pressing it into Ivy's hand. She takes the cup of tea from her and places it on the coffee table.

Ivy is crying again. This place! It has brought up emotions that were long ago buried.

'Oh, I'm being silly,' she says. She forces a laugh. 'I got carried away to the past, as I often do these days.'

'Oh no, you shouldn't do that,' says Mhairi. 'The past is where regrets and mistakes live. The future is what you need to concentrate on.'

That's easy for her to say. She is thirty years younger. Ivy doesn't have a whole lot of future left. 'I was thinking about the rocking chair test,' she says. 'You know, when you sit in your rocking chair when you're old...'

'Like us?' laughs Barbara.

'Yes, like us, and you look back on your life and see if

you have any regrets.'

'What's the point in that?' asks Mhairi. 'You could torment yourself to an early grave. You do what you think is right at the time, don't you? There is no use in beating yourself up afterwards.'

'Well, I think you're supposed to do the rocking chair test before you get too old,' says Ivy. 'You're meant to do it in your twenties or thirties, so you can plan how your life should be. Then, when you do the real rocking chair test in your senior years, you should have no regrets. That's the theory, anyway.'

'I see,' says Mhairi. 'If only life were that simple.'

Ivy wonders what she has done in her life and what regrets she has. She doesn't know anything about her, other than she is Andrew's mother and she loves the theatre. But there will be plenty of time to get to know her properly when she visits London.

'I think it's about things like sky diving and parachute jumping, and visiting exotic places,' says Barbara. 'It's a justification for the young people to spend all their wages on frippery, telling themselves they want to live life to the full rather than getting a job and settling down. Ordinary things like that are seen as boring nowadays.'

'So how's your rocking chair test, Barbara?' asks Mhairi.

'As a woman who has spent ninety percent of my life on this island, and a huge percentage of that in this very house, I am happy to say I don't have many regrets. I would have wanted another child, but I was happy. Very happy, actually, and very fortunate.'

'That's lovely,' says Ivy.

She swallows down the instant regrets she has about not having been here to see Barbara's son grow up. Each summer when she visited, she could have remarked on how much he had grown since the last time she saw him, as she showered him with kisses and expensive gifts from London that Barbara would roll her eyes at, as she laughed at how much he was being spoiled. Ivy would have liked to have been that glamorous aunt from the big city, who floated around Hollow Pines in designer clothes and killer heels (not that she ever did that), telling tales of her exciting life in the theatre, of how she mixed in celebrity circles and never got to bed before five in the morning. That would have been her dream if she and Barbara had kept in touch.

The reality is, it wasn't all glitz and glamour – as an actress, there were some periods of unemployment, and many long months when the play was boring, each night repetitive and tedious, and sometimes Ivy couldn't wait for it to end. But still, it would have been nice to share that with Barbara and Hugh.

'Apart from losing Terence at such a young age, you've had a good life, haven't you, Ivy?' says Mhairi. 'Well, from the outside looking in. Obviously, I know that the papers don't always paint a true story, so I can only go on what has been written about you.'

'Losing Terence was the worst thing to have happened to you, wasn't it?' says Barbara. 'And you were both so young. It was awful.'

Ivy shakes her head, tears coursing down her face now, uncontrollably. 'The worst thing was that Terence's death was preventable,' she says. 'We shouldn't have gone out in the rain, or stayed so long that it went dark. Terence's death was my fault.'

The book resting on Ivy's knee falls to the floor. She bends down to pick it up, brushing imaginary biscuit crumbs from the cover, her fingers moving quickly. Brush, brush, brush.

Barbara is silent. The whole room seems to have gone silent, apart from the ticking of a small wooden clock on what used to be a working fireplace, and the howling of the wind through the pine trees, which seems to be whispering *It was your fault. It was your fault.*

## Chapter Thirty-Two

## Ivy

'How could you say such a thing?' says Barbara.

'I said some terrible things to him that night,' says Ivy.

'We all say things we don't mean in the heat of the moment,' says Barbara.

'But I pushed him.' Ivy's words are so quiet, as though she is frightened of saying them too loudly in case that confirms them as true.

'You pushed him,' says Barbara. It isn't a question. It is a statement, as though Barbara has always known.

'I didn't mean to,' says Ivy. 'It was a terrible accident. It was dark, and I didn't see how close he was to the edge.'

'You pushed him over the cliff?' Barbara's wide eyes flick between Ivy and Mhairi as she waits for someone to tell her it isn't true.

'No, of course not. I didn't push him over the cliff,' says Ivy. 'Not like that. But when we argued, I poked him in his chest with my finger and pushed him backwards. That's why he was so angry and didn't come back to the house with me. It was my fault he fell. It's no wonder he lost his footing in the dark. If he hadn't stayed out, if he hadn't been so angry, it would never have happened. It's my fault.'

The look on Barbara's face tells Ivy that she has made a

mistake. She thought Barbara would take her in her arms and absolve her from her sin. She expected all guilt to evaporate as Barbara comforted her and assured her that everything was forgiven. Surely she knows Ivy didn't mean it.

Can they change the subject now? Can they chat about trivial things, go back to normal, without the truth imposing on their party like an unwanted gate-crasher?

'Did you see him fall?' Mhairi breaks the silence and asks the question that Barbara is afraid to ask.

'No,' says Ivy. 'But it was almost dark…'

'That's it then. Let's hear no more about it,' says Barbara. She reaches across the table and strokes Ivy's arm. 'Terence fell after you left him, after it had gone dark. His death was no more your fault than it was mine.'

'Well, maybe you have hit the nail on the head,' says Ivy. 'We both should take some responsibility. Terence's death could have been avoided if a little more care had been taken by *you* that night, not just me.'

'Whatever do you mean?' says Barbara. She whips her arm back, as though from an electric shock. She looks frantically over to Mhairi, expecting Mhairi to jump to her defence when the crime she is accused of hasn't yet been clearly stated.

Ivy can see that Mhairi is as shocked as Barbara. She can see it in her eyes. She probably has no idea what her mother-in-law has, allegedly, done wrong. It is highly unlikely that Barbara would have admitted to anything. Mhairi's mouth falls open, and she stares at Ivy, then quickly looks down, examining the crumbs on her plate with great interest. The poor woman has found herself caught up in this vortex of grief and sadness, when all she wanted to do was sip tea, read books, and munch on biscuits.

'I have never been here in the winter,' says Ivy. 'I didn't know how fierce the storms could be.'

'But it wasn't winter,' says Barbara, her eyes wide with shock. 'I can't believe what you are accusing me of. It was July. It was the middle of summer. I'm sorry, I don't understand what you're suggesting.' Barbara's voice quakes with unshed tears.

'I know it wasn't winter, but it may as well have been. It certainly felt like a winter storm. I would have thought that what I'm suggesting is quite obvious: that you should have warned us how strong the wind could be around here,' says Ivy. 'You're the one who lives here. Maybe you should have made it clear how dangerous it was to go outside. You didn't even insist on us taking a torch. In fact, you gave me a shawl so that we could stay out longer.'

The reality is, it wasn't Barbara's fault, not really. Terence was a grown adult and took responsibility for his own actions. He was the one who chose to stay out long after it had gone dark. He knew the clifftop as well as anyone. He knew how dangerous it was to walk close to the edge. The logical part of Ivy's brain has always known that. But the damaged, grieving part has always refused to accept it. In any event, the truth about how she feels is out now. It sits like a grenade between Ivy and Barbara, and there is nothing anyone can do to put the pin back and avoid the inevitable explosion.

'What?' Barbara is almost shouting. She is glaring at Ivy. Heated red circles have appeared on her cheeks.

Ivy wipes her eyes with a sodden tissue.

*Barbara looks so unexpectedly angry. No – disappointed. Can't she see I am crying? I thought Barbara was an empath. Why isn't she feeling sorry for me?*

A little voice inside tells Ivy to stop talking about Terence and the past, to sit back and enjoy this unexpected company, and to turn the conversation to lighter topics. But the thoughts she has kept to herself for fifty years, restrained and hidden in the deepest recesses of her mind, are running free. She has no control over them. She hasn't previously told anyone that she secretly blamed Barbara, as well as herself. There is no reason on earth why she should share her thoughts now, especially not with Barbara, someone who loved Terence almost as much as she did. Ivy's life is coming to an end. She can take the secret to her grave, quite happily.

But she dismisses the voice. She has had enough. She is tired of being the only one to bear the burden of guilt.

'Maybe Terence died because of our negligence, yours and mine equally,' she says.

Barbara glares at Ivy, her jaw set tight, her lips clamped together. 'All these years,' she says. She is shouting now. 'All these years, I have grieved for the two of you. Not just Terence. I grieved for you, for the life you should have had and which I thought was taken from you, so unfairly.'

'It *was* taken from me.' Ivy is shouting, too, matching the volume of Barbara's voice.

'And all this time you blamed me for what happened. I can't believe what I'm hearing.'

Ivy places her cup of tea on the arm of the chair, not caring whether it will spill, and pushes herself up. The book that was resting on her knee falls to the floor, again, but this time she leaves it where it lands. She dashes from the room, as quickly as her aged legs will carry her, dozens of pairs of eyes watching her as she makes her way to the door, negotiating past discarded handbags on the floor, legs sticking out from chairs, piles of books, and a young toddler kneeling on the floor piecing together a wooden jigsaw.

She pulls at the library door and escapes into the Great Hall.

'Hello, Miss Montclaire,' says Andrew from behind the reception desk. 'Is everything okay? Do you need more tea? More biscuits?'

'For goodness sake, Andrew, stop fussing,' she says. She marches through the reception towards the lift. 'And whose idea was it to put in that God forsaken door?' She throws up her arm in the direction of the revolving door. 'It's a monstrosity.'

As she waits for the lift, jabbing at the button as though that will bring it any quicker, she half expects Barbara to run after her, declaring that she didn't mean to shout and she is terribly sorry. Ivy will tell her she is sorry, too, and that those nasty, vile words slipped out of her mouth in a moment of madness. She didn't mean a single one of them. Of course, Barbara isn't to blame, she will say. Everyone knows that Terence's death was a tragic accident. Nobody should be blamed except Ivy herself. She has served her sentence well. Her penance has been loneliness. She hasn't been blessed with the love of another man and a child, like Barbara has. She has lived a lonely life, single, without a family of her own. Yes, there have been other men, but she hasn't loved them like she loved Terence.

Her life dragged on because Terence lost his.

But Barbara doesn't appear. Ivy again jabs at the lift button frantically, wishing her old legs could carry her up the stairs. She doesn't want to wait here a second longer than she needs to, but unfortunately, necessity dictates that she must wait for the lift. If this were 1976, she would have skipped up those stairs in no time. But it isn't. So she waits.

After a moment, the ding of the bell indicates that the lift is here. The door opens to reveal Simone and Troy.

'Going up?' asks Simone with a friendly smile. She steps out of the lift and holds the button with her finger, keeping the lift door open for Ivy.

'Yes, thank you,' says Ivy.

'Are you okay, Ivy?' asks Simone, keeping her finger on the button.

'Yes, I'm fine, thank you,' says Ivy, forcing a smile.

'It's just that your eyes look red,' says Simone. 'As though you're about to cry.'

Ivy rubs her eyes instinctively. 'Allergies,' she says. 'I think someone has smuggled in a cat.'

'No? Really?' Simone's smile widens at the thought. 'How cute. I love cats. Sorry that you're allergic, though. I wonder who it is. That's cheeky, isn't it?'

Ivy smiles, waves goodbye, and says that she will probably see them later for lunch, hoping that is the end of the conversation. She is desperate to be alone.

'You haven't seen Catrina, have you?' asks Simone. 'She isn't answering her phone.'

Simone shows Ivy the screen of her phone, providing evidence of missed calls, as though she wouldn't have believed her without it. But Ivy can only see a blur of colour without her reading glasses on. She reluctantly steps out of the lift. Simone lets go of the button, and the doors close.

'As a matter of fact, I saw her in the library earlier,' says Ivy. 'I was choosing some books for my friends.' She takes a deep breath. The last word *friends* catches in her throat. She doesn't suppose they are friends anymore, her and Barbara. They found each other again after fifty years, and Ivy has managed to lose her in less than twenty-four hours. The talked-of trip to London will now probably not materialise, either. That's a shame for Mhairi, she was looking forward to seeing a good West End show and doing her Christmas shopping in the famous department stores. There's not much Ivy can do about that now.

'Did she say where she was going?' asks Simone.

'Yes, she's going to meet Lucas at the beach,' says Ivy.

She pushes up the sleeve of her cardigan to peer at her wristwatch. It is approaching eleven o'clock. 'Just about now, actually.'

'She told me she wasn't going to go,' says Simone. 'She seemed quite adamant about it.'

'I hate to say it, but she was lying to you again, babe,' says Troy.

'I wouldn't go that far,' says Ivy. 'She wasn't lying, or at least she didn't mean to. Maybe she just changed her mind.' There is doubt on Simone's face. Ivy expects her to argue that she knows Catrina better than Ivy does, but she is too polite to do so. 'When she spoke to me, she was quite emotional. I don't think she knew her mind at all, not clearly. She feels very let down by Lucas, and I think she just wants some answers. I don't think she wants to rekindle their romance, but rather to draw a line under it. So, I can understand her wanting to speak to him, can't you?'

Simone shakes her head. 'No, not really. Well, I mean, yes, I suppose I can. But how come she confided in you and not me?'

'Sometimes it is easier to tell a stranger something close to your heart, isn't it? A stranger can't judge you, like your friends can, because we don't have all the facts. We can only go off what that person is telling us at the time, and when it is told in such a way that their point of view is reasonable and plausible...'

'Yes, I get it. That person then becomes a new friend who won't judge you.'

'Well, not a friend exactly. A temporary confidante, maybe. And yes, certainly without the judgement,' says Ivy.

'Come on,' says Troy. He pulls at the sleeve of Simone's jumper.

Simone shakes him off. 'What do you mean, come on?'

'We need to go to the beach. I wouldn't mind a word or two with Lucas myself,' he says.

'I think they need to be on their own,' says Simone. 'I know you're angry with him, too, but we need to leave Catrina to do her thing.'

Troy tuts and looks at Ivy, waiting for her to mediate, to take sides between him and his wife. Ivy has nothing to lose, so she decides to offer advice. Whether they listen is up to them.

'I think you should go to the beach,' she says. 'I appreciate that she needs time to speak to Lucas, but Catrina needs her friends now, more than at any other time. Believe me, I pushed a good friend away when I needed her the most, and it was one of the biggest mistakes of my life. Now, it's too late. I have ruined our friendship, and I don't think she will ever forgive me.'

'Oh, Ivy, I'm sorry to hear that,' says Simone. She strokes Ivy's arm.

*She's such a kind and understanding person. I can imagine her in front of a class of children. I bet she is one of those teachers whose pupils remember long after they have left school. One of the inspirational role models that you hear adults talking about years later when they reminisce about their school years. Someone who put them on the long road to success in life. Every school has one.*

'Is your friendship salvageable?' she asks.

'No, I don't think it is,' says Ivy. That lump is here again in the back of her throat, but she swallows it down and takes a deep breath. 'But don't make the same mistake with Catrina. I know you two are close. Don't let anything or anyone come between you, especially not a man like Lucas.'

'I agree,' says Simone. 'We are very close. We have been together since we were little children at school. That's why I'm a bit perturbed that she didn't speak to me, if I'm honest.'

'Well, like I said, she is pushing you away for complex reasons we can't understand. She thinks she is doing the right thing, but she isn't. She needs you.'

'Do you really think we should go?'

'Yes, if I were you, I would go to the beach and speak to her.' Ivy turns to Troy. 'Which also means you can see Lucas. You used to be friends, didn't you?'

'Yes, we used to be,' he says. Like Simone, he has the expression of someone let down by a close friend.

'So there you are. Killing two birds with one stone, as it were.'

'Thank you, Ivy,' says Simone. 'Come on then, husband. What are we waiting for?'

Ivy goes back to her room, pleased that Simone and Troy are on their way to support Catrina when she needs them.

As soon as she closes the bedroom door behind her, what she said to Barbara hits her. She is beset with regret, like a tide crashing in and pulling her under. She is drowning in sorrow. Not only has she lost Terence, but she has now lost Barbara after only just finding her.

The rain continues its relentless plan to ruin everyone's weekend. It weeps down the window, making Ivy want to weep along with it.

## Chapter Thirty-Three

## Catrina

Catrina bumps into Simone and Troy at the bottom of the hotel garden. When Simone asks her whether she has seen Lucas, there is no accusatory tone, just concern from a friend. Catrina says yes, but nothing happened between them. Lucas is well and truly in the past now. She doesn't want to talk about him ever again.

'I will call in on his parents when we get back home,' she says, 'and will tell them where he is. They deserve to know, but I'll be doing it more to annoy him than anything, as he doesn't seem to want them to know. The selfish sod. But after that, I'm done with him.'

'Are you really?' asks Simone.

'Yes, I don't want anything to do with him or his family.'

For a moment, Troy looks confused. He glances over Catrina's shoulders as though expecting to see Lucas, his old friend, trailing behind her. It is clear that he would like to see him.

'He'll probably still be around if you want to speak to him,' says Catrina. 'I left him on the beach, licking his wounds. I don't think he has ever been dumped by a girl in his life. I'm proud to be the first.'

'Yes!' shouts Simone, holding up her palm for a high-five. 'Did you put him straight? There's no ambiguity, is there? I don't want him creeping back to you because you didn't make it clear.'

'Yes, I told him in no uncertain terms that I never wanted to see him again, and I also told him I didn't believe he was in witness protection. I will tell you all about it another time, but first I need to see Ryan. Do you know where he is? I haven't seen him since last night. He is ignoring my messages.'

'No, we haven't seen him, sorry,' says Simone.

'He's in Room Five on the ground floor,' says Troy, sheepishly. He turns his back on Catrina, pulling his coat hood over his head. 'Come on, let's get out of this rain. I need a beer.'

'What? Never mind your beer. Why didn't you tell me that earlier?' asks Catrina. 'How long have you known?'

'Not long,' says Troy. 'Maybe about an hour. I didn't know at breakfast time, honestly.'

'Troy, I can't believe you,' says Simone. She pulls his hood down and glares at him, her head on one side, waiting for a valid explanation.

'He's my mate and he told me not to tell you if I thought there was anything going on between you and Lucas. But now I know that there isn't, I can tell you.' Troy shrugs, seemingly unable to see that he has done anything wrong.

Catrina doesn't know whether to be mad at Troy for keeping a secret from her or be impressed that he has his friend's back. She chooses the latter. She doesn't want any more bad blood or arguments. Simone and Troy are her closest friends, more like family, and the last thing she wants to do is to argue with them. Troy was only doing what he thought was right.

She runs ahead of them, telling them that she is going to find Ryan and will, hopefully, see them at lunch time with

Ryan by her side.

Now, as she stands outside Room Five on the hotel's first floor, about to knock on the door, her heart is racing. Ryan isn't expecting her. She thought he wouldn't answer the door if she told him she was coming. She takes a deep breath, trying to calm her nerves. This feels like a first date, but one where the outcome is unpredictable. Maybe the boy will like her and she will get a kiss. Maybe he will reject her. Maybe he won't make an appearance at all. She is desperate to see Ryan, whilst simultaneously dreading the conversation that might confirm to her that their relationship is over. She is hoping he will forgive her, but there is a chance that he won't. If that happens, she won't blame him. Not one iota. If one of Ryan's ex-girlfriends appeared in a hotel while they were having a weekend away, and he sneaked off to speak to her, and then kissed her... well, that would be it.

As she had walked back to the hotel earlier with Simone and Troy, she had asked Troy for some advice. As a man, could he tell her what she could do to make this situation right, to make Ryan realise how sorry she was? Troy pursed his lips while he thought a moment.

'Honestly?' he said.

'Yes, honestly,' she said. 'I'll do whatever I need to do.'

'If it were me, it would be game over,' he said.

'Would it? Aww, don't say that,' she said, as tears pricked her eyes.

'Yes, I'm sorry,' said Troy. 'Don't get upset. I hate to see women cry.' He pulled her into a bear hug and kissed the top of her head. 'That's just me. I'm stubborn and have enough pride to fill a football stadium. Ryan's different. You'll be able to talk him round.'

But Catrina knows that he isn't different, not that much. People talk of male pride as though it's a good thing, an asset for a man. But in this case, it is definitely a hindrance.

She knocks on the door. She can hear music coming from inside the room. She is about to walk away. He hasn't heard her. She is wasting her time. But then the volume lowers, and a second later, the door opens.

'Can we talk?' she says.

Ryan steps to one side and allows her in.

The room is similar to theirs, but much smaller. When they were booking the trip, Ryan said they should treat themselves and upgrade to a deluxe room, as they were celebrating Simone's birthday. Their room has a deep Victorian bath, a separate walk-in shower and a king-size bed. This one is only a double. Her heart aches that she has caused Ryan to miss out on their beautiful room, not that this one isn't beautiful – it has the same green and white tartan carpet and countryside paintings on the walls - it's lovely. But it isn't theirs.

This room is on the other side of the hotel, looking out towards the front. There is no sofa under the window, just a small dressing table with a forest green velvet-covered stool pushed underneath. For some reason, she doesn't feel comfortable sitting on the bed; it seems too intimate, so she pulls out the stool and sits down. Through the window, she can see the pine forest and the path that leads to the spa, blurred by the heavy rain.

She looks down at her hands. Was it only yesterday when she was having her nails painted in there? It seems a lifetime ago. When she returned with Simone and showed Ryan her new nails, he had kissed her fingers and told her she was beautiful. Now, he can barely look at her.

'Talk then,' says Ryan. He perches on the end of the unmade bed. He looks tired, his face marked with the strain of their argument. His hair is rumpled, and he is unshaven. His t-shirt looks like it has been slept in. Or rather, not slept in, if Ryan's night was anything like Catrina's.

Catrina is desperate to take care of him. She wants to comb his hair. She wants to iron his t-shirt while he showers. She wants to make him a coffee and straighten the sheets on his bed. But that right has been lost. Is she still his girlfriend? She isn't sure.

The tears she has been trying to hold in come suddenly. She runs to Ryan and flings her arms around his neck, sobbing into his neck. For a second, he doesn't react, but then he stands, and she is relieved to feel his arms around her waist. He strokes her hair and tells her not to cry, that everything will be okay. The relief of hearing those words makes her cry more.

'Here, sit down,' he says, gently pushing her onto the bed. He wanders into the en-suite bathroom and reappears with a handful of tissues. Catrina takes them with a sad smile and wipes her eyes and nose.

'I'm so sorry,' she says.

'I know you are,' he says. 'It just hurt, you know? The thought of you and him kissing, I can't bear it.' He sits beside Catrina on the bed, which she wants to take as a good sign, but she can still feel resistance from him. She restrains herself from touching him.

'And that kills me,' she says. 'I would do anything to turn back the clock. But you need to understand that I didn't *want* to bump into Lucas. I had stopped searching for him ages ago.'

Was that true? Strictly, no. Her head still shot up whenever the bell over the café door where she worked jangled. Each time a new customer walked in, there was a possibility it would be him. But it never was. She had had to deal with disappointment every day for months. She was used to it. As late as last week, when this trip was planned and paid for, and her bag was packed, during her last shift at work, she had still half-expected Lucas to walk through the door. If he had done so, would she still have come on this trip with Ryan? Yes, she decides. Of course, she would, because Lucas would still have lied to her about where he had been. He may not have told her about being in witness protection, but it would have been some other cock and bull story, difficult to accept without considerable speculation and doubt.

Simone had been right. She was better off without him. She was much better off with Ryan if he would give her another chance.

'I will do anything to make things right between us,' she says. 'Just give me another chance, please.'

Ryan looks at her with his beautiful blue eyes. But this time, they are not twinkling with mischief; they are dulled by despair.

She has ruined everything.

## Chapter Thirty-Four

## Ivy

After an hour or so in her room, Ivy can't stand the solitude any longer. She decides to go for a walk, not to the cliffs - that would be suicide in this raging wind - but just around the hotel garden. The rain has eased a little, but she could borrow one of the hotel's umbrellas. Maybe she could follow the path to the wildflower meadow. It doesn't matter that the flowers are past their best. It is the fresh air that she needs. She is missing her daily walks down Beckenham High Street. She pulls on her coat, pushes her feet into her shoes, and makes her way to the lift.

In the reception, she stops at the desk and offers Andrew an apology for being rude earlier. He accepts it like the gentleman she knows he is, like Hugh would have done, by telling her not to be silly and giving her a warm smile. Everyone is entitled to have a little rant without having to be sorry, he tells her. She thanks him profusely for being so kind and tells him she is going for a walk. Shame prevents her from telling him about her argument with his grandmother earlier. She can't bear to go down even further in his estimation.

'Are you sure you want to venture out?' asks Andrew.

'No, not really,' says Ivy. 'But I don't want to sit inside

all day, either. I'll just go out for ten minutes or so. I haven't yet seen the wildflower meadow.'

Andrew nods. 'Well, when you get back, I'll get you one of those coffees that you like with hot milk.' He hands her one of the umbrellas, which is large enough to fit four people underneath.

'Thank you. I will look forward to that,' she says.

The wildflower meadow is somewhat of a misnomer. It is much smaller than Ivy expected it to be, although she can imagine it would be beautiful in the height of the summer. Some poppies still survive, their heads pitching like tiny scarlet ships in a rough sea. They are interspersed with white oxeye daisies that bob like white-capped swimmers alongside them, their leaves and petals soaked. Terence would have loved to see them. Red flowers were his favourite. Everything he treasured was red – his car, his typewriter, his mohair jacket. Ivy loves flowers of any colour, but Terence always chose to buy her red ones - roses, tulips, peonies, dahlias or her favourite, carnations. Red is the only colour that truly signifies love, he would tell her. All the other colours are for friends and family.

After he died, she surrounded herself with red roses and carnations, wanting to cling to the love he gave her. She ordered bunches and bunches of them from the local florist. She filled the three vases she had in the flat and put the remaining flowers in whatever else she could find, milk bottles, lemonade bottles, and even some in a tall gravy jug. She scattered them about the living room, bedroom, and kitchen, pretending that Terence had bought the flowers for her. If she told herself that he was away on a writing retreat and had sent her some flowers to remind her of him whilst he was away, she could pretend that the worst hadn't happened. She could pretend that he was still alive and she wasn't living the nightmare where each day she woke and reached over to his side of the bed only to find it empty and cold. She wouldn't need to face the terrifying grief that crept up behind her, like a burglar about to pounce, to rob her of every last ounce of happiness she had, leaving her with nothing.

On the third day after her return from Holm Island without him, she awoke to find a few rose petals had fallen from the flowers. They lay on the kitchen table like delicate embers from a dying fire. She carefully picked them up with her fingertips, as though they were too hot to touch, and held them in the palm of her hand. Then it hit her how stupid and pathetic she was being. Surrounding herself with flowers, telling herself that her dead husband had sent them, was something a mad woman would do. She kicked open the back door and shook her hand, scattering the petals to the wind. Then she went back inside and, grabbing the vases one by one, hurled them into the bin. The shattering glass brought her crashing back to reality.

Her flat remained void of flowers for a long time after that, and even now, she avoids buying any red ones.

'Ivy! Ivy!'

She can hear someone shouting her name. She swivels around suddenly to see Barbara making her way towards her. She is walking tentatively, as though afraid of falling, and Ivy is immediately concerned for her safety. Neither of them should be outside. The paths are treacherous underfoot.

'Barbara, what are you doing here?' she says.

'I came to find you. I was worried about you. Andrew told me you might be here.'

Barbara is wearing green wellington boots and a dark grey, almost full-length raincoat, buttoned up to the neck. As she approaches, Ivy can see the buttons are misaligned, as though she fastened them in a hurry. The coat doesn't have a hood, and Barbara's hair is plastered to her face. The rain drips from her chin.

'Be careful, Barbara,' Ivy shouts. 'Slow down.'

'The last time you said that to me, I was twirling around the dining room in a drunken stupor, singing *Love to Love You Baby* at the top of my voice. You thought I would twist an ankle and told me to take my shoes off. I fancied myself as competition for Donna Summer, do you remember?'

'Unfortunately, I do,' Ivy laughs. 'That was a good summer, wasn't it?'

'They all were,' says Barbara. She has reached Ivy now and takes her hands in hers. Ivy holds the umbrella over them both with her other hand, offering shelter to her friend. 'Listen, I wanted...'

'Please don't tell me you are sorry for shouting at me,' says Ivy. 'You had every right. What I said to you was dreadful, truly dreadful. I am the one who is sorry.'

'My darling, I never knew that you felt like that,' says Barbara. 'Why didn't you tell me at the time? We could have talked about it.'

But Ivy was incommunicado then. As unreachable as though she were on an undiscovered desert island.

'I wasn't ready to face it back then. It's true, though. His death was so preventable, that's what I have struggled to come to terms with all these years. It was a silly argument, Barbara. I wish it had never happened. I would do anything to turn back the clock.'

'I know, I know,' says Barbara. 'I'm sure Terence knew deep down that there was nothing between you and that man, what was his name?'

'He was called Allan and he played my husband, Stanley, in *A Streetcar Named Desire*. I played Stella, Stanley's long-suffering wife. Terence knew the plot as well as I did. He knew that Stanley and Stella shared a passionate kiss on stage. But he said that the kiss seemed a little too passionate for his liking. I told him it was nothing of the sort, that we were acting, but he accused me of entertaining Allan in my dressing room. I didn't, you know.' Ivy grabs Barbara's hand and clings to it. 'I never did anything wrong, Barbara. I was always faithful to Terence, always. I took my marriage vows extremely seriously.'

'I know, darling,' says Barbara. 'I know how much you loved him.'

'When the rain started, suddenly and violently, we were soaked within minutes. We should have gone inside then. I honestly thought the end of the argument had reached us. But no, it had a long way to go. Terence said that he had seen me when I left the theatre after the final show. He said he saw me kissing Allan on the steps of the stage door. But we didn't kiss. Not like that, not like Terence thought. Allan was gay. We kissed on the cheek, that was all.'

'What happened then?' asks Barbara.

'I told Terence that I was sick of him. I said that I would not apologise for being a good actress.' Ivy pauses for a moment. 'Then I hit him hard in his chest with the palm of my hand,' she says. 'The hurt on his face has haunted me ever since. I said to him *I'm sick of this. I'm not going to apologise. I'm not going to stroke your ego.* As I spoke, I hit him in the chest each time. I walked away then. When it went dark, he must have stumbled too close to the edge of the cliff, and he fell. All because I left him.'

'My darling, I am so sorry,' says Barbara.

Barbara wraps her arms around Ivy, who sobs into the collar of her raincoat.

'I left him, upset and disoriented, in the dark after a terrible argument,' says Ivy. 'Why did I do that?'

'Shhh, it's okay,' says Barbara. 'I'm sorry for shouting at

you earlier, whether you want me to say it or not, I am. It was such a shock, what you said, it was…'

'It was completely out of order,' says Ivy, stepping back and looking her friend in the eyes.

Barbara shakes her head. 'But Mhairi made me realise that what you went through has left you traumatised, more than I appreciated. We didn't talk about things in those days like people do today, did we?'

'No, stiff upper lip and all that,' says Ivy.

'It's terrible. You were left all alone with your thoughts. I should never have let you travel home on your own so soon.'

'Do you think you could have stopped me?'

'I don't know, but we should have tried. We should have locked all the doors and windows. Put you in the attic like Mrs Rochester. It was obvious how deeply affected you were, lying in the road like that waiting to be run over. Goodness me, Ivy.'

'I have missed him so much, Barbara,' sobs Ivy.

'My dear girl, you worshipped him. I know that. And he knew that, too.' Barbara dabs at Ivy's face with a crumpled tissue from her pocket.

Ivy tries not to think about her train journey home without Terence. There was no First Class carriage on the small train from Fort William to Glasgow, but thankfully, it wasn't busy. On the train from Glasgow to London, she managed to secure a small table for two in the First Class carriage, and again was lucky that it wasn't busy. She didn't have any direct neighbours and was spared from having to make small talk. How on earth would she be able to tell a stranger that no, she didn't have a good holiday? No, it wasn't because of the awful storm. Yes, the storm was dreadful, wasn't it? No, she didn't experience any flooding, because Hollow Pines has an elevated position above the cliffs. Oh, the cliffs. Didn't she mention those? Yes, the clifftop was where her husband had just died. No, he didn't have a heart attack. He didn't die a sudden but a natural death. His death was very much unnatural, in fact. And yes, she does blame herself, now that you ask.

'Come on,' says Barbara. 'Let's go back inside. Andrew is organising some coffee. We have a London trip to organise, don't we? There is lots to talk about. Mhairi is keeping your seat warm in the library.'

# Chapter Thirty-Five

## Catrina

Ryan is back where he belongs, in their room, on the bed with Catrina. After an emotional conversation, she managed to persuade him that her kiss with Lucas was a huge mistake. She begged for forgiveness, which Ryan eventually gave. He told her that there was never any doubt that they would work it out. He loves her deeply, he said, but he quite enjoyed having the bed to himself for a night. She laughed at that, and the ice was broken.

Now she is watching him sleep. She wants to lean across and stroke his hair and kiss his face, but right now, she needs to let him sleep. He told her that he only had a couple of hours' sleep last night. He stayed awake watching films until the early hours of the morning, and then, when he turned the lights off, sleep seemed a million miles away.

Catrina picks up the book by Terence Nightingale, *The Swirling Sea Mist*. Ivy told her that this was his best-selling book and put his name on the map, as it were. Earlier in the library, as Catrina had turned the book over and read the blurb on the back, she asked Ivy whether the book was about her. Ivy's eyes had misted with tears, and she said perhaps there was something of her character in the protagonist, although Terence had denied it. He always told her that he found it easier to write about fictional characters, rather than people he knew, because he could make them say and do what he wanted; their stories were free from the constraints of the truth. Nevertheless, she liked to think that he was thinking of her when he wrote female characters, placing her in different locations and giving her exciting lives to live. Catrina thought that Ivy didn't need a more exciting life to live; the one she had seemed to be glamorous enough, but she didn't say anything.

She reads the blurb again to remind her of the story:

*Helen denies that she is experiencing a midlife crisis. She tells her friends that she isn't unhappy with her single life and her steady job as a bank clerk. This is the life she chose. But everyone knows Helen is lying to herself. When she abruptly resigns and moves to a Lancashire seaside village to take up a position as Postmistress, nobody is surprised.*

*For Helen, this isn't running away; this is going back. She spent three years in the village as an evacuee during the war and has always talked of returning there one day.*

*As the mist swirls in from the sea, it brings back memories of the people she lived with, old Alice and Bob Charmley - who already had a house full of children but found room in their hearts for one more - and Peter Denby, the boy in her class at school who became her best friend and first love. The boy she was devastated to leave when it was time to go home.*

*She begins her search for Peter, but what she uncovers is far more complicated than she imagined. Is there the possibility of a second chance at love in the place she once called home?*

The story sounds fascinating. The book is a hardback with a plastic protective dust jacket, which Catrina isn't a fan of. She would much prefer to hold the cardboard cover, so she gently pulls the book from its jacket and leaves it on the bed between her and Ryan. She is engrossed in the story when Ryan wakes.

'Hi,' she says. 'Do you feel better? You've been asleep for over an hour.'

'Yes, much better, thanks,' he says. He leans on his elbow and reaches over to her for a kiss. She wants to tell him again that she's sorry. But he knows she is. She keeps quiet, not wanting the spectre of Lucas to ruin this moment between them.

'Are you hungry?' she says.

'Starving,' says Ryan. 'Have we missed lunch?'

'No, they serve until two o'clock, but I thought I'd order some room service, if that's okay with you? Unless you want to go downstairs? Whatever you want to do.' She is tiptoeing around him, allowing Ryan to lead her in this dance, and set the pace of this new phase of their relationship. She has no idea how fast she should go. Are they back where they were this time yesterday? Or do they need to take things more slowly, step by cautious step, until they find their rhythm again?

Ryan laughs. 'You can stop this, right now,' he says.

'What do you mean?'

'Letting me have all my own way. This isn't us. Just relax.'

Catrina can't help smiling. 'I don't know what you mean. You always get your own way, and you know it.'

'Oh, shut up, woman, and order me some food,' says Ryan. He picks up the room-service menu from the bedside table and hands it to Catrina, who smacks him over the head with it. Ryan feigns injury and rolls around the bed, clutching his head.

'You could have killed me then,' he says, laughing.

As Catrina calls the reception and orders a cheese and pepperoni pizza and two beers, Ryan picks up the book cover and reads the back. 'There's something in here,' he says, opening the book's dust jacket and laying it flat on the bed. 'It's an old letter.' He pulls out a faded pale blue Basildon Bond envelope with the name *Barbara* handwritten on the front.

'That's the name of Ivy Montclaire's friend,' says Catrina. 'She's the one she used to stay with years ago, when Barbara and her husband owned this house.'

'Interesting,' says Ryan. 'I wonder how long this has been inside the book. A long time by the looks of it.'

'It does look pretty old, doesn't it?' says Catrina. 'I didn't notice it. It must have been tucked away inside the cover. Hey, Ryan, no, you can't open it. Don't read it, it's private.'

'Never mind that,' says Ryan. He holds the letter high in the air, out of Catrina's reach.

'Give it to me,' says Catrina. 'It could be an old love-letter.'

'All the more reason to read it,' laughs Ryan. 'If it is a love-letter, then I want to know who wrote it.'

'Fine,' says Catrina. 'But we can't tell Barbara that we've read it.'

'Of course,' says Ryan. 'We don't know her anyway, do we? Why would we tell her? We'll just put it back in the book where it was. I won't breathe a word, I promise.'

He pulls the letter from the envelope and begins to read, with Catrina leaning over his shoulder.

*My dearest Barbara,*

*I don't know how to begin. I shouldn't be writing this at all. My memory of last night feels like one of my stories, something fictional that lives only in my imagination. But I know it is true. Every part of me is screaming to bury it deep and never let it resurface, but the truth of the matter is, I can't stop thinking about you.*

*How will I be able to live through the next three seasons without you? Autumn, winter and spring will torture me until summer arrives and will once again allow us to see each other.*

*What happened between us was not planned, as you know. Alcohol played a large part in our decision making, but I can't regret what we did. If I did, it would ruin the memory of it, and I don't want that. I want to treasure the memory like the gold that it is.*

*I keep replaying every moment, like my favourite record, the sound of your laughter as I kissed your neck, the passion in your eyes when you looked at me, your cheeky smile as you pulled me up the stairs and into the unoccupied bedroom.*

*What does this mean for us now? Can we see each other again? Perhaps I can invent a book-signing in Edinburgh and you can meet me there? We can stay at The Caledonian.*

*Maybe this was only a one-off for you. Maybe that's where we should leave it.*

*Please let me know how you feel. Can we talk in the library after lunch?*

*Terence.*

'Oh my God, Ryan, that's Terence.' Catrina points to the signature. 'Terence Nightingale, the author.' She turns the dust cover over in her hand and points to his name.

'Yes, the man who fell off the cliff,' says Ryan. 'I remember Troy reading about him in that leaflet.'

'Not just that, but he was Ivy's husband and he only ever came here with her, so she must have been with him when he got together with Barbara. The dirty, cheating, liar.' As soon as Catrina says the words out loud, she realises how contradictory they sound. Luckily, Ryan doesn't react.

She wonders whether Ivy knows about his dalliance with Barbara. If she did, surely they wouldn't be friends.

The letter isn't dated, so she has no way of knowing when it was written. It could have been written in 1976. It could have been written the day before Terence died. In that case, his secret would have died with him. But what if it was written years earlier, and his affair had carried on?

Poor Ivy has dedicated her life to his memory. She has mourned him for fifty years, never moving on, never allowing herself to love anyone else. She remembers Ivy telling her the first time they chatted in the library that she never fell in love again. She never looked for anyone else, as nobody could live up to Terence. Yet all the time, he wasn't so special after all. He was an ordinary man, undeserving of his place on Ivy's pedestal. Cheating on her with one of her closest friends.

What an utter bastard.

## Chapter Thirty-Six

## Ivy – July 1975

Terence was as much in love with his Porsche 911 as he was with Ivy. His previous three books have sold extremely well, surpassing expectations, which had enabled his agent to negotiate the best advance he had ever had. No amount of warning from Ivy was going to deter him from spending virtually every penny of it on a new car.

'Can you remember that summer when we drove to Holm Island in the Morris Minor?' he said. They were in the car showroom on Brompton Road in Knightsbridge. He stroked the Porsche's roof with his fingertip. 'We have come a long way since then, haven't we, darling?'

'Yes, we have,' said Ivy.

'I never would have dreamed that I would be able to afford a car like this,' he said.

It was a beautiful car, although if Ivy had her choice, she would be happy to potter around in their old Hillman Avenger. She didn't need a sports car to feel good about herself. But Terence had worked hard, and he deserved it. Day after day, night after night, for months on end, he hunched over his typewriter, bashing out page after page until the manuscript was finished. Many times, Ivy had arrived home after the theatre only to find him still in the spare bedroom upstairs, which he used as his study, shoulders stiff and fingers aching from typing for so long. She had massaged his shoulders and told him to come to bed, but his deadline was approaching, and while he was focused, she knew there was nothing she could do to tear him away from his work.

'Have you eaten anything today?' she asked when he was working on his last chapter.

'A cheese sandwich,' he replied.

'Is that all? Do you want me to make you anything else?' He didn't reply, but continued tapping away, his glasses on the end of his nose.

She left him to it and went to tidy the kitchen. Crumbs littered the breadboard, the cheese had been left out to go hard and dry, and the washing-up bowl was filled with half a dozen dirty cups. She wrapped up the cheese and put it back in the fridge, washed the pots, and made Terence a fresh cup of tea. She left it on the end of his desk, kissed him on the cheek, and went to bed.

When the manuscript was finally finished, Terence could finally return to his old self. Conversation and laughter were back in the house. The door to Terence's study was no longer closed, trapping him inside. He occupied the other rooms, once again. He read his newspaper in the kitchen, listened to music in the living room, and went to bed at the same time as Ivy. They went back to being a couple again. They walked in the park, ate dinner in restaurants, and had friends round for drinks and nibbles on a Sunday afternoon.

When the summer arrived, Ivy's run at the theatre came to an end, and they were both free until September, when Terence would begin working on his next book.

'Let's spend more time away this summer,' Terence had said one morning over breakfast. Ivy had made boiled eggs and toast soldiers. 'If we get a decent car, we can take it to Holm Island. We will take...'

'Oh, Terence, really?' said Ivy, interrupting him. 'Don't you remember how many times the Morris overheated? How many hours we spent by the side of the road waiting for her to cool down?'

'How could I forget?' laughed Terence. 'But wasn't it romantic?'

'No, it bloody well wasn't,' said Ivy. She knew what he was referring to. That afternoon, when they were stuck in traffic on the M6 motorway. Steam had begun to rise from the car bonnet, so Terence had been forced to pull over to the hard shoulder, only a few miles north of Preston. As they waited for the car to decide she was all right to continue with the journey, they had kissed like a couple of teenagers who had nowhere else to go.

He tapped at the newspaper on the table with one of his toast soldiers, leaving a greasy butter stain on the page. An advert from the local car dealership showed that they had a beautiful Porsche for sale. A red one, which Ivy knew Terence wouldn't be able to resist. 'If we go in this,' said Terence, 'we won't need to worry about it breaking down.'

Ivy's concerns about being folded into a tiny sports car for ten hours were allayed by Terence's promise to split the journey into three. They could stay at nice places along the way. She could choose. City breaks, or a country house hotel. Whatever she wanted. They could take their time travelling to Scotland and enjoy the journey.

So the purchase was made, and on the last weekend of July, they arrived at Holm Island for their three-week stay. Barbara squealed when she saw Terence's car. She threw open the door and skipped down the steps as though the car was to be hers.

'What an absolute beauty,' she declared. 'Can we go for

a spin?'

'Let the poor man stretch his legs, Barbara,' said Hugh. 'He's been driving for hours.'

'Not really,' said Terence. 'Only from the ferry. We stayed at the Thistlewood House Hotel on the mainland last night.'

'Oh my,' said Barbara. 'I love it there. We stayed there for our anniversary last year. The rooms are divine. Did you have one with a sea view?'

'Of course. I'm just trying to even things out,' said Ivy. 'Terence has his car to keep him happy. Overnight stays in expensive hotels make me happy.'

The journey to Hollow Pines had taken a week. Ivy had insisted on staying at Oxford, Stratford-upon-Avon, Chester, and Kendal, in nothing less than a five-star hotel each time. Terence didn't attempt to argue. He had never been to any of those places before and was happy for Ivy to get what she wanted.

'Jump in,' said Terence. 'I will show you what she can do on these hills.'

Barbara ran around to the passenger door and climbed inside the car. 'Oh, I love it,' she said, stroking the dashboard and the cream leather seats. 'Hugh, I need one of these.'

Hugh took their suitcases out of the boot and carried them into the house. 'Come on, Ivy,' he said, 'I've got a lovely bottle of wine cooling in the fridge. Let's make a start.'

By the time Terence and Barbara arrived back at Hollow Pines, Ivy and Hugh had opened their second bottle of wine. They were both beginning to worry that the car had been in some kind of terrible accident. Maybe a tree had fallen on them. Maybe they had skidded off the road on a steep bend, and the car had gone tumbling down the hillside, landing on the roof. Maybe they had simply broken down miles away and had to walk back. Barbara was still wearing her slippers - pink, fluffy mules, completely unsuitable for outside walking.

Just as Hugh was considering telephoning the police station to ask if anyone had reported an accident, they arrived back. Neither of them was concerned that they had caused Hugh and Ivy to worry so. They breezed into the drawing room without a care in the world. Barbara looked at the clock on the wall and said they had only been out for an hour. Hugh told her it had been over two hours. He demanded to know where they had been and why it had taken so long. They must have travelled the length and breadth of the island four times at least. Barbara giggled - somewhat forced, Ivy thought - and kissed her husband's cheek.

'Don't be silly, darling,' she said. 'Time just seemed to pass us by, that's all. Now then, what's this bottle you have open? Shall we have a drink, Terence? I'll go and get us some glasses.'

Later, as they unpacked their things in their room and got ready for dinner, Ivy asked Terence again why they had been out so long. He was busy hanging his shirts in the wardrobe and didn't turn to face her when he spoke. He mumbled something about loving the car so much that he just wanted to drive it. He said he was sure the novelty would wear off soon, but right now, he couldn't get enough of it. He laughed and began to tell a story about when his dad bought him a set of toy cars for Christmas, igniting his love for them. You know what men and machines are like. Blah blah blah. Ivy stopped listening. He was waffling. Talking too much. The gentleman doth protest too much, methinks. Not that she had yet accused him of anything.

She told herself she was being ultra-sensitive. What was

wrong with Terence and Barbara spending a little time together? They had known each other for four years. They were close friends; they all were, the four of them. Except that, given the choice, she wouldn't want to spend another afternoon with Hugh on his own. It didn't seem right, being alone with someone else's husband.

That night, they were joined for dinner by four of Hugh and Barbara's friends, Pam and Arthur, and Janet and Stan. It was a beautiful evening, still and calm. There was the slightest summer breeze, not one strong enough to ruffle any leaves or blow napkins from tables, but just enough to keep them cool. They ate dinner outside in the garden. Barbeque spare ribs that had been marinating for twenty-four hours, homemade coleslaw, and corn on the cob, followed by Barbara's pièce de résistance, Black Forest Gateau. Ivy was more than a little tipsy by the end of the meal. Music was playing, the women were dancing, and she didn't notice initially when Terence began to clear away the plates from the table. Usually, they were left for the staff to clear, but Barbara had allowed them the night off due to one of the staff members turning twenty-one. They had hired the village hall for a party. She said she was happy to stack the plates in the kitchen, and they could be cleaned the next day.

'You've got him well trained, haven't you, that husband of yours?' said Janet, Barbara's friend from her book club.

She was dressed in a floaty halter-neck maxi-dress in royal blue, which perfectly highlighted her blue eyes. She was an attractive woman, Ivy thought, although a little too loud for her liking. She drank too much, smoked too much, and laughed like a hyena. Or was that unkind? Was Ivy being overly critical and bitchy because she had caught Janet staring at Terence for too long? Maybe. Janet hadn't noticed her looking, but when Ivy followed her gaze, she saw Terence leaning against the wall, a martini in one hand and a cigarette in the other. Barbara was next to him, whispering something in his ear, which was making him laugh. Ivy had ignored their closeness at the time. Terence was attractive and charismatic, and women loved his company. She had got used to it, but everyone knew he belonged to Ivy, and at the end of the day, he was going to bed with her, nobody else, wearing the gold band on his ring finger that Ivy had put there herself.

'I couldn't get my husband to clear the plates for love nor money,' said Janet.

'Terence is good around the house,' said Ivy. 'He has to be, as I'm out at the theatre sometimes five or six evenings week, so if he wasn't self-sufficient, he would starve.'

It was true. But tonight, Terence had no reason to be so conscientious about the pots. It wouldn't take Barbara five minutes to take them away herself. It wasn't as though she had to wash them. She had staff, for goodness sake. Everything would be dealt with tomorrow.

Ivy continued dancing, smiling, and chatting with Janet and pretending that she wasn't irritating the life out of her. But she couldn't take her eyes off the door, waiting for Terence to reappear. How long does it take to walk to the kitchen and back? The house is big, granted, but it isn't Buckingham Palace. After five minutes, she went to find him. She walked through the drawing room and into the Great Hall. He was there. On his way out of the kitchen, followed closely by Barbara.

'Darling, is everything alright?' asked Barbara.

'It is now,' said Ivy. 'Now that I have my man back.' She tucked her arm around Terence's waist and led him back outside.

# Chapter Thirty-Seven

# Catrina

At intervals through the evening, Catrina has been watching Barbara and Ivy across the dining room. There doesn't seem to be any animosity between them. They are laughing, sipping wine, and chatting as old friends would, who have got together after so many years apart. They must have plenty to talk about. She concludes that Ivy doesn't have a clue that Barbara has slept with Terence. If she knew, she surely wouldn't want to speak to her. In fact, she probably wouldn't have come to this hotel in the first place.

When Barbara leaves the table after the main course, Catrina gets up to follow her.

'Where are you off to?' asks Simone.

'I just want a quick word with Barbara,' she says. 'I won't be long.'

'Who's Barbara?' asks Simone.

'I'll tell you when I get back.'

Ryan grabs Catrina's arm as she passes his chair. 'What are you doing?'

'I just want to speak to her,' she says.

'It's got nothing to do with you,' he says. 'Babe, in the nicest possible way, keep your nose out of stuff that doesn't concern you.'

'What stuff?' says Simone.

If Beth-Ann had been sitting with them, Catrina wouldn't have said anything. She likes Ivy and doesn't want her to be the subject of gossip. But Beth-Ann is sharing an intimate table for two with a man she got chatting to yesterday evening in the bar. Catrina has faith that Simone and Troy won't gossip, so the secret is safe with them. 'I found a letter in one of the books I took out of the library addressed to Barbara, the woman who has just walked out.' She indicates the dining room door, where, through the glass, she can see Barbara making her way towards the ladies' bathroom on the other side of reception. 'She's Andrew's grandmother, and Ivy Montclaire's old friend from the seventies. The letter turned out to be a love letter to her from Ivy's husband.'

'Ivy Montclaire's husband?' repeated Simone. 'You mean Terence Nightingale? No way. He was playing away with her best friend?'

'I don't know,' says Catrina. 'I mean, yes, they definitely did it once, but whether or not they carried it on, I don't know. It may have been a one-off. That's what I'm going to find out.'

'You can't do that,' says Simone. 'Like Ryan says, it's none of our concern, and didn't he die like a million years ago?'

'Yes, but that's the point,' says Catrina. 'Poor Ivy has played the part of Miss Havisham for fifty years. Well, maybe not quite that dramatic, she has had a bit of a life, but she has mourned him way too long. He isn't worthy of that much angst, and Ivy deserves to know the truth. It's the only way she can move on.'

Ryan holds his hands up in surrender. 'Personally, I don't think you should say anything, but it's up to you.'

'I agree with Ryan,' says Simone. 'I'd say that if it

happened yesterday, the woman has a right to know, but it was so long ago. I think you should leave it. If anyone should tell her, it should be Barbara, but if she hasn't said anything in fifty years, she isn't going to. It isn't your place.'

Catrina sits back down. 'Okay, I'll leave it,' she says reluctantly. 'You're right, it's not my place at all, and I shouldn't get involved.' She takes a sip of wine. 'No, sorry, I can't do it. I'm going to speak to Barbara. I won't say anything to Ivy, though, I promise.'

Ignoring her friends' protestations, Catrina makes her way to the ladies' bathroom, hoping that Barbara is still there and that she will be alone. As Catrina pushes open the door, she sees Barbara standing at the sink putting on a fresh coat of lipstick. Barbara smiles.

'Hi,' says Catrina. 'I'm Catrina, do you mind if I have a quick word?'

'Of course, dear,' says Barbara. 'Shall we go and take a seat in the hall? Is everything alright with your room?'

'Yes, yes, great. It isn't about our room. The room is lovely.'

'Oh, that's good. Are you at the back? I do find the rooms at the back have the better view, although I wish you'd had better weather.'

Catrina takes Terence's letter out of her bag and thrusts it towards Barbara. 'I found this letter in a book by Terence Nightingale,' she says. 'It's yours, I presume.'

Barbara's face turns pink and then immediately white. She is so pale that Catrina fears she might faint and regrets her decision to confront her. This is an old lady. What on earth has she done? Why did she feel it necessary to bring up something from fifty years ago? Ryan and Simone were right. It isn't her place, and she shouldn't be here. She wants to tell Barbara to ignore her, but it's too late now.

Barbara snatches the letter from Catrina's hand, folds it

in half and pushes it into her handbag, which is resting on the side of the sink.

'Have you read it?' asks Barbara. 'Yes, you must have, otherwise you wouldn't be accosting me in such a manner. I suppose you're here because you want me to explain why Terence would be writing such a letter to me?'

'Well, I...'

'I'm afraid you are going to be disappointed, because I will do nothing of the sort,' says Barbara. She puts her lipstick in her handbag, squashing the letter further down. 'What happened between me and Terence is in the past, and is none of your business. Now, if there is nothing else, I need to get back to the table. My guests are waiting for me.'

Barbara lifts her chin and marches out. Catrina is under the impression that she would have slammed the door behind her, had it not been attached to a spring that gives it a soft closure.

It is only then that she realises one of the cubicles is occupied. Someone else is here. Someone else would have heard their conversation. But it doesn't matter, because they didn't mention Ivy's name. Everything is fine.

The toilet flushes. The door opens, and Ivy walks out of the cubicle. Catrina didn't notice her leave the table.

'Hello, Ivy,' says Catrina brightly. She forces herself to smile, as though nothing is wrong and she hasn't just lit an unexploded bomb from the past.

'So it's true,' says Ivy.

'What is true?' asks Catrina, pretending she doesn't know what Ivy is talking about.

'I suspected that there was something going on between Terence and Barbara. The letter you gave her, was it an intimate letter from Terence? Is that what you wanted to question her about?'

Catrina sighs. She wants to cry. She should never have

said anything. 'Yes, it was,' she says. 'I'm sorry.'

'I don't want to hear details, but was it clear from the letter that something was going on between Barbara and Terence?' asks Ivy.

'Well, not really.' Then, 'Yes, it is very clear. Ivy, I'm sorry, I should never…'

Ivy shakes her head. She leans her hands on the sink and looks at her reflection in the mirror. 'Look at me, Catrina,' she says. 'I'm at the end of my life. I might have a good few years left in me, but my best years are behind me. I've wasted them, beating myself up for something that was beyond my control. I realise that now. What happened to Terence was not my fault. A combination of factors meant that he was in the wrong place at the wrong time.'

'Oh, Ivy, of course, his accident was not your fault. Is that what you have been thinking?'

'I did, yes. I have punished myself for such a long time. Too long, in all honesty. But not anymore. Terence was a grown man, and on the night he died, he could have followed me back to the house if he wanted to. It was his choice to stay behind. Even if I had got down on my bended knees and begged him, I don't think he would have gone back with me. He needed space to calm down after our cross words. I left him there on the cliff because he wanted to be left.'

'So why would you ever think that it was your fault?' asks Catrina.

'Because I believed that he lost his footing when we argued.' Ivy takes a deep breath. 'And I pushed him in his chest. No, no, before you ask, I didn't push him over the cliff. But…'

Catrina holds up her hand to stop Ivy's words. 'Ivy, please. I don't for one minute think that you pushed him over the cliff. You don't need to justify anything to me. It was a tragedy. And it certainly wasn't your fault that it went dark and poor Terence lost his footing and fell,' says Catrina.

'No, I know that now,' says Ivy. 'I don't know why I thought he fell when I was with him. I would have heard him fall. I would have seen it.' She turns on the tap and washes her hands. Catrina passes her a paper towel to dry them. 'I have blamed myself for his death my whole life. It has taken this trip to make me realise that it wasn't my fault.'

'It was never your fault.'

'Thank you,' says Ivy. She smiles at Catrina through the mirror. 'Was that letter inside *The Swirling Sea Mist?*' asks Ivy.

'Yes, it was tucked away in the dust cover,' says Catrina. 'But I hate those things, so I took it off to read the book, and the letter fell out onto the bed. I'm sorry, I shouldn't have read it.'

'And you're sure it was addressed to Barbara?'

'Yes, it was in an envelope with her name on, but it wasn't dated.'

'I know when it was written,' says Ivy, nodding to herself. 'It was the summer of 1975, the year before he died. I suspected something was going on between them that year. He had just bought a new fancy sports car, a bright red Porsche, and we drove up in it from London. He gave Barbara a signed copy of that book on our last night here, together with a bottle of her favourite Champagne, as a thank you for having us. The book had only just been released the month before and he had hardback copies to give to all of his friends. He must have hidden the letter inside the book.'

'Or given her the letter some other time, and Barbara left it in the book.'

'Yes, either way,' says Ivy. 'It's of no matter now. It is so far in the past that it isn't worth bothering about.' Ivy throws the paper towel into the waste paper basket underneath the sink. 'What's done is done.'

'Is that it?' asks Catrina. 'Aren't you going to tackle her about it?'

Ivy smiles, but her face is filled with sadness. 'I'm not as shocked by this revelation as you might think,' she says. 'Like I said, I suspected something was going on. You haven't told me anything I didn't already know deep in my heart. You have simply confirmed it. That summer, Terence and Barbara seemed to spend a lot of time together. They went for walks on the beach, had whispered conversations here and there, and when we first arrived, he took her for what was meant to be a quick spin in the car, but they ended up being out for over two hours. He had guilt written all over his face when he got back. I thought something was going on, that's what my instinct was telling me anyway, but I told myself not to be so stupid.'

'I'm not surprised,' says Catrina. 'You wouldn't suspect your close friend, would you?'

'Barbara wasn't a very close friend,' says Ivy. 'We only saw each other once a year. Sadly, it has been confirmed tonight that she wasn't a friend at all, in fact.'

'I agree,' says Catrina. 'Real friends don't sleep with your husband.'

'The sad thing is that the argument Terence and I had before he fell was because he was accusing *me* of kissing a man too passionately on stage. He was jealous of a man who was acting a part in a play and who, I am almost a hundred percent sure, was gay. He had given me the cold shoulder for two days, and when he finally told me what was bothering him, I became angry because I knew he was being unreasonable. The irony. Given how he had been the year before with Barbara, he had a cheek accusing me of anything, when he was the one who had been unfaithful.'

'And that's why you shouted at him?'

'Yes, I was so cross. The double standards.'

'But did you tell him that you thought there was something between him and Barbara?'

'No, I didn't,' says Ivy. 'I was hoping I was wrong, so I kept my fears to myself. I didn't want to know the truth.'

'I can understand that,' says Catrina. 'So what are you going to do now?'.

'Nothing, dear,' says Ivy. 'What's done is done.'

# Prologue

## Catrina – December 2025

'That's it,' says Catrina. 'The last of the Save the Date cards. I'll post them out tomorrow.'

'This is your final chance to change your mind,' says Ryan. 'Once those cards have arrived through people's letterboxes, you're committed.'

Catrina shakes her head. 'I'm not committed until that wedding ring is on my finger.' She points to the ring finger of her left hand, where a beautiful solitaire diamond engagement ring shimmers under the kitchen light. She leans across the table and kisses her husband-to-be.

Their wedding is booked for the following April. They are keeping the guest list small, just close friends and family. With Catrina's new café, which opened a couple of weeks ago, having taken most of their savings, they need to keep a tight grip on their purse strings.

Since the wine tasting weekend at Holm Island, Catrina has kept in touch with Ivy. They have spoken on the phone many times, and when Catrina told her about Ryan's proposal, Ivy said that it was the best, most romantic proposal ever.

They had been walking on the promenade at Lytham. Ryan had taken Catrina away for the weekend to celebrate her birthday. The night before, they had eaten a three-course meal in the hotel's restaurant and had far too many cocktails. On the Sunday morning, he suggested a walk before breakfast, and although Catrina was reluctant, Ryan persuaded her that some fresh air would help to alleviate the hangover symptoms.

He promised that they wouldn't be out for more than half an hour, and then they could enjoy their breakfast.

Holding tightly to her hand, Ryan dragged her across the road to Lytham Green, a stretch of grass between the main road and the promenade next to the beach. They walked towards the two-hundred-year-old windmill, where Ryan got down on one knee and asked Catrina to be his wife. She burst into tears and said yes immediately.

'Remind me to give Ivy a call tomorrow night,' says Catrina. 'I'd like to know how she got on this weekend.'

'Is this the weekend Barbara and Mhairi are visiting her in London?' asks Ryan.

'Yes, she said she has a whole itinerary ready for them, including an afternoon tea at The Ritz and front row tickets for a show tonight. Mhairi is a huge fan of the theatre. Apparently, she once saw Ivy play Lady Macbeth at Stratford. I can imagine she was outstanding, back in the day, can you?'

'Yes, I can actually,' says Ryan. 'Why don't you go and see her in London one day? You could take Simone and stay in a hotel in the city and take her out for dinner.'

'Yes, that would be good,' says Catrina. 'But maybe not when Barbara is there. I don't ever want to see her again.'

Ryan laughs. 'Not that you're holding a grudge or anything.'

'No, not really,' says Catrina. 'Just a small one, I suppose. I'm glad that Ivy can forgive her, but I don't think I would have been able to if Barbara had been my friend.'

She remembers the conversation she had with Ivy on the ferry from Holm Island to the mainland. They were travelling back from the hotel a day later than planned, thanks to the storm that had caused the cancellation of the ferry.

'I can't wait to get back to London,' said Ivy. 'I used to love visiting Hollow Pines, we really did have some fantastic parties in that big old house. But even then, when I had enjoyed myself tremendously and had Terence by my side, I was always happy to get back home.'

'Do you think you'll ever go back?' asked Catrina.

Ivy shook her head. 'I don't think so.'

'Well, at least you don't have to see Barbara ever again.'

'I've invited her to stay with me in London, actually,' said Ivy. 'She will be coming down with Mhairi in December for a weekend of shopping and a trip to a show.'

'Really? After everything?'

'Life is too short, don't you think?' said Ivy. 'You know, in those days we all had too much to drink. The holidays would pass in an alcoholic blur. I suspect some of the guests took some of the hard stuff, too, although I never did.'

'You mean drugs?' asked Catrina, astounded.

'Yes, you young people didn't invent hedonism, you know.' They both laughed. 'What I'm trying to say is that things happen when people are drunk that wouldn't happen when they are sober. Barbara shouldn't have flirted with Terence, but he shouldn't have encouraged it, either. It takes two to tango.'

'You're a special person, you know that, Ivy,' said Catrina.

'No, I'm not,' said Ivy, laughing. 'But I was with Terence every day after we got home that summer. He never saw Barbara alone again, so I'm almost certain that whatever happened between them was a one-off. Then the following year, well, that was the year he died.'

'Well, if you can forgive her, then I suppose that's commendable.'

'It isn't really about being commendable,' said Ivy. 'It's about making the most of every day I have left. I don't want to sit in my rocking chair when I'm old – I mean older than I am now – and have regrets. Instead, I want to remember the lovely times I had with my friends.'

Catrina threw her arms around Ivy and hugged her. 'And you're not going to blame yourself for anything?'

They both knew what she meant. 'No, I am not,' said Ivy. 'I know it wasn't my fault.'

As she spoke, a glistening of tears in her eyes, Catrina could almost see the burden of guilt being lifted from Ivy. She seemed lighter than the woman who had arrived on the island three days ago. It may have taken fifty years, but at least she got there in the end.

THE END

The Author's Wife

*Author's Note*

I hope you enjoyed the story of Ivy and Catrina. How would you have reacted if you'd found out that one of your close friends had slept with your husband? I certainly wouldn't have been as forgiving as Ivy, but then again, maybe you view life differently in your eighties. Life is too short for aggro, isn't it?

Holm Island is a fictitious island off the coast of Scotland. When writing it, I pictured the Isle of Mull in my mind, with those beautiful pastel coloured houses in Tobermory. I haven't ever seen the cliffs on Mull, so that part of the book came from my imagination. I imagined cliffs that weren't too steep, so you could negotiate your way down to the beach via the steep steps, but they were steep enough that any fall would have been tragic.

Initially, I wrote a book called Murder on Holm Island, in which Ivy had pushed Terence on purpose. She had covered up his death and lied about what happened, until she confessed on her return journey fifty years later, as she held a gun to her head, threatening to kill herself. I know, I know, you probably can't imagine her doing it, can you? She's such a gentle soul. That's why we writers do more than one draft.

If you have enjoyed my book, please could you leave me a review on Amazon? It helps more than you know, especially for an independent author like me. The more reviews that are written, the more Amazon will push my book to new readers. So, thank you!

Do you like murder mysteries? If you do, continue reading a sample of The Murder of Mrs Chadwick, which is set in 1976 in a Lancashire village. Poor Mrs Chadwick is found dead in her kitchen. The story is told from the perspective of three suspects and the detective inspector.

# THE MURDER OF MRS CHADWICK

Thursday, 7th October 1976

*Jack*

Jack Chadwick has been in the police station interview room for more than an hour. He watches the hands on the wall clock count down the passing minutes unbearably slowly. He asks Detective Inspector Holt when he will be able to go home. He needs some air. He needs some sleep.

Call me Elena, she says with a smile. He has never met a woman policeman before. She seems kind and Jack wonders whether she has been trained on when to show compassion, or does it come naturally to her? So far, her smile has never faltered, even on the journey from the house to the police station, when she twisted around in the front seat of the car and told him he would have to stay somewhere else tonight, she continued to smile. She felt sorry for him, he could tell. As he peered out of the back passenger window of the blue and white Ford Cortina, his breath steaming the glass, he wanted to ask her to stop the car. He needed to run back into the house and tell them to be careful. His train set is delicate; some of the pieces are quite expensive. They shouldn't knock the table, otherwise the signal office will dismantle. He hadn't had time to glue it properly this afternoon, and the house was so busy. There were people everywhere. But Detective Inspector Holt had interrupted his thoughts. It's unlikely that the forensic team will be finished this side of midnight, she had said. She could arrange a hotel room, or he could stay at a relative's house? She posed it as a question, although she knew Jack didn't have any other family. He had already told her that.

Now, Elena assures him that they are almost finished. Just a few more questions. Jack sighs and leans back in the vinyl armchair, the colour of rust and decay, resting his head on the back cushion.

Elena tells him that his tiredness is probably caused by the trauma. It's his body's natural response. But if he wouldn't mind answering a few more questions, it will help them to catch his mother's killer. Jack flinches at her choice of language. *Killer.* His eyebrows come together in a frown. He wants to tell her he can't take much more. It is almost ten o'clock. He is always in bed by now, and he hasn't eaten for hours, since he made himself a snack this afternoon, a couple of cream crackers and a slice of cheese. It's important that he eats regularly, otherwise he has trouble thinking properly.

He tells the inspector he has never seen a dead body before. His mother's is the first, and she agrees that would be a traumatic experience for any person.

Elena is particularly interested in Jack's relationship with his mother. Did he love her? Did she love him? Didn't he find it difficult still living at home when he was, how old? Twenty-nine years? Jack can't fathom why these questions are important. What relevance do they have? But he assures the inspector that yes, he was very happy, and, no, the thought of leaving home had never occurred to him.

They looked after each other, him and his mother. Why would he want to live anywhere else?

Until now. Now, she is gone, and now he doesn't have anyone to look after, or to look after him.

Jack tells the inspector that he can't believe she has gone, as he sobs into his hands. She tells him to take his time, and Jack sips more stewed tea from a tired brown mug. He runs his fingers over the chip on the rim and the crack that meanders from the handle down to the bottom. He wants to point it out to the inspector and warn her of the dangers of hot tea. The mug could break at any moment and scald him.

His mother would have told her. His mother would never drink tea from a chipped mug, and she wouldn't have put up with stewed tea, either. She would have asked for a fresh one. She would have pushed it back across the table with derision and refused to speak until a 'proper brew' was made. She liked things to be 'just so'. Each night, as she dragged her tired feet along the path to their front door, Jack would dash into the kitchen and put the kettle back on the stove. By the time his mother had shrugged off her coat, kicked off her shoes, and hung her handbag on the hook at the bottom of the stairs, the pot of tea was waiting for her, fresh and perfectly brewed. A silent gesture of her son's enduring devotion.

'You're not stewing my tea, are you?' she would inevitably complain.

'No, Mum,' Jack would answer, as she inspected the tea, peering into the pot as though it contained the secret to life itself. 'It's just how you like it.'

Elena asks Jack where he was all afternoon. Jack tells her he was at home, as usual, except for the time he went to the corner shop. He has already explained this to the officer who attended at the house, how he had returned from the shop and dropped the cigarettes his mother had asked him to buy on the floor when he fell to his knees to check whether his mother was still breathing. He is pretty sure that she wasn't. She was a strange colour and very still. He admits he had moved her, in order to check. He apologises, saying he knows he shouldn't have done. The police officer, the one in uniform who came to the house, told him that you shouldn't disturb a crime scene. But at the time, he didn't know, and he wasn't thinking straight. It was such a shock, he says, to find his mother on the floor like that.

Jack watches Elena whisper something into the ear of her colleague, who promptly leaves the room. No doubt they will be checking his story about the corner shop. Jack is sure the woman behind the counter can vouch for the fact that he has been in there. Less than two hours ago. It feels like a lifetime ago.

'She's off to Spain in a couple of weeks, Angela and that live-in boyfriend of hers,' his mother had told him earlier. They were in the kitchen, standing near the stove. She had taken her cup of tea from Jack with one hand and picked up the saucepan lid with the other. 'What's in there?'

'It's potato hash,' he replied. 'We had some corned beef that needed using up.'

Mrs Chadwick dropped the lid onto the saucepan. 'You stupid boy. I was going to have that on my sandwich tomorrow. What am I going to have now?' Without waiting for a response, she marched into the living room, tea splashing from her cup onto the saucer with each pound of her heavy feet. 'You've over-filled it again, stupid boy. Here.' Jack followed her into the living room, taking the tea from her outstretched hand. 'Tip a bit down the sink.'

Jack did as he was told, while wondering how many times a day she called him a stupid boy. He returned the cup to her when she was settled on the sofa, and pushed the footstool towards her legs. He lifted one of her legs, and

## The Author's Wife

then the other leg, onto the footstool. He plumped a cushion and placed it under the arm holding the cup, and then stood back waiting for her to tell him that she was comfortable.

'Whereabouts in Spain?' he asked. Knowing that his mother loved to talk about the people she cleaned for, he thought a chat about Angela Bennett's future travels would snap her out of this grouchy mood.

Last week, his mother had arrived home with tales of the exciting and exotic food Angela had bought from the new grocers in Wellington – they called it a delicatessen - avocado pears all the way from Mexico, kiwi fruit, prawns, and oil made from olives in Italy that his mother had the pleasure of putting away for her, as Angela had chatted excitedly about what meal she was planning to make for her dinner party, and the show she was going to watch at the theatre next month in Manchester. His mother had enjoyed listening, stealing away little snippets as though they were golden coins to pay for future opportunities to gossip.

But Angela now seems to be out of favour and her planned trip had touched a nerve, for some reason, and had made her angry.

'I didn't ask,' she said. 'She wanted me to, but I told myself, no, I'm not pandering to her.'

'Quite right,' agreed Jack. He hoped that he was saying the right thing. Agreeing with his mother was his usual appeasing course of action.

'She stood leaning against the worktop, getting in my way when she could see me trying to clean the kitchen, flicking through her magazine, pointing out this, that, and the bloody other that she wants to buy. Her wardrobe is already fit to bursting. I thought to myself, you don't need a new outfit for every day, do you? I don't care how many stars the hotel has got. You're just showing off, telling me you want to buy all them things just to make a point. She was doing it to annoy me. As per usual.'

His mother continued to complain about Angela. Jack tried to keep listening. He didn't think Angela was a particularly annoying person, but maybe she was sometimes. He simply agreed with his mother. The sooner he could pacify her, the sooner they could begin to enjoy their evening together.

'You know where she was off to yesterday afternoon?' his mother had asked. Jack shook his head. 'Having lunch in Wellington, again. There's something going on there. She's probably got another man stashed away somewhere, you mark my words. She had painted her nails bright red. You know that kind of woman has red nails, don't you?' His mother held out her hand and inspected her own short nails, at the end of dry, cracked fingers. 'What are you looking at?' she shouted.

'Nothing, Mum,' said Jack.

'We can't all be born a princess, you know. Some of us can't afford to put nail varnish on, just for it to chip the next day. We have to work for a living.'

'We can go to Spain,' Jack had said to his mother. He wanted to distract her attention away from her fingernails, to calm the storm of anger. 'One day, when I get a job, we can go away. You'd like Spain, wouldn't you?'

'Who's going to employ you? Look at the state of you. When was the last time you put on a clean shirt?' said his mother.

Jack, perched on the edge of the sofa next to his mother, looked down at his shirt. 'This was clean on this morning,' he said, pulling it away from his body and inspecting it.

'Liar! Stop lying to me!' his mother shrieked. She pushed him away from her and lifted the cushion under her arm.

'And where did you put my library book?'

'I don't know, Mum,' said Jack. He jumped up, lifting the rest of the cushions in turn. 'It's not here. I don't…'

'I'll find it myself, you stupid boy,' she shouted. 'Get out of my way.' She batted him away with the back of her hand.

'I can't think when you shout, Mum.' Jack put his hands over his ears and scrunched his eyes closed.

'I'm not shouting,' she had said. She was. 'Now, go and check on that potato hash. You're not burning it, are you?'

'No, Mum,' said Jack. He lowered his arms and trundled off to the kitchen. Why did his mum have to ruin his mood? Every day was the same. Every day she grumbled and moaned and picked at him, as though it was his fault that she was miserable. All he did was try to make her life as comfortable as possible. He cleaned the house, cooked her food, and washed all the clothes. The only thing he didn't do was work. But one day he would. One day he would get a job that would pay enough to take them on holiday. Maybe to Spain. Maybe somewhere else. Anywhere she wanted to go.

The inspector is still looking at him. She asks him again to recount his afternoon. She tells him to take his time. She has already asked him so many questions, one after the other. How many more can there be? He wants to go home. The walls of the police station interview room, the colour of weathered bricks, are giving him a headache.

He doesn't want to admit that he and his mother had a falling out. It doesn't seem right now, besmirching her memory. Not now she isn't here to tell her side of the story. He bites his bottom lip. He doesn't want to tell the police that his mother was grumpy every day and that her face wore a persistent deep frown. Jack can't remember the last time he saw her smile.

Elena asks Jack if he is ready to continue. Jack's eyes

flick once more to the wall clock. Is this almost over?

*Angela*

Angela Bennett's blood-red Porsche 911 skids around the corner into Southgate Drive and comes to a sudden stop under the shelter of a large oak tree. The old roots push their way through the concrete flags of the narrow residential pavement where two of the Porsche's wheels now rest. The last of the autumn leaves, bending under the pressure of the recent rainfall, plummet down onto the roof of the car.

Through the windscreen, Angela watches the police activity at number eight, Miriam Chadwick's house. Blue flashes from the parked police car at the bottom of the footpath spin around the dimly lit cul-de-sac, mixing with the amber light from the open front door as it spills out onto the front step. An officious-looking uniformed policeman, chin held high, back straight, stands guard, feet hip distance apart, ready to glare at any inquisitive neighbour who dares to peer out from behind half-drawn curtains.

A sharp siren wail introduces another police vehicle as it pulls into the cul-de-sac and stops across the road from the first one. She watches two police officers jump out and hurry to Mrs Chadwick's house. A middle-aged plain-clothes policeman appears at the front door, hands thrust into the pocket of his trousers. He steps onto the path, where he waits for his colleagues to approach him. Angela recognises Detective Sergeant Miller. She would know his bald head and protruding stomach anywhere. She knows all of the detectives from Wellington Police Station. There isn't a single one who hasn't given her house or shop a visit at one time or another. Angela watches them talk. Presumably, DS Miller is giving the newcomers a synopsis of the events, as far as they know. The new arrivals nod as they listen, their heads bobbing up and down. Eventually, they follow the detective to the front door, before wading into the house.

Angela reverses her car out of the cul-de-sac and drives off. If she was religious, she would pray that DS Miller has not spotted her car.

www.ingramcontent.com/pod-product-compliance
Lightning Source LLC
La Vergne TN
LVHW041622060526
838200LV00040B/1401